THE LAST SEPTEMBER

Also by Nina de Gramont

BOOKS FOR ADULTS
Of Cats and Men: Stories
Gossip of the Starlings

BOOKS FOR YOUNG ADULTS
Every Little Thing in the World
Meet Me at the River
The Boy I Love

The Last September

A NOVEL BY

Nina de Gramont

ALGONQUIN BOOKS OF CHAPEL HILL   2015

Published by
ALGONQUIN BOOKS OF CHAPEL HILL
Post Office Box 2225
Chapel Hill, North Carolina 27515-2225

a division of
WORKMAN PUBLISHING
225 Varick Street
New York, New York 10014

This is a work of fiction. While, as in all fiction, the literary
perceptions and insights are based on experience, all names, characters,
places, and incidents either are products of the author's imagination
or are used fictitiously.

LIBRARY OF CONGRESS CATALOGING-IN-PUBLICATION DATA
Gramont, Nina de.
The last September : a novel / by Nina de Gramont.—First edition.
pages ; cm
ISBN 978-1-61620-133-3
I. Title.
PS3557.R24L37 2015
813'.54—dc23   2015004228

10 9 8 7 6 5 4 3 2 1
First Edition

To Peter Steinberg

THE LAST SEPTEMBER

PART ONE

My Life had stood—a Loaded Gun—
In Corners—till a Day
The Owner passed—identified—
And carried Me away

— EMILY DICKINSON

1

Because I am a student of literature, I will start my story on the day Charlie died. In other words, I'm beginning in the middle. *In medias res*, that's the Latin term, and though my specialty is American Renaissance poetry, I did have to study the classics. Homer, Dante, Milton. They knew about the middle, how all of life revolves around a single moment in time. Everything that comes before leads up to that moment. Everything that comes afterward springs from that moment.

In my case, that moment—that middle—is my husband's murder.

WHEN I LOOK BACK now, it hurtles toward us like a meteor. But at the time we were too wrapped up in our day-to-day life to see it. Charlie and I lived in a borrowed house by the ocean.

Our daughter, Sarah, was fifteen months old. September had just arrived, emptying the beaches at the very moment they became most spectacular: matte autumn sunlight and burnished eel grass. Cape Cod Bay was dark enough to welcome back seals but warm enough for swimming, at least if you were Charlie. He made a point of swimming in the ocean at least one day every month, including December, January, and February. I used to joke that he was part dolphin.

But this was late summer, and unseasonably warm. You didn't need to be a dolphin to go swimming, and on Charlie's last day he had already been in the water by the time Sarah woke up from her morning nap. At eleven thirty, he carried her into the extra bedroom I used as a study. If I'd run my hand through his hair, I would have felt the leftover grit of salt water. But I didn't run my hand through his hair because I was too angry. I was generally angry at Charlie that fall, and it didn't help, his tendency to wander into the room where he knew I was trying to work. Sarah still wore nothing but a diaper, and obviously not a clean one. Between jobs since his restaurant failed, Charlie had spent the morning working on reshingling the house, which belonged to his father. Like Sarah, he was half naked; he wore khaki shorts and no shirt. Ignoring my pointed glance, he lay down on the worn, woven rug, crossing his long legs at the ankles. His curly blond head rested on his hands with his elbows pointing toward the ceiling. Sarah squatted about six inches away, her gaze focused on her father, concentrating in that intense toddler way—almost as if she knew these hours constituted her last chance to see him alive. Remembering that look, I like to think of Charlie's face imprinting itself on her subconscious, the memory as intrinsic as the strands of his DNA. Sarah was a thoughtful child who already had an impressive vocabulary—twenty words that she said regularly, more popping up here and there. But she was slower to walk. She hadn't begun crawling until past her first birthday; she often stood up on her own, her face scrunched in a grimace as if she were *planning* to walk, but she had yet to risk a step.

I sat at my desk, reading a collection of Emily Dickinson's letters to her sister-in-law. My dissertation was on these letters, their hidden code. Charlie had promised to watch Sarah but instead was letting his parenting time spill into mine—lounging with only one halfhearted eye on his daughter. I tried not to move my eyes from the text. If I indulged in my usual gaze out at Cape Cod Bay, it might imply availability. I'd spent the early morning with Sarah and would have her again in the afternoon. Now was the time for Charlie to remove himself and our child from my work space. Staring down with unnatural concentration, I marked a line that I had already underlined many times, grooves surrounding it so deeply that you could almost read a sentence on the next page through the wear. *Sue, you can stay or go.* I dragged my pen beneath it, drew another large star in the margin, then put down my pen and sighed.

Just as Charlie raised his eyes to mine, Sarah teetered to her feet. She pushed up with one hand on the teepee of her father's crooked elbow. Then she let go, picked up one bare foot, and stepped closer to him. I pushed my book aside. This was the moment I'd been waiting for, checking milestone charts, harassing the pediatrician.

"Did she just take a step?" I asked, as if I hadn't seen it myself.

Sarah broke into a smile. Her fat little legs began to shake with the effort. Charlie and I froze as she lifted her foot to step again, then collapsed in a triumphant, diapered heap on his chest.

"Step," Sarah said, her voice filled with the finality of the achievement, and the prospect of a new world of movement.

Charlie got to his feet and swooped Sarah over his head in one fluid motion, so her white curls grazed the exposed beams of the sloped, second-story ceiling. Two identical pairs of blue eyes smiled at each other. Everywhere Sarah and I went people asked, "Is she yours?" assuming I must be the small, dark-eyed nanny.

With a smile that mirrored his rosy mirror self, Charlie pretended to take a congratulatory bite out of Sarah's cheek. Not a giggler, she didn't laugh, but just looked quietly and enormously pleased. Clearly she understood her accomplishment and all that it presaged. She had spent months thinking it through, and finally the road lay passable before her. We cheered, Charlie bringing her down to his chest so I could step in for a family hug. His bare skin felt warm against my forearms. Sarah's spicy baby scent bonded the three of us into a single entity. We could hear the flutter and chirp of swallows outside our open window as they staged for their journey south. The Saturday Cove church bells chimed the half hour, mingling with the salty breeze off the ocean. Our home's musty disrepair transformed, as it sometimes did, into something almost magical.

"My God," Charlie said. "I love you so much."

He squeezed his hand at my waist, a degree of fervency, as if he had something to prove to me. So I said the only possible thing, reflecting the dominant, if not sole, emotion: "I love you, too."

Charlie kissed my forehead. And Sarah—who deeply approved of any kind of affection—put one hand on her father's bare shoulder and one hand on my T-shirted breast. Then she laughed.

I hope I'm not just being charitable toward myself but am remembering correctly, because it seems to me now that in that moment, I thought: if Charlie left for work every morning in a coat and tie, we might have enough money to pay our bills or move out of his father's summer house. But we wouldn't have been in the same room, all together, to witness Sarah's long-awaited first step.

And that moment is what should have remained of the day—happy and indelible, an entry in a pale pink baby book. If the phone hadn't rung two hours later, I never would have known to regret using up our luck so early. When I think about the rest of that day, and how it unfolded, there are too many stretches of time that would require rewriting, if ever the chance presented itself: to do everything over again.

2

I was at the post office when Eli called Charlie. All traceable moments were carefully detailed later, in police reports, so I know that at the precise instant the phone rang back at the Moss house, I was standing in the vault of mailboxes staring at a postcard from Ladd Williams. Sarah had one sticky hand wound into my hair and she stared down at the note intently, as if she could read it, too. Ladd had funny, distinctive handwriting—all sharp angles and cubes. I recognized it without having to look at the signature.

I turned the card over. On the front was a picture of a toucan. *Honduras*, it read, under the bird's otherworldly green, red, and blue beak. *Todo Macanudo*. Ladd had gone there with the Peace Corps, but apparently he was back—the card was postmarked

Saturday Cove. The note, which I'd already memorized, read: *Dear Brett. Staying at my uncle's cottage. He has some books you used to want, you can stop by to borrow if you like. Best wishes, Ladd.*

I closed our box, leaving the rest of the mail—bills we couldn't pay—untouched. As I pushed through the door into the sunlight, Sarah plucked the postcard out of my hands. "Cat," she said, looking at the bird. *Cat* was her standard word for anything new. Then, as if she knew this wasn't quite right, amended, "Kitty."

How like Ladd, I thought, not to include a phone number or tell me the titles of the books. If I wanted to know, I'd have to show up on his doorstep. The last time I'd heard from him was just before he left the country, a little more than two years ago. He'd written a sort-of love letter intimating that I was the reason he needed to go away. But it was a convoluted piece of writing, filled with erasures and apologies and semisarcastic jokes, and I didn't know how seriously to take it, or if I'd interpreted it correctly in the first place. I'd also never mentioned it to Charlie.

Sarah brought the postcard to her lips, nibbling delicately on one corner. Part of me wanted to take the bait immediately and drive over to his uncle's compound. I wondered if anyone had told Ladd that I'd had a baby. I buckled Sarah into her car seat and pried the soggy postcard out of her grip. Instead of putting it in my pocket, I just tossed it onto the backseat, where Charlie could find it if he had any interest, which he probably didn't. Charlie never got jealous.

And that's what I thought about on the short drive home: a postcard from an ex-boyfriend. My husband's general lack of jealousy, and how it was probably founded. If Ladd could see me now—with my hair unwashed and sweatpants doing nothing to camouflage the still-leftover pregnancy pounds, not to mention the child all but sewn to my hip—he probably would not be writing cryptic love letters.

What did I know about the way my life would change in a matter of hours? Absolutely nothing. *Murder.* It's a word out of potboilers and film noir. It leaps from the TV screen during police dramas or the evening news. It doesn't sound real. It's nothing you ever think will have to do with you.

AT HOME, THE HOUSE smelled rich with wine and garlic. I walked into the kitchen and plopped Sarah on the floor, then opened the lid on the stock pot and breathed in the damp steam. Coq au vin, to celebrate Sarah's first step. Charlie would let it simmer all day so that it would be falling off the bone by the time we sat down to dinner. Which was lovely, but he had also left the kitchen a wreck. The sauté pan still sat on the stove with olive oil burnt into its copper bottom. The cutting board was exactly where he'd used it, with a garlic-encrusted knife next to it on the counter. I saw the hours of my day tick away with child care, errands, and now this toppled kitchen. I pictured my study upstairs—compromised enough with the baby accoutrements that spread into every room in the house—and decided to go outside and ask Charlie to attend to his appointed parenting duties.

I followed the sound of the hammer to the back deck. Charlie's father planned to come for Thanksgiving; reshingling the house was a surprise for him. In a week of laboring—the stop and start tempo of our life—only one wall had been completed.

"Hey," Charlie said, barely looking back at us.

Seeing her father, Sarah lifted up her arm as if it were an elephant's trunk and trumpeted. "Arrrooo," she said. "Arooo." Charlie laughed and turned, then did the same. Thanks to Babar, Sarah was fascinated by elephants, and this was their customary greeting.

"I got a postcard from Ladd," I said. "He's back in Saturday Cove."

Charlie still hadn't put on a shirt. Broad freckles speckled his fair shoulders and sinewy back. His stomach sloped outward, a healthy and muscular version of distention. In a typically strange but successful act of vanity, he'd tied a leather shoelace around his neck. My resolve to confront him weakened, and I thought—as I often had in the years since I first kissed him—that he was put together exactly right.

"Ladd's home?" Charlie said. "Seems like he just left."

"I guess it's been two years. He says he has a book I might be interested in."

Charlie turned his head half toward me, raising an eyebrow, but the response was more reflexive than agitated. "That's good," he said. "Are you going over there?"

"Maybe later."

"Oh yeah? Think he'll show you his etchings?"

"Sure," I said. And then added, in the baiting tone a marriage counselor had recently warned me against: "Then we'll make out on his chaise longue while Sarah takes a nap on his bed."

Charlie was better at following the counselor's advice. He put down his hammer and turned toward us, reaching out to touch the top of Sarah's head, then mine. He let his palm stay there for a moment, cradling my skull, conferring the warmth of apology, instead of saying anything.

The battered old squirrel we called One-Eyed Wally scrambled across the deck's rail and stood up on its back legs. Sarah pointed and said, "Wally." The squirrel was the closest thing we had to a pet since my cat had been hit by a car in July. Even during Tab's reign, Wally used to sit on the deck's railing waiting for the birdseed or bread crusts we fed him in spite of ourselves. Sarah reached her hand closer to him; instead of running away, he skittered a little closer.

"Shoo," I said mildly, waving my hand at him. "Get away from here."

Charlie climbed off the ladder and headed inside, motioning with his head for me to follow. I adjusted Sarah on my hip and trailed into the kitchen, where Charlie lifted the lid of his simmering pot and stirred. His brow furrowed as he stared into the garlic-scented steam.

"Eli called," he said.

I'd started to put Sarah on the floor—giving her a chance to repeat the earlier steps—but instead picked her up and held her closer.

"How did he sound?" I asked. Last time we saw Charlie's brother, he'd dropped an enormous amount of weight and begun scribbling notes on his jeans and forearms.

"He wants to come by tonight," Charlie said. "Get out of the city for a couple days."

"Did he sound like he'd been taking his meds?"

"He didn't sound too bad."

Charlie brought the wooden spoon to his lips and tasted his sauce. I stood there, balancing Sarah on one hip. In my whole life, there had never been anything in the world I wanted more than a home with Charlie. Not so long ago I wouldn't have cared if that home were borrowed from his father, or if the sink were piled with dishes, or if Eli lived there permanently. I would have lived with Charlie in a cave, or a tepee. I would have followed him anywhere.

"I told Eli it would be okay," Charlie said.

"But Charlie," I said. "If he's off his meds."

"His roommates kicked him out," Charlie said. "He's got nowhere else to go."

I started to nod and then stopped, not wanting Charlie to interpret the gesture as agreement that Eli should come to us. Every other year or so, these phone calls would begin. Sometimes they'd come from Eli or from the animal-control office where he worked. Sometimes the calls would come from his roommates, or new friends—people who'd only known him since his latest recovery and couldn't understand the change.

"Do you know why they kicked him out? Did he do something? Were they frightened?"

"No," Charlie said. "They weren't frightened. They kicked him out because he's behind on the rent."

"That's what Eli says."

"True," he admitted, still stirring, not looking at me.

"If he can't pay rent, does that mean Kathy put him on leave again?" Kathy was Eli's supervisor at the Angell Animal Shelter. "Have you called her?"

"I left her a message," Charlie said.

"Well, why don't you talk to her before you let him come here?"

Charlie let his shoulders tense. He turned toward me and leaned against the stove. I worried about hot liquid spattering onto his bare back. "What are you saying?" he asked. "You want me to tell him he can't come?"

"You know I'm always happy to see Eli. Except when he's off his meds."

"But Brett," Charlie said. "That's when he needs us most."

The words worked, for a moment at least. Guilt silenced me. But the weight of Sarah in my arms let me recover. "It's different now," I said. "It's not just us." Charlie didn't respond—his form of shouting. So I kept talking. "We told him the rules when we moved in here. No visits unless he's medicated."

"It's Eli's house as much as mine," Charlie said. Infuriatingly. It had been his idea to move to his father's house, in the eighth year of my PhD—when my teaching appointment had run out and my last possible fellowship could barely cover our expenses even if we lived rent-free. I had foreseen this moment—Eli's encroachment—since Charlie first formulated the plan. Charlie had sworn it would never be an issue.

"You promised," I reminded him.

He turned his gaze out the window and crossed his arms, the wooden spoon still in his hand, warm sauce dripping to the floor. Sarah squirmed, anxious to practice her new stepping skills. "Down," she insisted. I tightened my grip and she let out a squawk of protest.

"I'm sorry," I said. "But it sounds like Eli's off his meds. So if he comes here, Sarah and I have to leave."

Charlie's face looked placid, but I could see the veins in his neck pop up. Once, he told me a dream he'd had about his brother, where an adult Charlie walked along the beach and stumbled upon seven-year-old Eli building sand castles.

"Eli," Charlie said, in the dream. "Are you all right?"

"Yes," Eli told him. "I am. I'm all right." And they'd danced along the shore together, in celebration and relief.

I put Sarah down on her precarious little feet. This time her attempt at a step failed and she teetered onto her bottom. A good sport, she grabbed the baggy fabric at my knee and pulled herself back to standing. Then she let go and executed one, two, three steps, exhibiting the wisdom of waiting till you can do a thing right. Charlie and I were too absorbed to congratulate her.

"One night," Charlie said, lowering his voice to imploring. It felt strange and unnatural not to relent to that tone. Before Sarah's birth, he always won our arguments. I would rather have capitulated than have him be angry at me. But circumstances had shifted these past fifteen months. Before, I'd only been mildly aware of my physical limitations. Moderately athletic, I considered myself in good strong shape, but Sarah's helplessness had made me acutely aware of my size. I tried to comfort myself by remembering I had the ability to protect her from all the usual dangers: deep water, oncoming traffic, her own unsteady footing. But my imagination— the ability to conjure up more extraordinary evils—made me wish for the claws and strength of a mountain lion, a grizzly bear, a wolf. Evolution, I thought, had shortchanged human mothers, giving us nothing but brains to protect our babies.

"He's my brother," Charlie said to my continued silence, his voice not exactly pleading, but defeated in its matter-of-factness.

"I'm your wife," I said. "This is your daughter."

Charlie's eyes narrowed, as if that implication—that he didn't take our connection to him as seriously as Eli's—pained him too much to warrant a response.

"Goddamn it, Charlie," I said.

His eyes narrowed, breath gathering as if gearing up for a fight. He lay the wooden spoon across the top of the pot, steam rising up, soaking the porous fibers. Charlie adjusted his shoulders, softened his face. It was one of his talents, halting a disagreement suddenly, harnessing his ability to see the larger world through the mountains of time he would have later, to manage it all.

"Look," he said. "If you're worried, take Sarah over to Maxine's for the night. I'll get a feel for how things are with Eli. And we can take it from there."

Which would mean saying good-bye to all the work I had to do. I felt the familiar anger start to bubble up and fought against it with a deep and steadying breath. Charlie's face looked pleading, waiting for me to shift into reason—meaning, waiting for me to shift into agreement with him. I let the words form in my head as if they were my own ideas: Eli could be in trouble. And days would spill forth on the other side of this difficulty, plenty of room for my dissertation. I didn't want to fight.

"Okay," I agreed, on an exhale. "Will you let me know how he seems?"

"I'll call," Charlie said.

He put both hands on my shoulders, warmth radiating from his palms, the nearness that was second nature to both of us. He kissed me good-bye. When I went upstairs to call Maxine and pack for Sarah and me, I could hear him out on the deck, the sound of his hammer, pounding one more new shingle into the outside wall.

3

Sarah fell asleep on the drive to Maxine's. In the driveway, I unbuckled her in slow motion, easing her out of her car seat with the most careful possible movements, leaving the passenger door open as I hoisted her over my shoulder. Maxine walked out onto the porch looking coolly put together, strands of blonde hair swept off her forehead with a small tortoiseshell clip—the kind of careful details I couldn't be bothered with anymore.

"Hey," she said, her voice full of sympathy, the way you greet someone who has an illness in the family.

I walked past her and lay Sarah down on the daybed by a wide, sunny window. She emitted the tiniest hiccup of a waking breath, eyelids fluttering, then sighed back to sleep. I went outside to shut the car door, then came back. The expensive hush of Maxine's remodeled saltbox felt like a bubble of unexpected calm. Maxine had won the house in a settlement from her second husband; it had vaulted ceilings and spectacular water views of Alden Lake. In a couple weeks, Maxine would head back to her winter house in Newton. I'd never been there but suspected it was at least as lovely as this place and wondered for a moment what it would be like—to live balanced between two such well-appointed homes.

"Can I get you a cup of coffee?" Maxine asked.

"What I'd really love is a shower," I said. "I didn't get a chance to take one this morning."

"Of course!" She gestured expansively toward the upstairs; then her eyes fluttered toward the daybed as she realized I wasn't asking for the guest bathroom so much as babysitting services. "Not to worry," Maxine said, trying not to sound dubious. "I'll watch her. There are clean towels under the sink."

STANDING BENEATH THE RUSH of hot water in the lilac-scented guest bathroom, I thought of the postcard from Ladd and wondered which books he meant. When I'd packed to come to Maxine's, I'd made a conscious decision to leave my work behind, but if I had new books—important books—I could at least start looking through them. I turned off the water, half expecting to hear Sarah crying downstairs but happily hearing only the settling of water.

Ten minutes later I came down the stairs in a tank top and long, crinkly skirt, toweling off my hair. Maxine sat in an armchair nearby, leafing through a magazine. Sarah still snoozed safely in the middle of the bed. "Hi," I said. Maxine looked up, clearly proud that Sarah still slept.

"Look at you," she said. "All clean."

I rolled my eyes. "That should not be a compliment for a thirty-three-year-old woman."

"Thirty-two," Maxine corrected. "You've still got another two weeks."

"Barely." I ran my hand over the nubby back of her couch and said, "Listen. I need to pick up some books at a friend's. Do you mind watching Sarah for a little bit longer while I run out and do that?"

Maxine looked over at my daughter. The small, napping stretch of time had given her a false sense of confidence. "Absolutely," she said. "You take as much time as you need." Sarah made a small, gurgling sound in her throat and Maxine amended. "Thirty minutes should be no problem at all."

Now when I examine that day—going over it again and again in my mind—I don't collect the books from Ladd's cottage. Instead I realize that if Sarah and I need protecting, then so does Charlie. So I drive back home.

"Look," I remind Charlie. "I love Eli, too."

I never say this in the past tense, because I do love Eli, even now, after all that's happened. That day, in my reenvisioning, I invite my husband back to Maxine's.

"Eli can stay at the house for a few days," I tell Charlie. "He doesn't even have to know where we are."

Charlie listens carefully. He hears me. He packs a bag and

comes along with me to Maxine's, where he will be safe. Where he will continue.

But that's not what happened. Instead I went to see Ladd, who had found some books I'd been pining after for a long time, *The Years and Hours of Emily Dickinson*. The volumes were impossible to find, as they'd been stolen from every library, even Widener. I'd tacked my name and phone number to bulletin boards of rare bookstores across New England, in case one or both volumes ever appeared. It was so like Ladd, to remember that I wanted them. Leaving his place, I let the car idle at the end of Eldredge Lane. The dashboard clock read 3:36, but it felt much later. One thing that continually astonished me in my life as a parent was how much *day* I had now that a child demanded my waking before first light. It seemed, today, I had already been up for so long, so much had already happened.

The sun moved a little lower and a little stronger, as if settling into the late afternoon. I could feel its heat, an Indian summer sort of warmth that raised the hair on my forearms, and I lowered the driver's-side window. At the same moment, I caught a glimpse of myself in the side view mirror. My skin had a pinkish glow. I thought, for the first time in ages, that I looked passably pretty.

Seven years ago, I had left Ladd Williams. With only the smallest bit of encouragement, I had run away from everything my life was supposed to become. Driving away from him now, with the dusty volumes resting on the passenger seat, I remembered one of the earliest of those days. This is not hindsight or revisionist history. I remember it absolutely, thinking as I drove, about walking on the beach with Charlie in the days when we were first together. That day—the day I remembered—I didn't have a bathing suit. So when Charlie went out to swim I stood on the sand and watched him. Staring out to sea, I didn't expect Charlie to stop or wave to me any more than I'd expect that from a porpoise. It felt like enough just to stand there, watching him, knowing he'd swim back to me before too long. And my chest swelled with a very specific sort of joy.

Charlie dove into the waves, disappearing, then reemerged. He stopped for a moment, getting his bearings, searching the sand. Looking for me. Across the water, I could sense more than see him smile. I thought of a stanza from an Emily Dickinson poem, which— if you believed my dissertation—had been written for Sue:

> She beckons, and the woods start—
> She nods, and all begin—
> Surely—such a country
> I was never in!

At that moment, the world settled in around me. Mist off the ocean draped itself over my skin. I could smell beach plum, rotting snails, and festering seaweed draped over rocks. Not so far away, Charlie dipped and dove under a sun that still insisted on summer. And I didn't just love him. I loved him enough to stop caring about anything else. I loved him enough to wreck my life. I loved him the way you dream about *being* loved, when you don't even know you're dreaming.

LATER, THE POLICE TOLD me that Eli arrived a little after five. A neighbor saw his VW Golf pull into the driveway. A few hours later, I was putting Sarah to bed. She sprawled out in the middle of the queen-sized mattress—a fortress of pillows and sofa cushions surrounding her. Charlie and I had never been able to get Sarah into a crib. The first four months of her life, we'd traded off sleeping with her on our chests. Since then, she'd slept snuggled blissfully between us. Once I was sure she'd fallen asleep, I tiptoed down Maxine's staircase. Walking into her kitchen, I could see the moonlight shine off the lake through professionally washed windows. Everything seemed peaceful and clean. Maxine poured me a glass of white wine and topped off her own while I placed the baby monitor on the kitchen table.

"So, have you talked to Charlie?" Maxine asked. She and I had met a few years before at the antique shop where she worked in the summer, making her the only person I knew in Saturday Cove whose original connection wasn't to my husband's family. Or Ladd's.

"He hasn't called yet. I'll call him in a bit if I don't hear from him."

Maxine nodded. "It must be so hard," she said. "The whole thing with Eli."

"It's the worst," I said, taking an especially deep sip of wine. A book Charlie and I had read, *Surviving Schizophrenia*, called it "the death of a living relative." The phrase had seemed exactly apt until the day Eli read the same book and held out the page where I'd underlined that sentence, his face wounded and broken. *Brett*, he'd said. *I'm right here. I'm very much alive.*

"Do you think Eli's dangerous?" Maxine asked.

"No," I said, then paused. Because it sounded dishonest. If I didn't think Eli was dangerous, what was I doing here?

"It's all . . ." I put down my glass, gathering the right words in my head. And there were no right words, really, for the heartbreaking and complicated mess of it. I settled on saying, "It's just not something for a child to be around."

Maxine nodded and put her hand over mine. Despite the conversation topic, it felt so nice, just sitting in someone else's clean house, someone else's uncomplicated life, talking to a friend, drinking a glass of wine. Funny how Sarah always seemed so paramount, and then the rare moments without her could feel like the most natural thing in the world. As if on cue, a disgruntled moan peeped through the monitor. Maxine and I stared at it, holding our breath, to see if it would evolve into a full-on wail.

Which it did. I took the steps two at a time to reach Sarah before she could roll over the cushions and onto the hardwood floor.

I MEANT TO GO back to Maxine and my wine. But it took so long to calm Sarah from waking up alone in a strange place. And she felt so plush and loving—warm insistence on wrapping her little body into mine. At some point I lulled down along with her. When I opened my eyes, the bedside clock read eleven, and it took a moment for memory to catch up with my anxiety.

Maxine must have already gone to bed. I got up and tiptoed to the landing, but downstairs was dark. I pictured her, hours earlier, rinsing out my wine glass before turning out the lights. I went back to the guest room and checked my phone. No messages. I pressed 1 on my speed dial.

"Hey," I said, when Charlie's voice mail picked up. "It's me. Call right back, okay?" I hung up and waited a few seconds, then dialed again. "Charlie," I said. "You said you would call. So please call as soon as you get this. Okay?"

My phone lay silent in my hand. Beside me on the bed, Sarah slept on her back, her arms spread wide as if she'd been making snow angels. I thought about calling back and leaving another, nicer message. Maybe he and Eli had gone out together. The idea of Eli well enough to socialize cheered me and at the same time riddled me with self-doubt for abandoning both of them. I crawled back under the covers.

SARAH WOKE THREE TIMES that night, and each time after I calmed her back to sleep, I tried to call Charlie. He must be sleeping, I told myself after the second call. But the phone didn't go straight to voice mail. It rang. Charlie usually turned off his phone before he went to sleep.

Three a.m. Even if they had gone out, all the bars and restaurants were closed now. What could be keeping him from answering, from calling? I tried dialing the home phone. The old answering machine didn't pick up, and I just lay there, listening to the endless ringing and watching the first strands of sun reach through the linen curtains.

"I HOPE EVERYTHING'S ALL right," I said to Maxine while she ate breakfast. I couldn't stomach any food. Sarah perched on my knee, chewing on a toasted bagel.

"Maybe he's sleeping in," Maxine said. "Or maybe Eli's really bad and he doesn't want to tell you."

"Oh, that's comforting," I said, and Maxine laughed. "It's just not like Charlie," I went on, "not to call when he said he would."

Maxine looked away, out the window, as if she weren't so convinced of Charlie's reliability. Sarah wailed as I attempted to wipe her face. When she quieted, I called the landline again; its un-answered rings sounded canned, old-fashioned, as if I were calling Timbuktu rather than two miles away.

"I'd better go over there," I told Maxine. "Do you mind watching Sarah for half an hour?"

Maxine was way too polite to point out that this was the same time frame I'd suggested yesterday. She and Sarah eyed each other warily.

"Okay," Maxine said, her voice displeased but resolute. "But really just half an hour this time."

I left quickly, not realizing till I was halfway there that I'd left my phone on Maxine's breakfast counter.

CHARLIE'S PARENTS HAD BOUGHT their house and its oceanfront acre years ago. A two-story, cedar-shingled cape with picture windows looking out on the bay, back then it had been a modest old house in a modest seaside neighborhood. These days there was no such thing as a modest seaside neighborhood, and his father routinely battled the temptation of selling. The only people who could afford to buy beachfront property had too much money to spare. While neighbors succumbed and trophy houses rose up like skyscrapers, the Moss residence stood low to the ground in rebellious disrepair. Other than the ocean view, it boasted nothing in the way of luxury except the wide green lawn where Charlie and I had been married. As I pulled in behind his battered old Golf, I could see Eli pacing back and forth across the grass, the bay clear and calm in the distance. It seemed odd that his little dog, Lightfoot, wasn't following at his feet.

My tires rumbled over the seashell and pebble driveway, and

I thought of another time I'd rounded a corner and stumbled upon Eli, my sophomore year of college in Colorado, another September day. My birthday, in fact. I'd gone home the back way to find Eli outside, blowing up a package of balloons one by one, and floating them into my open bedroom window. Eli had stood there in the sunlight, concentrating on his task, then looking up at me—caught—his cheeks puffed with air. "You were supposed to go in the front door," he said. His fair, straight hair stood slightly on end from the static electricity, and his face was pink from exertion. We walked around together, through the front door and into my bedroom, where balloons rolled around at our feet and floated inches above the floorboards, filling my room with color and air. I remember the happiness at the center of my throat, bubbling up, that someone would do this for me. I remember it happening, and I remember remembering it, over and over so many times that it feels like just that—a continuing moment that happened over and over again. It occurs in a series of cartoon infinity bubbles.

But on this other September day, New England's sunlight shone dimmer, more nuanced than Colorado's, and the years had rendered Eli a less welcome sight. At the same time, he was so familiar that in person I didn't feel afraid of him. I left my keys in the ignition as I waved broadly. Without Sarah, my mother-lion hackles receded. Eli and I had been young together. We had climbed Long's Peak. We'd eaten pancakes at midnight in cheap diners. He had filled my room with balloons on my nineteenth birthday, and given me away at my wedding.

Eli's blond hair, bright and unfaded like Charlie's, hung past his shoulders. He wore a white T-shirt with a funky batik design—more like something that would belong to his brother—and faded jeans that were covered with his tiny, slanted handwriting, rows and columns that looked almost like Asian characters. There was a pen in his right hand, and for a moment he stopped to scribble something new onto his jeans. Then began pacing again. The last time I saw Eli he'd been wearing his animal-control uniform, a khaki polyester blend that stretched over his medication-bloated stomach. Now he looked gaunt, lean, and agitated—almost like a second entity, broken loose from the foggy bulk of compliance. I'd seen him in this state often enough to know that up close his eyes would be a clear, electric blue, echoing the boy I'd known in college. But I'd also see deep grooves in his brow. Elaborate lines spiderwebbed around his eyes. If the two brothers had been standing together, Charlie would easily have appeared the younger of the two.

"Eli." I waved my arms over my head. "Hey."

He stopped short, then held his palm up toward me like a crossing guard. "Stop, Brett," he said. "Stop right there."

I walked a few steps closer. And then I stopped, but not because of his gesture or command, but because I was close enough to see that Eli's shirt did not actually have a funky design. It was just plain white, spattered with what looked like brick-colored paint. Lots of it. I tried to remember where such a color would come from, what he and Charlie would have been painting. The only project I knew of were those pale brown shingles, which would soon enough fade to gray in the salty Cape Cod air.

"What's on your shirt?" I said to Eli.

"Stay back," he said. "It's not safe here." The words sounded anguished and completely sincere. As if the old Eli—somewhere inside this pacing madman—called out to me in warning.

"Where's Charlie?" My voice seemed to come from somewhere involuntary: behind me, or above. I could feel my throat constrict, and despite one instant of wondering, I knew that this was not a dream. In a dream, I wouldn't have been able to speak at all.

Eli lifted one arm, wraithlike, and pointed to the back of the house. "Charlie's right where he's always been," he said, his voice rising, not making any sense. Eli never made any sense when he was like this.

I have never been good at dealing with agitated people. Charlie, on the other hand, was excellent at conferring his own self-possession. He had a knack for calming people in distress. As I walked around the house, obediently following Eli's still-outstretched point, I found myself desperately wishing for my husband to step forward and intervene.

Because I knew already that he couldn't. Although my back was to him, Eli's aged and bloodless face loomed clearly in front of me. And I knew that Charlie wouldn't walk out of the house to help. I wouldn't have been able to articulate it or explain my exact thoughts as I headed toward the back deck. My emotions had gone AWOL. I forgot to be frightened of Eli or worried for Charlie. I didn't even think about Sarah. I just floated across the lawn, my eyes flitting habitually out toward the water. I squinted at a cluster of cormorants on a tall rock, holding their wings out to dry, then turned my eyes back to the house. And if I had paused in that moment and closed my eyes, I think I would have been able to conjure up exactly what waited for me.

Everything in my life so far had led to this point. If I'd done one thing differently—slept an hour later last Sunday, voiced a complaint I'd suppressed four years before, worn my hair up instead of down on a Friday night. If I hadn't picked up those books yesterday afternoon, or made love to Charlie the first night I met him. Certainly if I'd never known Eli: this morning would have played out differently, if it had ever occurred at all.

THE FIRST THING I saw were the bottoms of his feet, close together but flayed out in V formation. They looked calloused and dirty—Charlie's long, bony feet, tough enough to traverse the rocky bluff without sandals.

Behind me, a spectral and disturbing noise: Eli, beginning to weep. My flip-flops thwacked across the deck. A chickadee let out its seven-note cry. My body operated in jerky, oafish movements and I tripped over Charlie's hammer. I looked down to see blood and hair caked on its claw and kicked it aside with instinctive revulsion.

"Brett," Eli yelled from the lawn. "Is he still there?" The question, his voice, was still tinged with weeping. And I knew I would have to answer eventually, because we were in this together. The three of us.

Charlie's eyes stared wide, a glassy and expressionless blue. Not surprised or wounded—simply vacated. His jaw had fixed into a rodentlike and grossly uncharacteristic overbite. Blood and what may have been bone matted his curls against the left side of his head. But what caused the most blood—still wet enough to soak through the knees of my jeans as I knelt beside him—was an injury I didn't understand: his throat, slit wide open. For a moment, I mistook the gash for the leather shoelace he'd tied there yesterday; but the makeshift necklace was gone, in its place this crude and horrible injury.

Charlie. I pressed my hands over the wound on his neck as if I could staunch the blood, but it was cold as yesterday's coffee. I scrunched my nose against the scent of minced garlic.

"Brett," Eli called again. "Do you see him?"

"Yes," I said, surprised at the clear, unshaking way my voice carried. "He's still here."

"Is he dead?"

I couldn't answer, I couldn't say it. It must have been shock. Even in that moment, the word formed in my head, *shock*, and I knew it as the cause of this strange emptiness. I also knew my responsibility as first person to arrive on the scene. Charlie had no carotid artery left, so I pressed my thumb against his wrist, searching for a pulse.

"He's alive," I lied, my voice raised in that unnatural calm. "You better stay back."

I looked down to Charlie's feet and then to his shoulders, trying to ascertain whether I could pick him up and carry him to the car. I put one hand under his ruined neck, one hand under his waist. We used to joke about my being strong enough to piggyback him. He would climb up onto my back and I would pitch forward, staggering under his full weight. Once I hurt my knee, hauling him up a slope on Mount Washington. When we got back to our hotel, Charlie had fixed me a drink and an ice pack. I'd elevated my knee on his lap, and we laughed at the ridiculousness of my injury. Now my hand sloshed against the slickness under his neck, and his head slapped against the deck as if I'd broken something. My body let out a noise—a whooshing gust of air. The sound of panic surprised me; my brain hadn't yet recognized my body's terror.

"Brett," Eli called again, his voice agitated but oddly normal, as if I were taking too long bringing him a beer. "What's going on?"

My mind sifted through possible answers. I didn't know what was going on. My eyes fell on that hammer and then the knife—the two murder weapons, still here, still handy. I wondered how many seconds it would take Eli to stride across the lawn and use them on me. And instead of fearing for myself, I had the most primal vision of being gone forever, following Charlie, the clouds overhead parting to let us both through. From my perch, far up above, I could see Maxine walking Sarah through the gorgeous, sterile rooms of her house while my child screamed with anguish and loss, having no idea these emotions would become permanent. For a child to lose her father was horrible, awful. But for a child to lose her father *and* her mother: nothing could be worse, an orphaned grief that would stretch through the end of her days.

I let go of Charlie and slipped out of my flip-flops to crawl across the deck, my hands and knees smearing his blood across the unstained wood. When my hands touched the stones of the driveway, I stood up like a toddler, pushing up off the ground. Then I ran. Shells and stone bit into the heels of my feet, nowhere near as conditioned as Charlie's to take the beating. Behind me, I could hear Eli's footsteps on the deck. I could hear him scream—as if this were his first glimpse of Charlie. And I thought for a minute that perhaps someone else had done it, that Eli had arrived and found Charlie murdered. Maybe he had leaned over him, the same way I had, and that's how the blood had managed to decorate his shirt.

But my body wouldn't take that chance. It hurtled away fast as possible and threw itself into the car and locked the door. It gunned the motor and flew out onto the road—leaving the past, and flesh of its flesh—behind, and cold, forever.

SARAH'S CRIES CAREENED THROUGH the windows as I ran toward Maxine's house, a steady stream of, "Mommy, Mommy, Mommy." I threw open the front door.

"Hey," Maxine called from the kitchen. Her usually perfect hair flew in every direction, bouncing my distraught child on her hip. "Are we glad to—"

When she stepped into the hallway, her relieved smile disappeared.

"Brett," she said, pulling Sarah closer to her as she stopped crying and reached out for me. "Jesus Christ. What happened to you?"

I looked down at myself. Blood dried and caked in the cracks of my palms. It soaked my T-shirt and my shorts. Behind me, my bare feet had left prints on her wood floor. I pulled off my shirt and bent over to wipe them clean.

"God, don't worry about that," Maxine said. "Tell me what happened, Brett. Are you hurt?"

I pictured Charlie's mortal injuries. His unblinking blue eyes. Before today, I hadn't even known the definition of hurt. Now I didn't know what to say. I had made my modest academic career out of a reverence for the power of words. So I knew that the second I said it aloud—engineering the metamorphosis from trauma to statement—the events would become permanent. If I said, "Charlie's dead," he would be dead. The world would have no choice but to continue without him.

"Mommy," Sarah said, shaking her arms insistently.

I looked down again at my shirt—my arms, hands, knees, feet. What Sarah saw was my not reaching back toward her, and the cries began again. I lifted my arms to hold her, then pulled them back. How could I hold my baby when I was soaked with her father's blood?

"Maxine," I said. "We have to lock all the doors. We have to call the police."

She nodded and began to hand Sarah to me—then stopped, equally unsure how to cope with the blood. "Should we hose you off?" she asked.

"Not outside," I said, hearing—more than feeling—the panic in my voice as it occurred to me for the first time that Eli could have followed me in his car. My strongest impulse, running from the Moss house, had been to get to Sarah. I remembered a story I'd found in my research, of a nineteenth-century Amherst mother who'd accidentally lit herself on fire with a kerosene lamp. As the fire engulfed her, she'd reached for her infant in a reflexive, protective grab, and they'd both gone up in flames. *What if the killer had followed me.* I turned around and bolted the front door shut.

"What else," I shouted at Maxine. "Show me all the doors." She followed me to the back door, while Sarah wailed in her arms. We dead bolted the door to the cellar.

"I think that's all of them," Maxine said. We ran up, into her bedroom. "What should I say?" she asked, picking up the phone. "I don't know," I said. "Just tell them to come here."

"Not to your place?"

"No," I said. "I want them here first." Maxine dialed obediently, awkwardly, as Sarah struggled in her grip, reaching her arms out to me.

"I'm sorry," I said. "I'm sorry, my sweet. But Mommy has to take a shower."

Maxine jutted her chin toward her bathroom. "There's an emergency," I heard her say as I turned on the hot water to full blast. I wondered how they would hear her over Sarah's crying. In the next room, I could only just make out her explanation as tears started to grip her voice: "I'm not sure. But it's bad. It's very bad. My friend is covered in blood."

She hung up and came into the bathroom as I rasped a loofah over my bloodstained knees and feet. The stream of hot water scalded my back. Charlie's blood poured off me, eddying in spirals before fading and disappearing into the drain. I dropped the sponge and pulled the shower curtain aside.

"Lock the door," I told her, and she pressed in the doorknob's button—a flimsy apparatus designed for avoiding embarrassing intrusions, not keeping out murderers. I turned off the water and wrapped a towel around myself. Finally, I took my sobbing daughter from Maxine and sat down against the wall. The Spanish tile felt cool and soothing on my parboiled back. Sarah's cries subsided into wounded hiccups. Finally in my arms, exhaustion took over. Her tired little eyelids blinked as warm water dripped off my shoulders and onto her face.

"Did you call them?" I asked Maxine, though I knew she had.

"They're on their way." She sat down next to me, and I saw tears standing in her eyes.

"Brett," she said. "Please tell me what happened."

"I can't."

Maxine nodded and placed one hand on my knee. We listened for a while to Sarah's snuffling breaths, waiting for the police to arrive. Years ago, Charlie and I met with a family therapist for help in navigating his brother. At the time, Eli had been in one of his worst states—manic and unreachable. I asked the therapist what we should do if he seemed dangerous. "Just dial 911," she had said, with a blithe wave of her hand. "They'll be there before anything can happen." Sitting in Maxine's bathroom, I could feel the minutes tick away, and I wondered how many times someone could have killed Charlie—could have killed any of us—in the time it took for the police to appear.

"Will they ring the bell, do you think?" I asked, after a few minutes.

"I guess so." The words were barely out of her mouth when the doorbell rang.

"God," I said. "How do we know it's them?"

"I'll go to the front window and look down," she said. She stood up and unlocked the bathroom door, then turned back toward me, obviously afraid to go alone.

"We'll come with you," I said. Maxine handed me the plaid flannel robe from a hook on the door. I tied it around Sarah and me. From the upstairs hall window, we looked down at her front door. A police cruiser parked in the driveway, its lights blinking.

"What can I do for you?" Maxine whispered as we turned to go downstairs.

Nothing, of course. But instead of brushing the request aside, I did the oddest thing. I lifted my free hand and touched Maxine's cheek. As my palm pressed against her skin, I noticed a small, rust-colored smear staining the back of my wrist.

I said, "Tell Charlie I love him."

Relief fell across her face like color returning after a shock. "I will," she promised. "Of course I will."

Underneath Maxine's robe, Sarah's head rested—almost asleep—on my shoulder. I closed my eyes, existing for a moment in the warm breath against my neck. And then I pictured Maxine: standing on our deck, her hair tousling in the autumn breeze. Charlie perched on his rickety ladder, the unblemished hammer in his hands.

"Brett loves you," Maxine would say.

And Charlie would smile—that slow, easy and face-changing expression. "I know," he would say, taking a nail from his mouth.

I see it clearly as I've seen anything in my entire life. I see Charlie, tapping in that nail. The world around him buzzes with seasonal changes—monarchs and birds swirling in migratory preparation, the sun dipping down earlier and farther east. The world around him quietly poised for my uneventful return—fulfilling promises as a matter of course, and utterly lacking violence.

I see this moment, again and again. I try my hardest to will it into being as I go over the past, trying to make things turn out differently, trying to make things lead, instead, to Charlie, alive and smiling on that deck.

. . .

BUT I CAN'T. THEY don't. It never does. No matter how many times I relive it, we always end up—Maxine, Sarah, and I—standing in that upstairs window, staring down at those twirling police lights. While back at the house on the bay, Eli leans over his brother's bloody and vacated body. He watches Charlie, for how many minutes nobody knows. And then he disappears, escaping on an invisible tightrope wire that leads to the rest of his ruined life, and prevents mine from possibly ever moving forward. Unless I can take all the pieces and unravel them into clear formation, making sense—a pattern, an answer—where none can ever be found.

PART TWO

It's all I have to bring today—
This, and my heart beside—
This, and my heart, and all the fields—
And all the meadows wide—

—EMILY DICKINSON

4

The first time I saw Charlie Moss I was eighteen years old. A blizzard had just swept through the front range of the Rocky Mountains. I called my friend Eli from the phone booth outside my dorm room. The west-facing window at the end of the hall had lost its view except for a thick, whorled crust of ice.

"Is the party still on?" I asked him.

"What do you think?" he said. I laughed. Eli loved parties. He would never let a mere three feet of snow interfere with a social event, especially one of his own. "You can meet my brother," Eli said. "He was supposed to leave this morning, but the storm closed down DIA."

A few hours later, I walked through deserted, unplowed streets.

A typical Colorado storm, it had hit fast and furiously and then moved on. The sky above me loomed clear as summer, boasting a thousand stars or more. I felt too warm in my heavy down jacket. Still, there was that sense of reprieve inclement weather can bring. As if all ills—crime, taxes, homework assignments—had been suspended for the sake of the storm. In the forgiving snow-lit night, the ramshackle Victorians—these days rented by destructive and unappreciative students—looked more like the comfortable miners' homes they'd originally been. Soft lamps shone behind curtains. Wood smoke trailed up from chimneys.

In all that quiet, I could detect the pulse of Eli's party from a block away. As I headed up his walk, I saw the door was propped open; the thicket of people must have overheated even his drafty old house. The front path was littered with skis, snowshoes, and boots. I entered sideways and slid off my coat but didn't bother removing my boots. The hallway was already caked with melting ice and snow.

"Hey, Brett," Eli shouted.

He was leaning in the arched doorway to the living room. Three other roommates lived here, but Eli was the one who positioned himself to greet every guest, gregarious and mannerly, with too-long hair and a beer buzz already evident at first glance. Not wanting to distract him from his hosting duties, I waved and continued toward the kitchen, where I knew the keg would be. I planned to get a beer and then go station myself beside Eli. That was my standard strategy at parties, to let him do all the talking, laughter the only noise I'd have to make. In the kitchen, my Sorrels skidded slightly across the crooked, snow-muddied wood floors. And there was Charlie: standing by the stove, stirring something in a large, warped tin pot, his lean form haloed by steam. A few girls sat at the table, talking loudly and throwing back their hair— probably for his benefit. I didn't recognize him as Eli's brother, though I would have if I'd looked carefully. They shared the same angular jaw, fair hair, and round blue eyes. Charlie's handsomeness registered in the crowded room as a matter of course, so intrinsic as to be almost secondary. He looked too old to be here, and I wondered what he was cooking.

"Hey," he said to me, as I took my place in line for the keg. "Bring that cup over here. This is better suited to the weather."

At eighteen, I was nothing if not obedient. I walked over and held out my red plastic cup. He filled it with what looked like hot cocoa, but the steam smelled thickly of rum and Frangelico. I saw a box of Ghirardelli chocolate squares on the counter. I'd never seen anyone make hot chocolate out of anything but powder. I lifted the cup to my face, bathing my skin in the fragrant steam. I drank the hot liquid while chunks of snow melted and dripped toward my ankles.

Over the years, I would ask Charlie repeatedly: why did he single me out in that moment? He always gave the same, unsatisfying answer. "I just happened to look up, and there you were."

What I remember is Charlie's curly blond head, bent in concentration over his steaming brew. Without particular design or awareness, I stepped into the only place available, waiting to get a beer. And true to his own recollection, just at that moment Charlie looked up. And there I was. That day, the first day I ever saw him, he had three days' worth of stubble. He wore a thin black thread around his neck, beaded with a smooth lapis stone that matched the color of his eyes. When I looked at him, his lips slid upward at the corners. My heart lurched. I don't know why. It just did. It lurched toward him and refused—stubbornly—to ever lurch away.

"I'm Brett," I said.

"Brett," he repeated, instead of telling me his name. He added a cheerful, staccato sound to the t's, making them really sound like two. "Like Lady Brett Ashley."

I stared at him. "That's who I'm named after," I said. "My parents were English professors. It was either that or Claudine, after the Colette novels."

His face went slightly blank, and I knew I'd lost him but I kept on talking. "Mom wanted to be a writer. She said that Colette's husband used to lock her in a room until she'd written however many pages he wanted. That's how the Claudine books got written."

"So your mom wanted to be locked in a room?"

"I think she just wanted to be encouraged. Have you read a lot of Hemingway?"

"No," Charlie admitted. "I didn't even read *The Sun Also Rises*, to tell you the truth. I just listened to them talk about it in class."

I laughed. If I were him, having already impressed me with the reference, I would have lied. In fact, because I wanted a point of commonality, I lied in the opposite direction. "I haven't read it either," I said, and he smiled.

It should have bothered me that Charlie hadn't actually read the book. My mother was an English professor. My father had been, too. The little house I grew up in had book-lined walls in every single room. What's more, I'd just finished a course on the Victorian novel that had electrified me. Fresh from a high school career that had gravely disappointed my mother, I wasn't used to getting excited about anything academic. As a freshman, I imagined my primary focus in college would be exactly this: standing on a sticky floor in a crowded kitchen. Drinking beer and talking to a cute boy. But last semester, I had actually foregone parties to stay in my room and read through the thick paid-by-the-word novels. I had slogged dutifully through subplots and unfamiliar language. I had forgiven the coincidence in Dickens and aspired to the moral imperatives of Eliot. In other words, I had lost myself in the *stories*, falling asleep every night anticipating the next evolution a book would bring.

Charlie's intelligence, I would discover years later, lay more in the realm of the physical. He had an intuitive and sometimes uncanny understanding of what would feel good, taste good, look good. My mother used to say he dressed like a European, with small flourishes that should have looked feminine but never did. He could glean obscure details about people just by looking at them.

That first night, after telling me he was Eli's brother, Charlie asked me my last name.

"Mercier," I told him.

And he said, "Ah, French."

"Mais oui," I said, very nearly the only two words I spoke of the language.

Charlie touched my jaw with the underside of his knuckle. "I should have known," he said. "I studied cooking in Paris. This curve here: very, very French." We stood on the back porch now, still wedged between everyone else's shoulders. Our breath spiraled upward like the wood-smoke trails.

"You know, it's too bad," Charlie said, "to waste this night crammed in such a mob scene."

I laughed, recognizing a come-on when I heard one. Still, that heart stayed lurched—affixing my feet exactly next to him. "Where else would we go?" I asked. "In case you didn't notice, there's three feet of snow out here."

"Which makes it perfect for a moonlight ski," he said. "Eli's got plenty of equipment in the garage."

We worked our way around the side of the house and opened the garage door. A pile of equipment tangled itself together in one corner. I had to jam the inserts of my Sorels into the smallest pair of boots to make them fit. Charlie wore Eli's gear.

"Where's your coat?" he asked. Pathetically, this small moment of concern made the inside of my chest swell open. He cared about me! I thought of my thick down coat, tossed over Eli's banister. "It's too warm," I said, though all I had on was a skimpy lamb's-wool cardigan. "We'll just keep moving."

Charlie dug into an old barrel and found a musty oatmeal-colored scarf and mittens for me, a moth-eaten wool cap and mismatched leather gloves for himself. As I wound the scarf around my neck, the door from the house struggled open, casting a slant of light and a burst of noise into the garage. Eli stood on the landing.

"Hey," he said. "What are you two doing?"

"Going skiing," Charlie said. For a second, I worried he'd ask

Eli to come along, and I realized how much I wanted to glide away from the crowd, just the two of us, Charlie and me.

"Skiing," Eli repeated. As if we were both crazy. He closed the door behind him to block out the noise. "When did you two even meet?"

"In the kitchen," I said. "Charlie made hot chocolate."

Eli's usually animated face looked quieted, dismayed. Not that he was jealous—Eli and I were strictly friends. I recognized a kind of protectiveness, but it was already too late to turn back, so I didn't consider the possible reasons.

"Brett's one of my best friends," Eli said to Charlie, the slightest note of warning.

"Cool," Charlie said. "I'll take good care of her."

Dismissed, Eli sidled back into the house as we put on skis. I could tell he was trying to catch my eyes, to communicate something, but I didn't want to communicate with him just then. I wanted to follow Charlie, so that's what I did. Once we had stomped through the footsteps leading to Eli's party, we hit pristine, glistening snow. We didn't talk, just glided and shuffled through the back streets, heading uphill until we reached Chautauqua. The snow shimmered, untouched, over the rises that led up to the flatirons. I had loved Colorado since I first arrived—the day I stepped off the plane to start college and walked out of the airport to the immense and jagged vista of the Front Range. My hometown in Vermont had close green hills. Endless winter snowfall and clear, starry nights. Here, living closer to the sky made it seem all the more far away—thin, exhilarating air. The ground beneath us felt flat despite the slopes, so much nearer than the closest mountaintop, towering whitely against the night's clear backdrop.

Charlie leaned on his poles and admired the untouched hilly between us and the Bonnie Blue trailhead. "Perfect," he said. We broke trail, the snow collapsing through its crust into sifted granules. Charlie glided between the trees first. The scarf itched my neck and I could feel my ears burning red. The fabulous night silence—our labored breath and our skis whooshing through the snow.

Charlie saw the bear first, sitting just above the entrance to the Mesa Trail, only fifteen feet from us. I heard his breath draw in. "Stop," he whispered. "Bear." As if my survival instinct were duller than my curiosity, I skied closer so I could see. I let one ski slide to the inside of Charlie's and linked my arm through his elbow. The material of my sleeve was thin enough that I could feel the lanolin squeak of his fisherman's sweater, and for the first time that night I felt cold. No grizzlies lived in Colorado, so despite the darkness I knew it was a black bear. He sat chewing on a stick with animal absorption. I couldn't tell whether he'd seen us.

"Shouldn't he be hibernating?" Charlie asked. I shrugged. There was the bear, wide awake and in our path, whether he should be hibernating or not.

"I don't know anything about bears," I whispered.

"What are we supposed to do?" Charlie asked, as if he hadn't heard me. Our only light was the glare off the snow, but I saw the bear's ear twitch.

"I think we're supposed to wave our arms and make ourselves look taller," I said, remembering something I'd read on a forest service sign.

"Doesn't that seem like flagging him down? I don't think he's even seen us yet."

"I just know we're not supposed to run." I slid back, untangling my skis from his.

"Shit," Charlie said. We both slid backward a foot or two. The bear didn't move.

"I'll race you," Charlie whispered. We turned away from each other with fluid synchronicity. I skated a few strokes, then curled myself into a tuck. Freezing snow flew up to plaster my face as I whooshed too fast to wobble. I could hear Charlie panting behind me, but no thundering ursine footsteps.

I kept going—gliding across Baseline Road without looking for traffic, continuing down Ninth Street—until I couldn't hear Charlie behind me anymore. When I tried to stand, I lost control and smashed into a snow-banked curb—snow packing itself into my sweater, my jeans, my ill-fitting ski boots. Charlie glided to an elegant stop beside me while I lay on the ground, poles flailing.

"I win the speed prize," I said as he extricated me from the snow, "but you get points for grace."

"You're soaked," he said. "You're shivering."

The itchy scarf crackled with ice as he unwound it from my neck. Then he pulled me in and kissed me, almost as an act of charity—a Good Samaritan performing mouth-to-mouth resuscitation. I could feel my blue lips returning to pink against his; I could feel a raspberry stain, pixeled from the cold, spreading across the base of my collarbone. I could feel the tug of the future—even if in that moment, all the future meant was a place to curl in closer.

• • •

A WEEK LATER, ELI and I met for breakfast at Dot's Diner. He ordered a Belgian waffle, which took a good thirty minutes to arrive at our table. We talked about his party and his Russian Literature seminar.

"Goddamn core curriculum," he said. Eli was premed, acing bio and chem classes but struggling with the written word. The opposite of me. I offered to help him write his term paper.

"Could it come to that?" he said, digging into the finally arrived waffle. "A freshman writing my papers?"

"*Helping you* with your paper," I corrected, not out of any particular moral high ground; I just didn't want to write an entire twenty-page essay. We split the bill and stepped outside into high-altitude sunlight. A warm stretch had hit, and dingy, hardened clumps of snow huddled against the curb—the only remnants of the storm. Eli slipped on Vuarnets, but I could tell from his brow he was still squinting.

"So," I finally said, after battling against it the past hour. "What do you hear from your brother?"

His eyes weren't visible, but he let out a little sigh. "Not much, Brett," he said. "Not much at all."

I waited for something more, and when he didn't provide it I elbowed him lightly in the ribs. Charlie and I had spent our night together in the single bed in my dorm room. The next day we came here, to Dot's Diner. I had slid into my side of the bench, expecting him to sit across the table, but instead he slid in right beside me. We spent most of that day leaning into each other, clinging to each other. It never occurred to me that our imminent separation— after such transcendent and life-altering togetherness—was any less painful for him. When Charlie left that afternoon, he'd told me that he didn't have an email address, and neither of us had cell phones. Not everybody did, back then, the late nineties. I told him not to call me on the dorm phone.

"Write instead," I said. "Nobody writes letters anymore."

It had been almost a week and I hadn't received a letter yet but was determined not to despair. Charlie wouldn't have written his first day home in Hyde Park, where he was going to culinary school. He would, I thought, have written his first letter to me the next night and mailed it the following morning.

"Eli," I said now. "Is that all you're going to say?"

"For the moment, yes."

I pushed him again, hard enough that his shoulder banged against the window at Nick-N-Willy's. The pizza baker paused, catching his dough in midair to glance over at the thud. Eli righted himself and brushed off his coat.

"If I hear from him," he said, "I'll tell him to call you. Okay?"

"He said he would write."

Eli nodded, unreadable, his eyes still hidden behind dark glasses. We turned and started heading up Ninth Street. Usually after a big brunch Eli and I liked to hike up the Sanitas Trail off Mapleton. I had my hands in my pockets, staring at my feet as they alternated on the crooked sidewalk. Obviously Eli was doubting it, the connection between Charlie and me. As worry fluttered, I tamped it down by remembering the way Charlie had looked at me and the fact that he was the one who'd had set the whole thing in motion, back in Eli's crowded kitchen. Why would he have done that if he hadn't wanted to be with me? My concentration on these matters was so complete that when I lifted my head to look at Eli, he wasn't walking next to me anymore. I stopped short.

"Eli?" I said, more to myself than calling for him.

He must have bolted away from me at warp speed, because I could see him, more than a block away, standing on the lawn of an imposing brick house, doing some kind of battle with a German shepherd. Eli loved animals, so it was hard to work out the nature of this interaction, whether it was playful or antagonistic. From where I stood, I could see he had his hands on the dog's head. The dog itself was tensed, haunches higher than its shoulders, as if it were trying to wrest something from Eli's grasp.

"Brett," Eli yelled. "Help me out here!"

I should have run, I know. But it was hard to conjure the motivation to get into a fight with a hundred-pound dog. My steps may have picked up a little bit, but tentatively. Halfway there I could hear the dog growl.

"Eli," I said. "What are you doing? Leave the dog alone!"

By the time I got there the owner had emerged from the house. Eli wouldn't let go of the dog's head, and I saw that he actually had a legitimate reason for what he was doing: the dog had a kitten in its jaws. When the owner—a frazzled gray-haired man in a plush bathrobe—grabbed its collar, the dog spat the kitten onto the ground at Eli's feet. Eli knelt to scoop it up, holding the ball of fluff protectively to his chest. The kitten was soaked—shiny with the dog's slobber, encased, as if it had just been born. I didn't see how it could be alive.

We walked away from the house and sat down on the curb. Eli

rested the kitten on his knee to examine it for damage. It was still coiled into the shape of a half-moon, and to my surprise it opened its eyes and blinked at Eli. I could see the imprinting taking place, from both directions, two sets of blue eyes refracting sunlight and each other.

"I think she's okay," Eli said. God only knows how he'd determined its sex. Maybe a lucky guess. Eli pulled the cat back to his chest, cradling her, wiping her clean with his shirt, and I knew there would be no FOUND KITTEN signs posted around the neighborhood. He placed her back on his knees and she shook herself off, little whiskers making themselves parallel, reclaiming dignity. Eli stroked her with a brisk kind of gentleness, and she arched her back into his palm.

"Look," Eli said. "People think we domesticated animals with food. But really, it's our hands." He drew her back to his chest, two fingers scratching under her chin, her eyes half closed in newfound bliss. "Cats might be able to clean each other," Eli said, "but they can't do this. It's people, we're the only ones who can pet and stroke and scratch bellies. That's why they love us. They can get their own food. But we're the only ones who can pet them."

"Hey," I said. "Eli. Did you ever think maybe you should be a vet instead of a human doctor?"

Eli smiled, his eyes still on the cat. "When I was little, that's what I wanted to be. A vet. We had this girl who used to take care of us during the summer, Sylvia, she was so great with animals. I always said my plan was to be a vet and marry Sylvia."

I reached over and touched my fingers to the kitten's head. Her fur was still spiky with dog slobber. She opened her eyes and glared at me with an adult cat's disdain.

"Maybe you still should," I said. "Be a vet. You love animals so much."

"I like people, too," Eli said. "I want to help. More than just animals. You know? The world."

"Well," I said. "What you just did was brave. Saving this kitten. That was helping the world."

Eli smiled. "Maybe I'll do both," he said. "After Harvard Med I'll go to vet school. Open up a whole family practice—people on one side, pets on the other." We stood up and started walking back down Ninth Street, the idea of a hike abandoned.

"What are you going to name her?" I asked.

"I don't know," Eli said, then started listing possibilities. But my thoughts had turned back to Charlie. Remembering his face, the way his fingers grasped my upper arm as he kissed me good-bye, I told myself I wasn't worried. Tomorrow at the latest: the letter would be in my hands. I walked all the way home with Eli, stopping at Delilah's to buy kitten food, barely talking at all.

TWO WEEKS LATER, NO letter from Charlie had materialized. I checked my mailbox twice a day and started to wonder if I'd given him the wrong address. Or maybe Charlie had lost it in his travels. I tracked Eli down at a Thursday night Pub Club, a weekly party thrown by the Deltas. It took me a half hour to find him. At ten o'clock, in the basement of a packed fraternity house, Eli had just poked a hole in the side of a beer can and was about to bring it to his lips.

"Hey," I said, tugging on his sleeve.

"Brett," he said, visibly happy to see me. "Want to do a shooter?"

I could barely hear him over the music. I stood on my toes and yelled into his ear. "I need to get Charlie's number from you," I said.

Eli paused and looked around like he wanted to put down his beer can. But he'd already poked the hole, and as soon as he let go it would spurt everywhere. So he shrugged and went ahead with the shooter while I waited patiently. Then he took my arm and led me over to a corner.

"Brett," he said, yelling over the noise. "Charlie wasn't even supposed to be there for the party. I didn't think you would meet him. And you know, there's a reason I didn't plan on introducing you two. I wish I'd been there when you did meet, I mean, I wish I'd gone into the kitchen with you."

The other day, at Dot's, I hadn't wanted to hear anything Eli had to say about Charlie. Now I felt like I needed to, but at the same time my heart knocked in agitated protest against everything I immediately knew he'd say. I didn't want it shouted, here at this party.

"Can we go outside?" I said.

We moved through the crowd together. Eli kept his hand just at my back, not touching me but letting it hover there, like he was guiding me. We stepped through the back door into the parking lot that bordered an alley. People milled about in thinner numbers, and we sat down on the curb. When Eli spoke, it was quiet, cautious, like he knew I didn't want anyone else to hear.

"I love my brother. He's a very cool guy. But he's not reliable. And with women he's not . . . he doesn't follow through."

With women. In my mind, an endless stream of us unfolded, before me, and after. Eli said, "I would have told you before if I knew, if I had any idea you two would get together. But by the time I found you guys—"

"It was too late."

"Yeah." He shrugged. "He's a helluva handsome guy, Brett. And decent. I mean, he doesn't mean any harm. But he's just not so keen on commitment. You know? He kind of lives in the moment."

I stared at the pockmarked pavement. Eli ruffled my hair, a brotherly gesture.

"Wow," I said. "I feel so stupid."

"Don't. It's not your fault." He let his hand rest there on top of my head. "It's Charlie. This is what he's like." A beat before he added, "I should have told you. He's sort of a womanizer."

This almost made me laugh. I'd never heard anyone except my mother use that word.

Eli went on. "He doesn't mean to be, I don't think."

"Except we just throw ourselves at him." The words sounded more bitter than I meant them to, and even as I spoke them I thought: had I thrown myself at Charlie? It hadn't felt that way. More like, I'd just made it easy as possible for him to reel me in, not the barest struggle on the line.

"What would you do if I asked for his phone number?" I said. "What if I asked you for his address?"

"I would give it to you." Eli's voice sounded very quiet, concerned, and a little bit reproachful. I could picture him—fifteen years from now, a doctor, with a soothing but faintly admonishing bedside manner, telling his patients not to smoke or eat fatty food.

That subtle admonishment helped me face the fact that if Charlie wanted to reach me, if he wanted to keep me in his life, he would have already done so. If Eli gave me his phone number, all I would do was humiliate myself further. Still, I brought my knees up to my chest and leaned my head into them, not able to prevent my teenage heart from asking, *Why? Why don't you love me?*

THAT SHOULD HAVE BEEN that, but over the next days I couldn't help waiting. Part of me waited to stop wanting Charlie to write. Another part waited for him to change his mind. Every day, I checked my campus mailbox, which only stood empty or held a magazine or a letter from my mother. In a particularly weak moment, I called Information, but there was no Charlie Moss listed in Hyde Park.

One evening Eli called. He'd won a BURST award to do research work for a biology professor and wanted to celebrate. I met him at the Sink—he'd already ordered a large veggie pizza and a pitcher of beer.

"Congratulations," I said, sliding into my chair. Eli filled my beer mug as I grabbed a slice of pizza.

"Thanks," he said. "I'm very stoked. This will look great on my med school application. Even if I do fail Russian Lit."

"Good to know," I said. Eli was still resisting my attempts to help, holding out for my writing the entire paper. He picked up the plastic teddy bear on our table, tipped back in his chair, and squirted honey onto a shred of pizza crust. We drank the pitcher of beer and ordered another. A few people from school joined us, including a girl named Wendy whom I thought had a crush on Eli. She had applied for the same BURST award.

"I'm glad you got it if it wasn't me," she told him.

Eli ordered more beer and poured her a glass. I watched them through fuzzy eyes, wondering if he would take her home, if she would fall in love with him, if he would blow her off. "No," I said out loud. "That's Charlie."

"Brett?" Eli asked. "Are you okay?"

Wendy looked over at me. I expected a glare for interfering, but she mostly just looked sympathetic. She would be a nice girlfriend. I thumped my head onto the table. Eli patted my arm.

"Do you want me to walk you home?" he asked.

"No." I pushed back from the table and stood up, hoping Eli would pick up on Wendy's cues and go home with her. Someone should fall in love, if I couldn't.

Back in my dorm room, instead of passing out, I stayed up late with Yeats and Coleridge, determined to erase Charlie's memory with poetry. But the next day in class, the pages of my text were soggy and tearstained and blurred before my eyes as I remembered the sorrows of Charlie's changing face. I'd thought he loved the pilgrim soul in *me*. But it turned out only the reverse was true.

Until that moment I had resisted poetry, my mother's specialty. But right then I gave in. Novels need a logical arc, a progression of events, whereas all poetry requires is a moment, a feeling, a complex and unreconciled reaction. In other words, all I ever had of Charlie. Without the ability to write poetry myself—my critical faculties already overdeveloped—the only thing left was for me was to study it.

"Why?" I used to ask Charlie, years later. "Why do you think that one night made such an impression on me?"

"I don't know," he always said, sometimes with a shrug. "Maybe it was the bear."

IT WASN'T THE BEAR. And it wasn't my youth, or the fact that I'd been a virgin, though certainly all those details played their role. When I think back to that night—or really any night with Charlie—it was the way he could be so utterly *convincing*. That he felt exactly the way I'd been waiting for someone to feel about me. Smitten.

That night, after we'd escaped the bear, we left the skis back at Eli's house and walked to my dorm, holding hands. My mouth still carried the chocolate-tinged remnants of Charlie's spiked cocoa, but I wasn't drunk, not at all, except on his nearness. We walked through the overlit halls of my dorm, and into my small, dark room, and although I'd said no to more than one boyfriend, I didn't utter a word of protest as Charlie eased my sweater over my head, and I knew I wouldn't, not even a token one. Light from the courtyard spilled through the blinds, illuminating his serious face, his blond curls, the fair stubble across his jaw. How could I even consider letting a word like *no* intrude upon this moment? Instead I told him, because I thought it was information he needed, that I had never done this before.

"Well, then. We don't have to do this."

"No. I want to."

Charlie stroked my hair away from my face, staring at me long and hard before kissing me softly, gently. It was all I could do not to say *I love you, I love you, I love you*, over and over again. It never occurred to me that he wasn't employing the same struggle. His face, his eyes, his tenderness—completely absorbed and entirely believable.

LIKE THE GENTLEMAN HIS brother wasn't, Eli persisted in our friendships with phone calls and invitations. When he started dating Wendy, she didn't object to our continued friendship, but it made me sad to be around them sometimes—Eli was a sweet and solicitous boyfriend, pulling out chairs and picking up checks.

"You can ask me about Charlie, you know," Eli said. "If you want to."

A Saturday, the two of us were in a classroom in Muenzinger. I had my own core curriculum worries and couldn't pass Psych 101 until the rat I'd been assigned learned to get through a maze.

"Thanks," I said. "But I'm trying to leave it behind me. You know?"

"It's a good plan," Eli agreed. He scooped up the rat gently, repositioning it midway in the maze. "If he can remember from here," Eli said, "then maybe he'll remember from the beginning."

"Wait," I said. "Which is the good plan?"

"Leaving it behind you. But I think the rat would do better if you gave him a name."

"The rat doesn't know if he has a name or not," I said as the rat found himself faced with yet another tiny wall.

"Maybe he does," Eli said. He picked the rat up and returned him to the middle. "I think you should try it." As I was about to speak, he said, "And don't name him Charlie."

I laughed. "Fine. How about Templeton?"

"Something less expected," Eli suggested. "Something smarter."

"Templeton was smart."

"Something nicer."

"What's Latin for rat?"

Eli cradled the animal and raised it to his nose. Its whiskers twitched, and its long, furless tail wound around his hand. I shuddered a little.

"Julien," Eli said, feeding him a piece of the cheese we'd placed at the finishing point. "It's a good, smart name."

He put Julien back at the beginning of the maze, installed a new piece of cheese at the end, and let him go. Newly christened, Julien executed the maze once, twice, three times. So of course I had no choice but to write Eli's term paper on the homicidal fickleness of Count Vronsky. In fact, on the day Charlie died that very paper lay upstairs in a box in their father's house, its edges curled and yellow, its print faded except for the clear, red, encircled A.

AT SOME POINT THAT spring, Eli and Wendy broke up, and I acquired a boyfriend named Franc, a Swedish chemistry major who dressed, I would realize years later, like Charlie—in batik T-shirts and crinkly Indian button-downs. I told myself that I didn't think about Charlie anymore, but truthfully his disappearance lived on—tucked somewhere between my ribs as a palpable and continuing ache. Although Franc had a jealous streak and often objected, Eli was still my main friend, the person I spent the most time with when I wasn't studying. Eli was quick to laugh but also willing to be silent; the two of us could walk for miles together without ever saying a word, and at the same time, when we wanted, we could talk about anything. Only the topic of Charlie was a strange blank between us—Eli careful since that day in Muenzinger to omit his brother's name when discussing future plans, or telling me stories about his past.

"You don't have to pretend he doesn't exist," I said one day in April. We were playing hooky to ski on the last day of the season at Monarch. On the chairlift, our legs dangled heavily as we rode up over the slopes, rocks peeking treacherously through the snow that remained.

"Who?" Eli said, and we both laughed. Then he said, "It's too bad, though. If it weren't for all that, you could come to the Cape this summer for a visit."

He'd told me about his house there, right on the bay, the summers sailing and swimming and building sand castles. "I like to build them out on the rocks at low tide," he said, "and then watch the water swarm around them, so they look like they're floating. They look like ancient ruins."

"Sounds beautiful."

I was half hoping he'd invite me anyway. Maybe if he did, Charlie would realize that he loved me. The chairlift slowed down and we glided off, slightly different directions, before turning our skis and meeting at the top of Ticaboo. Eli did not mention the Cape again—not that day or any other time. I understood that he didn't want to exclude me but protect me.

That summer, living at home in Randall, Vermont, I waited tables at the new French bistro and did some research work for my mother. An old high school friend and I drove to Maine to hike up Mount Katahdin. On the way back, when we stopped on the rocky coast, the water was too cold to contemplate swimming, and I wondered how it was on Cape Cod this time of year, if Eli and Charlie were swimming. I got a few emails from Eli but none inviting me to visit and none mentioning his brother. I wondered if they talked about me at all or if my name was something to be carefully avoided.

In the fall, Franc and I picked up more or less where we'd left off, and for the first couple months of school so did Eli and I—to the extent that Franc could bear it. "He hovers too close to you," Franc would say, and he wasn't a fan of Eli's birthday gesture, filling my room with balloons. I tried to explain it wasn't romantic, just whimsical, but with the language barrier I had a hard time explaining the difference between the two words. It became easier to spend time away from Eli, who was very busy anyway, with the work he had to do for his BURST grant. So by late October, when I ran into him at a Pub Club, it didn't seem strange that we hadn't seen each other for nearly two weeks.

"Brett," Eli called to me from across the room just after I'd poured my first beer. Franc was back in his off-campus apartment, studying for a sociology exam. I turned toward the sound of Eli's voice. The sight of him startled me. Two weeks didn't seem nearly long enough to justify his physical change. He had shorn his blond hair into a buzz cut and lost a considerable amount of weight, making his jaw appear pronounced and razor sharp. I remember thinking that the only way to lose so much weight so quickly would be to stop eating altogether.

"Eli," I said. "Your hair. And you're so skinny."

"Brett," he said again, intense and happy. He slammed his

red plastic cup into mine, a toast that made my beer slosh onto my shoes. We both looked down at the amber liquid, sinking into my white sneakers. Then Eli did it again, laughing. This time I didn't have enough beer left to spill. I stepped backward, attempting to smile, which ended up more as a grimace. On his jeans, which hung from his hips on the verge of falling, were scribbled words in different color pen.

"Are you okay?" I asked. "You look so different."

"I'm fine," he said. "I just need another one of these." He reached for my empty red cup. "Looks like you do, too."

"I'll get them," I said, escaping sideways into the crowd. As I waited in line for the beer, I glanced back over my shoulder. Eli stood, still watching me. I saw him take his sunglasses out of his pocket—Ray-Bans now, he must have lost the Vuarnets—and slip them onto the bridge of his nose.

I walked back and handed him his cup. He held it in his hand, not saying anything, just staring at me hard through his dark sunglasses.

"Why are you wearing those indoors?" I said.

Eli didn't answer. I lifted my hand and tapped lightly on one lens. Still no response. I decided to play along, staring back, until I couldn't stand it anymore.

"What?" I finally said. I punched him lightly in the solar plexus.

Eli grabbed my sleeve and said, "Come up to the roof." His voice sounded so furtive I almost worried he planned on making a pass at me.

"Why the roof?" I said. "Let's just stay here at the party."

"Come on," Eli said. "I have to tell you something about

Charlie." The buzz of the party seemed to halt for a moment. For so long, he had been careful to avoid that name. Now Eli and I stood in this private little bubble of my too-intense feelings.

"Why can't you tell me here?" I said. My voice sounded deeper. Grim. I didn't want anyone telling Franc I had gone up to the roof with Eli. And I told myself that I didn't want to know anything about Charlie, though at the mention of his name my focus had instantly sharpened. Worse, I felt like I wasn't talking to Eli, my careful friend, but to someone new, and not careful at all.

"The roof," Eli whispered, leaning in too close. His breath smelled muddy and acrid, as if he'd stopped brushing his teeth. I couldn't help scrunching up my nose. "The roof," he said again. "It's safe up there."

"It seems pretty safe down here."

Eli closed his fist tighter around my sleeve and pulled me through the crowd. I followed him, my friend after all. Truthfully I was curious. He was going to tell me something about Charlie. We climbed up the winding, beer-sticky stairwell to the third story, then pulled ourselves through a window to scale the sloping eaves until we reached a flat expanse. Settling next to Eli, my brain slightly fuzzy with beer, I felt glad I'd come. The sky hung heavy with stars, but the air tasted light in my lungs. That thin, high-altitude air—like diet air, not so full of oxygen. I sipped it in, my head clearing ever so slightly.

Eli scrunched his brow as if he were squinting into the night through his sunglasses.

"Take those off," I told him, tapping a lens again. "I don't know how you can see anything."

"I don't want to see anything," Eli said. "I can't stand the glare."

"What glare?"

"Shh," Eli said. "Just be quiet. Just shut up now."

I tried to laugh. He had to be joking. We sat there, silent, me waiting politely—as if I weren't allowed to say Charlie's name out loud even though Eli had used it to lure me up here. I swear that ten minutes passed, the two of us, just sitting. When my eyes had adjusted to the semidarkness, I tried but failed to decipher the garbled scrawl across his pants. The noise of the party pulsed through the roof, vibrating slightly. Arriving voices and slamming car doors traveled up to us from the parking lot.

"Eli." I finally spoke. "You said you were going to tell me something about Charlie."

He pitched forward, placing his forehead between his knees, and pressed his hands over his ears.

"Eli?" I said.

"Shh," he said. "Shut up. Don't say that name."

"Which name? Yours or his?"

He lifted his head and snatched off his sunglasses. I heard my own intake of breath; he looked so upset, so wired. His eyes were disturbingly beautiful even in this partially lit night; it made a kind of sense that he'd wanted to hide them.

"Eli," I said, my voice a whisper. "Are you all right?"

Another minute passed, maybe two. We stared into each other's faces. I thought how lackluster my own dark-eyed face must look in comparison to his. Then he turned in a jerky, agitated movement and slapped me across the forehead with the back of his hand. I couldn't tell if he'd done it on purpose or if it happened because he wasn't in control of his movement. Either way, the blow stunned me into a weird sort of calm—as if he'd smacked me right out of my body and now I could stand to the side, just watching whatever happened next.

"Shut up," he whispered fiercely.

I hadn't said a word. Eli stood, his eyes filling with water. I brought my hand to my forehead, which stung sharply. I pictured a quick, hand-shaped welt that would indeed take shape by the time I had a chance to look in a mirror. Eli drew his hand back to his own forehead and smacked it twice, harder even than he'd smacked me. The Ray-Bans flew out of his hand, skittered across the roof, and fell down to the parking lot.

"Eli," I said, regaining my voice, sharply aware of the distance between us and the ground. The trust required for me to come up here—in my own footing, in my companion—evaporated into the thin air. "Stop it," I said. "Stop it."

I could hear voices three stories below, halting. "Who's up there," a male voice yelled. I imagined him kneeling to pick up the expensive sunglasses that had clattered to his feet. Eli covered his face with his hands.

"Goddamn it," Eli said. "Don't you see what he's turned you into? Don't you see what he's making me do?"

"Who?" I said, though I knew exactly. I slid back a little, the tar shingles rough beneath my blue-jeaned thighs. I tried to calculate the distance and slope to that open window below. Eli moved his hands frantically across his head, as if discovering the lack of hair for the first time. He balled his hands into fists, and I thought he would start pummeling himself again. But instead he threw his arms out wide, like bird wings. The sky around us darkened in an elegant bow. Eli did a strangely graceful little hop, then ran down to the eaves with his arms outstretched and catapulted into the air. I swear that for a moment he hovered. It happened just after his feet grazed the gutters—his body hung flat, arms outstretched like a raptor about to swoop down on prey. But then that silhouette evaporated, and in less time than he'd been still, he crashed through the air to the pavement.

I heard male and female screams below, but I stayed silent. My arms hugged my knees close to my chest. A warm Chinook wind blew my hair off my sharply stinging forehead. I crawled down to where he'd lifted off, and peered over. Down below, three people—two girls and a guy—stood over Eli's body. He lay on his stomach, his arms splayed out, still like wings, though they would tell me later he'd managed to land on his feet before crumpling to the ground.

He's dead, I thought. Eli's dead. Then I remembered the kitten he'd rescued, how sure I'd been she couldn't possibly survive.

One of the girls looked up at me. "Are you all right?" she yelled, as if I were a victim instead of an accomplice.

"Is he alive?" I said, my voice such a froggy croak I didn't expect she would hear it.

But she called back. "Yeah. He's alive."

"Call an ambulance," I yelled back, my voice so loud and sudden it set off a little pulse behind my eyelids.

The girl brought her hand to her eyes, as if to shade them. "We did," she said. I crawled backward, over the roof, and climbed back through the window, heading dutifully if numbly to the place where he landed.

By the time I got to the parking lot, the whole street was engulfed in ambulance lights. Everyone knew that I was the girl who'd been up on the roof. I must have looked that traumatized, disheveled. Somebody, maybe the Delta who'd been standing below when Eli jumped, put a blanket around my shoulders.

I watched Eli rumble by on a stretcher, apparently conscious, his eyes opened and unfocused, staring blankly up at the sky. Without turning his head, he reached his hand out toward me. I grabbed it, relieved that his palm felt warm. The stretcher halted for a moment.

"Do you want to ride with him?" the EMT asked.

Remembering what he'd been like on the roof, I shook my head and let go of Eli's hand. It fell to his side with a sad flop and I immediately regretted saying no. By this time, the university police had arrived, too. The officers approached me as Eli's stretcher was loaded. I watched the ambulance pull away, already regretful. I should have gone with him. I should have been right there next to him, holding on to his hand.

"We saw the whole thing," said the valiant frat boy before they could ask a single question. "He was standing alone at the edge of the building and then he just jumped."

It hadn't occurred to me until I heard this defense that someone might think I'd pushed him. One officer scribbled on a notepad while the other looked hard at me.

"Was he drunk?" he said. "Acting strange?"

I nodded. The officer's pencil halted, expectantly, so I cleared my throat and said, "Yes, he was acting strange. Yes, he was drunk." That last word gave me a second of hope. Maybe that was all it was.

The officer lifted his eyes and squinted at me in the dimly lit parking lot, then reached out as if to push the hair off my face. I stepped back.

"Did he hit you?" the officer asked.

"No," I said, shaking the hair back in front of my face. "No, I'm fine."

His features sharpened as he paused, deciding whether to press the issue. Then he said, "Do you know how we can get in touch with his family?"

My opportunistic heart jumped, just for a moment, hovering like a raptor in the air. Then it landed splat on the pavement, worried and confused.

ON THE CAR RIDE over to Eli's house, the officers were sensitive and solicitous. Why wouldn't they be? Here I was, innocent, fragile, and quivering—the embodiment of everything they were assigned to protect. The redheaded officer sat in the back, giving me the front seat so I wouldn't feel like a criminal. When we arrived, Eli's house stood dark—his roommates were either asleep or back at Pub Club—but the front door was unlocked. I led the officers up to his room, expecting to find chaos. But when

I pushed his door open, the spare order took me by surprise: the bed perfectly made, the floor swept, the walls empty. It looked almost like a military barracks. The one thing not tucked away in a drawer was Eli's address book, the thin faux-leather kind that banks give away for free. As I picked it up, I caught my reflection in Eli's mirrored bureau: a dark-haired girl who looked dazed and much younger than nineteen, with a troubling red mark across her forehead.

"Moss," I said, handing Eli's address book to the redheaded officer. "His parents are named Moss."

"Are you sure you don't want to call?" the officer said. "It might be better if a friend tells them."

We walked downstairs to the kitchen phone. I dialed 1 and then the number written in neat, slanted handwriting next to the words *Mom and Dad.* I listened to it ring once, twice, three times, not sure if I would prefer a live human being or the answering machine.

"Hello," said a male voice, too young to be Eli's dad.

"Mr. Moss?" I said.

I heard an amused pause and could imagine Charlie's face, wry and smiling. "Sort of," he said. "Though probably not the one you're looking for. Can I take a message for him?"

"It's about Eli." I tried to pitch my voice lower, so Charlie wouldn't recognize it. Then I remembered all those weeks and months of silence. Why would he remember my voice after forgetting me so immediately, so resolutely? Something inside me hardened. "I'm sorry to tell you this, but Eli had an accident. He jumped off the roof of a fraternity house. He'll be okay, but somebody needs to come out here. Right away." The silence on the other end had stopped smiling. "I'm sorry," I said again.

Charlie spoke with a faint pause after each word: "Why would he jump off a roof?"

"I don't know," I said. "He was acting strange. He was acting wrong. I think there's something wrong."

"Brett?"

Charlie's voice suddenly steadied, as if his future self—the one who knew and loved me—had managed to reach backward in time to recognize my voice. "Is this Brett?"

My hand went numb. Maybe Charlie wanted to think this phone call was just a cruel joke, a sick way to get back at him for not loving me. Or maybe he thought I had pushed Eli off the roof. In that moment I felt almost as if I had.

"No," I said, scrambling for another name. I didn't want this to be about me and Charlie. Eli needed his family. I had to step back, invisible. In my dorm room, on the bedside table, lay Walter Jackson Bate's fat biography of John Keats, dog-eared and underlined. "This is Fanny," I said. "Fanny Brawne."

Charlie didn't say anything. What twentieth-century person is named Fanny? I wondered if he recognized this name from a class where he'd sat listening, not having read the text, or if he just computed the oddness. More likely he hadn't even heard me. I pictured Charlie holding the receiver and realized that I couldn't remember his face, not exactly, only its outline, and the color of his eyes: a dim reflection of Eli.

I gave him the name of the hospital where Eli had been taken, repeating the number that one of the officers recited. Then I said good-bye and hung up. The officers stood staring at me. One of them reached out to pat my shoulder, but to me the gesture didn't feel comforting. This was the first time I would experience it, the particular sense of trauma, Eli's madness still thrumming just below my skin.

But if Eli's family was now marshaling to come for him, this could be my only chance to see him again without running into Charlie. "Hey," I asked the officers. "Can you give me a ride to the hospital? So I can see how he's doing?"

"Sure," they said. "But they probably won't let you see him. Only family, I'd guess, at this point."

Which let me off the hook, an immediate combination of relief and disappointment. I remembered both ways Eli's hand had felt—slapping across my forehead and sliding out of my grip.

Over the next days and weeks and months, when Eli left Colorado and never returned, I tried to write a poem about that moment when he leapt off the roof and out of my life. Although it never materialized properly, it started to form in my head before we even left his house, the first lines interrupted by a creaky and mournful meow. Peering from behind a beat up armchair was the scraggly gray kitten, now a cat, brushed and plump under Eli's care. The officers gave me a moment to search for a cat carrier and supplies. I left the house with Tab and kept her with me for over a decade, till she died under the wheels of a car, just up the road from the Mosses' summer home.

5

For a while I tried to email Eli, to update him on Tab and find out if he was ever coming back to school. But he never answered. After a month or so went by, I helped his roommates pack up his things to ship back to his parents' winter house in New York.

"He's in some swanky hospital outside Boston," one of the roommates told me. "It's called McLean."

I knew about McLean from studying poets and listening to James Taylor. In my mind, it was like a boarding school with rolling green lawns and maybe even a swimming pool and tennis courts. I imagined Eli lying on a grassy hillside under a broad, blue sky, writing poetry in a spiral notebook. That image comforted me, even as the years unfolded without ever hearing from him. Eli went away. He had treatment. He was cured. Maybe when he got out he enrolled in a different college, went on to med school, got married. I pictured an understanding wife who he could be solicitous of the way he'd been with Wendy. My imagination restored him, created the life he should have had.

Which left my own life to unfold. I finished my BA and then waited tables in Randall for a couple years before entering the PhD program at Amherst. Where I met Ladd, who asked me to marry him and then—unwittingly—returned me to the Mosses.

IT HAPPENED LIKE THIS. Seven years after I saw Eli loaded into that ambulance, Ladd and I rode the Hy-Line ferry from Nantucket to Cape Cod. I hadn't been wearing his engagement ring a full twenty-four hours, and it felt new and heavy and noticeable on my finger. Ladd and I sprawled out on the life vest container at the stern. I wore a bikini top and shorts—at twenty-six, still too young to take skin cancer or premature aging seriously. Through the haze of early July—sunlight and milling passengers—I thought I heard someone call my name. Not sure if I made out the words correctly, I decided I didn't want to run into anyone, so I kept my eyes shut tight. Those days I felt happiest wrapped in a cocoon with just Ladd. Other people had become, by definition, intruders.

"Brett Mercier," the voice said again, insistent and determined.

Whoever it was, he lacked the social finesse to know he was being avoided. I peered to one side. Ladd lay asleep next to me. He and I both had dark hair, but in this bright sunlight, on the water, his skin revealed its northern European roots as opposed to my southern by getting redder by the minute. Ladd had thick eyebrows and narrow eyes, making his face look stern, almost craggy. Unlike Charlie's, it wasn't a face that everyone in the world would consider handsome. But I did. I knew I should wake him and tell him to put on sunscreen, a hat, something. I sat up, squinting into the sun, my hand coming down to rest on Ladd's bare leg.

It took several seconds to recognize Eli. In my mind, he had separated into two different people: the great friend who'd always had my back and the scary stranger who'd appeared one night, and then disappeared, taking the original one with him. Now there seemed to be a third one, barely recognizable across these distant years and miles. Not that I wasn't happy to see him; I just felt like it *wasn't* him, not exactly. Eli stood in front of me, blinking under blinding sun on a quiet Atlantic ocean. The most striking similarity to his old self—that last self, anyway—was his hair, cut very short.

He looked dejected that I wasn't more excited about this chance meeting. Involuntarily, I touched my forehead with the tips of my fingers. Eli was the only person in the world who'd ever hit me. For the first time in ages I found myself wondering again, if it had been an accident.

"Eli," I finally said, to his goofy and increasingly awkward grin.

All his angles had gone soft. A potbelly balanced on top of long, skinny legs. Despite the heat, he wore khakis and a striped oxford shirt, sweat stains visible under his arms. Somehow I knew without asking that he had not gone to med school.

I reached out my hand and Eli took it, then turned my palm

over and brought it to his lips. The gesture seemed so natural and sweet that I found myself smiling. Ladd's eyelids fluttered open and he propped himself up on his elbows, squinting into the sun.

"Hey," Eli said. "Ladd Williams?"

"Yeah," Ladd said as Eli's identity registered. "Hey, Eli."

It had never occurred to me to ask if Ladd knew the Moss family. How many thousands of people spent summers on Cape Cod? I'd imagined visiting Eli at his summer house, but if I ever knew the name of the town I'd long since forgotten it. Eli pointed at Ladd. The pudgy finger seemed nothing at all to do with the lithe, charismatic boy I remembered.

"You know Brett?" Eli said to him. And then, picking up on the unmistakable currents between us: "Are you, like, *with* Brett?"

"Yeah," Ladd said. "How do you know Brett?"

He had directed the question at Eli but clearly meant for me to answer. So I said, "We went to college together."

"We were best friends in college," Eli said.

For me, college had lasted four years. But Eli's time had been cut short. If things had happened differently, we would have stayed best friends. I wanted to tell him that I still had his cat—that at this very moment she was probably sitting on my pillow at home in a patch of sunlight. If he'd seemed more like the old Eli, I would have. But it was a little like running into the identical twin of someone you know very well. He was enough Eli that I thought he might want Tab back, and at the same time he wasn't enough Eli that I would trust him with her.

"Damn," he said. "Another girlfriend in common with Charlie. He is going to laugh."

Ladd turned his head toward me sharply. "You went out with Charlie Moss?"

"Not exactly," I said, trying to remember if the incident with Charlie ever came up in Ladd's and my debriefing of past romances. Generally he did not respond well to discussions of other men, so I tended to give him Cliffs Notes only. I put my hand over his.

Eli said to Ladd, "I saw your uncle Daniel last week. He said you went back to school."

"Yeah," Ladd said. "Finally." Ladd had scandalized his family by dropping out of Cornell after some girl broke his heart. He spent six years on a fishing boat in Alaska before he went back to finish at UMass. "That's where I met Brett. She was the TA for one of my classes."

I could feel Ladd's jumpy insecurity pulsing through his fingers and into my palm and knew he wouldn't go back to normal until we could be alone, and I could fill him in about Charlie. But Eli wasn't going to let that happen anytime soon. He sat down next to me. I pulled on my T-shirt and asked what he was up to these days.

"Spending the summer with Mom and Dad," he said. "You're back in school, huh? Advanced degree? PhD or something?"

"Yes," I said, with a pang of survivor's guilt that my brain hadn't robbed me of that opportunity.

"That's great," Eli said. "Really great." He turned his gaze out toward the bow of the boat, the blue waves, the mainland in the distance. Ladd finally put on a baseball cap, and the three of us rode together all the way to Hyannis.

• • •

AS THE FERRY PULLED into port, I excused myself and went into the bathroom. I splashed my face with tinny water and stared hard into the warped, filmy mirror. When I came out, the boat had nearly emptied. All the passengers spilled into the parking lot, collecting luggage. Back on land, the day seemed overly infused with color—the blues of the water and sky, the white of the boats, the green lawn, and the reds and yellows and pinks of cheerful summer clothing. By the time I walked down the metal plank, Ladd stood waiting for me with our luggage—his good leather valise and my faded canvas duffel bag.

"Where'd Eli go?" I asked, when I got down to the parking lot.

Ladd gestured sideways with his chin. "Disappeared into the crowd."

"Oh," I said. "I wanted to say good-bye."

"Small world, huh?" A slight edge to Ladd's voice, as if it might be my fault, the size of the world.

I shrugged, and not just because I didn't want to take responsibility. In my experience, the world was infinite. Only this very particular world, of summer homes and private schools, could accurately be considered small.

"I never knew Eli very well," Ladd said. His voice had gone back to normal. Ladd rarely stayed angry long. Typically a flash would rise, visible, and he would squelch it himself before it could fully erupt. I always found the process—the effort to protect me from his negative emotions—touching. Several months before, Ladd and I had gone to an exhibit of Marsden Hartley's paintings, mostly landscapes of Maine. But for a long time Ladd had stood in front of a portrait of Abraham Lincoln. The title of the painting was *The Great Good Man*, and I knew Ladd well enough to understand: that was what he aspired to be. A Great Good Man.

Now as I slipped my arm through his, he said, adding to his previous thought, "But Charlie and I were friends when we were kids."

"Are you still friends?"

"We still run into each other here and there. But no, I wouldn't say we were friends."

"Why not?"

Ladd didn't answer, just moved his arm out of mine and placed his hand at the small of my back, drawing me into his body. I felt his chin against my forehead as I stared out into the crowd and saw Eli getting into the passenger's seat of a wood-paneled station wagon. The driver was a lean, middle-aged woman with pale curls like Charlie's.

Ladd and I walked over to the Raw Bar for chowder, and when we sat down he said, "Why don't you tell me about you and Charlie?" He kept his eyes on the menu, his body falsely still.

"There's not much to tell," I said.

"Eli said you went out with him."

"I didn't. Stayed in with him. Just once. One time."

"Really?" Finally he returned his eyes to me. "I have a hard time imagining that, you having a one-night stand." He didn't say this in a judgmental way. He wasn't thrown by my loose morals, it just didn't jibe with his perceptions of my emotional capacity, and of course he was right.

"Well," I said, "I was only eighteen. And I didn't exactly mean for it to be just that one night."

Ladd nodded, jutting his chin toward me and then abruptly away. "Typical Moss," he said. His voice was angry, but I felt my shoulders relax, knowing the anger was toward Charlie, not me. I wanted to ask him about the other girlfriends he and Charlie had in common but decided to save it for later.

"What about you?" I said. "You spent summers with them here? In the same town."

"Yeah. My family has been friends with the Mosses for a long time. You know about my uncle Daniel's wife, Sylvia?"

"The one who died?"

"She was Charlie and Eli's au pair, in the summers. That's how Daniel met her. Did you know Eli went to McLean?"

I nodded.

"Daniel paid for that," Ladd said. "Because of Sylvia. She really loved Eli."

I nodded again, as if this were something any ordinary person could do, though I couldn't even imagine what that must have cost. The wealth of Ladd's family alternately perplexed and embarrassed me.

"So," I said. "Do you know what was wrong with him? When he went away?"

"Schizophrenic, I think."

"But he's better now." As if my words could make it so. "The Mosses, they couldn't afford it? The hospital?"

"Who knows," Ladd said. "Eli's father has always had strange ideas about what to spend his money on."

I felt a little flare of defensiveness. Ladd had no idea what it was, not to afford something. But I stayed quiet.

Ladd's face settled back into its regular ease, and he raised his hand to signal for the check. I could almost see the mental gesture, a broom in his mind, pushing the Mosses aside.

WE DROVE WITH THE top down in Ladd's convertible Saab, through the dingy streets of Hyannis, on our way to tell his family about our engagement. The seafood restaurants with lobster traps on the roofs gave way to the grassy, shore-scented highway of Route 6, and then off the highway, passing the increasingly wide lawns, houses farther and farther back from the road until each driveway became its own dusty dirt road. Ladd drove past the one that led to his uncle's compound, and I found myself turning around in my seat, staring, feeling newly connected to the place.

"Maybe one of these days we can stay with him," I said. "Your uncle Daniel."

Ladd looked over at me. The skin across the bridge of his nose looked singed from the boat ride. He placed his hand, palm up, on my lap. I gathered it up in both of mine, regretting my T-shirt and cutoffs.

"Hey listen," I said. "Can we actually turn around and sneak into one of those guest cottages? I wouldn't mind changing before we get to your parents."

Ladd checked his watch—the clock on his dashboard didn't work—then turned the car around, and we drove back to Daniel's. There were no cars at the main house other than the blue Chevy pickup that lived there permanently. Preparations for the annual Fourth of July party Daniel would be throwing that Saturday had begun—the round tables and folding chairs had been delivered and were stacked against the detached garage. We parked behind the Chevy and carried our bags down the path to the smallest guest cottage.

We passed an hour or more inside before finally attending to our original mission—showering and changing—so that by the time we walked back down the path the sun had sunk low but was still stubbornly bright in the sky. Refreshed, the two of us were combed and dressed and festive; my engagement ring sat snug in the pocket of Ladd's Nantucket Reds so as not to give anything away before we could tell his parents. As we headed across the lawn to the car, Ladd's uncle Daniel called to us from the deck.

The Williams family owned several houses in Saturday Cove, and although Daniel was years younger than his brother he had inherited the best one. It sat on a hill overlooking a beachside bluff. The summer before, when Ladd and I spent a week at his parents' house, nearly every day found us at his uncle's, which had its own long stretch of private beach. Now Ladd and Daniel shook hands, and Daniel bent to kiss me on the cheek.

"I left my phone in the car," Ladd said after greetings had been made and drinks offered. "I just need to go inside and let my parents know where we are."

Daniel walked inside with Ladd, then returned with a glass of white wine for me. He hadn't poured a drink of his own. Like Ladd, Daniel was tall, over six feet, which always made me want to stand on my toes, even when I wore my highest heels. I liked Daniel. He had a careful way of being and looking, a mix of intensity and kindness, and the news of how he'd helped Eli had only increased my admiration.

"You happy to be back on the Cape?" Daniel said, in a formal, making-conversation kind of voice.

"Yes," I told him in the same tone. And for no good reason other than a kind of panic, at being left alone with nothing to talk about, I said, "Ladd and I just got engaged. We're telling his parents tonight."

Daniel smiled. The polite, obligatory stance disappeared. He had dark blue eyes like Ladd, and his hair had grayed in a distinguished, silvery way. "I'm happy to hear it," he said. "I hope you'll get married here."

At first I thought he meant Cape Cod, but as he gestured at the deck I realized he meant this spot, his house. It made me worry that I shouldn't have said anything, upset the natural order of the announcement, without even consulting Ladd. My face felt a little hot, and I wished I hadn't left my sunglasses on the dashboard of Ladd's car. It was such a magnanimous offer, but saying "thank you" would feel like accepting. Which wasn't exactly my place.

"Sylvia and I were married here," Daniel said, graciously ignoring my silence. "I suppose Ladd's told you about Sylvia?" I hesitated before nodding. "You remind me of her," Daniel said.

Again, I wished for sunglasses. I searched my brain for a reply. Before I found one Daniel said, "Would you like to see a picture?"

He walked through the sliding glass door, which Ladd had left open. I thought he was going to bring the picture back to me, but he paused in the doorway long enough for me to realize I was meant to follow him. So I did, trying to remember a framed portrait hanging over a fireplace from my previous visits. Instead Daniel stopped by the main stairway and opened the single drawer of a small occasional table. We could hear Ladd's voice as he talked on the phone, coming from the kitchen.

"Look," Daniel said.

He handed me a small leather envelope. I opened it to see a head-and-shoulders picture of a young woman with hair damp-ened by the ocean. The blue sky stood behind her, and though I couldn't tell whether she wore a bikini or a maillot, I could tell from the straps she was in her bathing suit. She was very fair and freck-led, with narrow eyes the pale blue of a Siberian Husky's. She had a strong jaw, and short blonde hair. She looked athletic and patri-cian. Apart from age and the geography of the moment, I couldn't pinpoint anything the two of us had in common. Still, since he'd just compared us, it seemed wrong—self-congratulatory—to say that she was pretty. So instead I said, "She looks so young."

"She was young. This was taken a few years before she got leu-kemia, before we were married. She was only twenty-eight when she died."

"That's terrible," I said, as if hearing the story for the first time. "I'm so sorry." Not able to bear the brief silence that followed, I added, "My father died of leukemia when I was five." Actually my father had died of Hodgkin's lymphoma. As the words left my mouth, I realized Ladd might have told Daniel this, and my face reddened over the small lie. It would be splitting hairs to correct myself now. Daniel reached out and took the picture from my hands. He studied it for a moment, then snapped the envelope shut and returned it to the drawer.

"I took all of the framed pictures away," he said. "The first few years after she died they used to take me by surprise. I'd come around a corner finally feeling normal and then there she'd be, staring out at me from the top of the bookshelf. Now I keep pictures of her in drawers around my houses, so I can look at them when I want to. I thought of this one when I saw you standing out there on the deck. She was very sweet, Sylvia. And very smart. Layered. Always thinking."

"I'm sorry," I said again.

Daniel nodded, staring over my head toward some unknowable point. There was a sadness there that made me like him even more; it made me want to reach out and pat him on the shoulder, though of course I didn't. I wouldn't have used the word *sweet* to describe him, but everything else he'd just said about Sylvia also applied to him. And I supposed there was a sweetness, too. A kindness. The sort of man who stepped in and helped when help was needed. When he brought his eyes back to mine, I blinked and looked away.

"It was a long time ago," he said, polite, excusing me from the need to comfort him.

At their summer house, Ladd's mother—Rebecca— stood in the doorway, holding the screen door open.

"Darlings," she scolded, as if Ladd hadn't called. "We expected you hours ago."

His mother frowned at Ladd as she kissed him but then smiled at me and kissed me on both cheeks, not air kisses, but sincere and motherly ones. I smoothed my hair off my forehead as I walked past her to Ladd's father, Paul, who gave me a hug. He didn't hug or kiss Ladd but shook his hand warmly, then thumped him on the back. Even though Ladd's parents seemed genuinely fond of me, the bulk of my contribution to the evening had already taken place—showering, putting on a dress, combing my hair, and saying hello. Before long I would be basking in their good wishes and excitement. My own one-parent household was much lighter on enthusiasm than Ladd's. I always enjoyed the congeniality of his family but never quite knew how to respond in kind.

The next morning when I came downstairs wearing my engagement ring, Ladd sat with his mother at the wide oak table in the kitchen. They both looked toward me with the sort of startled, blank faces that told me I'd interrupted a private conversation. I knelt down to pet their little dog. His mother—better at rearranging her face than Ladd—pushed back her chair and smiled. I thought that she looked a lot more like Sylvia than I ever would. She was tall and fair and raw-boned, like she'd stepped out of an Andrew Wyeth painting. I imagined Ladd's mother, going out to play tennis, or to a party, while Sylvia watched Eli and Charlie. And then later, the brief period they'd had as sisters-in-law. Part of me wanted to ask her what Sylvia was like.

"Good morning, Brett," his mother said with genuine warmth. If she ever wondered why her only son wasn't marrying a woman who freckled after a long day of wind surfing, she never did a thing to show it. "Can I pour you some coffee?"

"I can do it," I said, giving the dog one last pat and standing up. I moved apologetically toward the coffeepot and poured the steaming liquid into the mug that sat there waiting for me. I stood against the counter for a few minutes, waiting to see what conversation they would invent, to continue.

Ladd tapped the spot next to him at the table, and I sat down. He said, "We can't go to Uncle Daniel's beach today. They're getting ready for the party tonight."

"It looks like rain anyway," his mother said, and as if on her command gentle drops began pattering against the window. We all looked in that direction as they increased their speed.

"You two should go into Chatham," Rebecca said. "Shop. Walk around. Have lunch." The rain picked up. We could hear it on the roof, three stories above our heads. Ladd's mother clucked her tongue. "I hope it clears up in time for Daniel's party."

OBEDIENTLY, WE WALKED DOWN Main Street in Chatham, huddled in our raincoats. Ladd and I stared through the rain-streaked windows, not buying anything, not even entering shops except for Cabbages and Kings, the bookstore. Finally we found ourselves walking past the slew of stores and restaurants, past the quaint, restored homes off Main Street, and on the beach—not the tamer bay side of Saturday Cove but the wide Atlantic ocean, roiling with waves nearly as large as we'd seen on Nantucket. Despite the fact that it was the Fourth of July weekend, and the streets of Chatham had been crowded, we had the beach nearly to ourselves if we didn't count the many seals resting out on the sandbars or the one man who stood in the water with a young child of indeterminate gender on his shoulders. He had valiantly rolled up his jeans and waded into the waves, presumably to get a better look at the seals. Ladd and I watched as the child extended a chubby, raincoated arm, damp fingers pointing.

"That'll be me and our kid one of these days," Ladd said. He pushed off his hood and let the rainy mist gather in his hair. Ever unoriginal, I did the same. Ladd put his arm around my shoulders. I stared up at his face—strong-boned like his mother's—and thought how I admired his willingness to commit, to look ahead, to *be* with me, minus any of the personal guardedness I had seen in other men.

"So," he said, in a different tone. It sounded businesslike, and aware of an unpleasant task ahead. "I was talking to my mother this morning. About the wedding."

"What's wrong?" I said.

"Nothing's wrong." Ladd's eyes flickered a tiny bit, ever so slightly unnatural. "Everything's perfect. It's just my family, it's stupid, but, I can't get married without a prenup."

A small laugh burst from my throat and Ladd frowned a little. I realized it annoyed me that he was still looking out toward the water, instead of at me. Did he always do this? Look away in the most important moments? Is that why he'd missed the fact that I counted his money against rather than for him?

"A prenup," I said.

"Yes," he said. "A prenuptial agreement."

"I know what it is," I said.

"It's just a formality." I could feel his arm tense behind my neck, the fingers slack over my shoulder. His words marched out in the manner of someone who's planned a conversation ahead of time. "My mother signed one."

I pictured a young Rebecca in some plush Boston office, leaning over a shining oak desk, her blonde hair pulled off her high forehead. Doing what needed to be done. Practical woman, dressed just right.

But that's not me, I thought. I wasn't practical, or well dressed.

I wasn't that kind of person. For the first time in years I did something I'd assiduously trained myself not to do: I thought of Charlie. Obviously his family wasn't as wealthy as Ladd's. But no matter how much money Charlie had, I knew he would never do this, ask me to sign a document, ask me to prepare for the end of something before it even began.

I could have told Ladd that his money didn't interest me. I could have expressed surprise that he didn't know this until now. I could have gotten angry, and refused. Instead I just said, "Okay."

"What does that mean?" His voice sounded not so much tense but released from tension. He'd come here braced for battle and maybe now he could move forward with it.

"What does okay mean?" I said.

"Does it mean, okay, you're listening? Or okay, you'll sign it?"

"I'll sign it."

I could feel his arm relax, then stiffen, as if he didn't quite believe it could be that easy. "It's not me who wants it," he said, too fast, not himself. Embarrassed at the premature outburst. "It's them. It's not even them. It's just the machine. I know we don't need it."

It would have been nice if he'd said that first. My gaze remained outward, toward the seals. I could feel the tension rising again in Ladd, his arm twitching as if he wanted to remove it from me. He was sticking to his side of the script. But I didn't know what my lines were. The words that felt most natural—any kind of argument—might ruin everything.

He said, "It's very standard."

I knelt down and picked up a small gray stone, then flung it, hard as I could, toward the water. It skittered, disappointing, just short of the breaking waves. Because I'd already peered down that rabbit hole, I went ahead and thought that Charlie would never say something like that, *It's very standard*. Then I reminded myself, Charlie would never ask me to marry him in the first place. He'd never even asked for a second date.

"Okay," I told Ladd. "That's fine."

A full minute passed. We watched a seal roll sideways off its rock. I could see its sleek head, bobbing in the water, staring at us. I took a step toward it, and the seal disappeared, under water. The rain picked up, not just misting but steady and torrential. Without speaking or putting our hoods up, Ladd and I ran up the beach, to the slick sidewalks, back toward town.

On the drive to Saturday Cove, sunlight slanted rays onto the pavement, making the puddles of water look like puddles of gasoline, streaked with black and violet. Clouds began to disperse. Ladd's knuckles looked red and chapped on the steering wheel. His hair was soaked and slicked back, his jaw set and irritated.

"I don't see why you're angry," I finally said, as if I weren't angry myself. "When I said I'd do it."

"I'm not angry." His teeth set the barest bit, biting back the emotion he couldn't contain or admit to. I sympathized with the struggle, and wanted to run my finger over the sunburnt skin across his cheekbones.

But I didn't. Instead I said, "This is good news for your uncle's party. The sun."

Ladd's face settled into a kind of relief, his eyes widening back to their normal size. He reached across to close his hand around both of mine. His hands were big enough for that.

"Yes," he said. "It's good news."

I NEVER GOT AROUND to asking the reason Ladd's father hadn't inherited Daniel's beach house. Maybe he didn't want it? The house he did have was significantly larger than the one that belonged to his younger brother. I suppose to make up for the fact that it wasn't on the beach, it had a swimming pool—a long, gleaming swimming pool, with a diving board, surrounded by white lounging furniture. I had never seen so much as a leaf floating on the surface of that pool, and I had never seen anyone swim in it. Late afternoon before the Fourth of July party, I stood staring out through the French doors at that pool. Ladd was their only son, and as Daniel had no children, there were no cousins. It would be up to me, then, to give the pool the life it needed. I tried to rearrange the placid scene before me, fill it with splashing children, the diving board always quivering.

From the staircase, I heard footsteps: definite, male, not Ladd's. I didn't turn, though I knew it was rude. Ladd's father stood there quietly and I imagined I could feel joy emanating from him. Ladd had delivered the news, how easy it had been. Not the barest whimper of objection. When I did turn around, he wouldn't say a word about that, but just say my name, and tell me I looked pretty. What else does a man say to a woman dressed up for a party? What else does a man hand to a woman who's agreed to marry him but a gold pen to sign a legal document?

Would John Keats have signed a prenup? Would Emily Dickinson?

My constitution could only handle ignoring him for so long. I turned around. The red dress I wore had been purchased for the party, on sale at Filenes. It had spaghetti straps. The hem grazed my ankles.

"Brett!" His eyes looked ever so slightly glossy with sympathy. He likes me, I reminded myself. He is prepared to love me. He wants me to marry his son. "Don't you look pretty," he said.

"Thank you."

Ladd came down the hall to stand next to his father. The two were dressed almost identically, in blue blazers and khakis. "Well," Paul said. "Should we announce the engagement tonight? At the party?"

"No," I said quickly. Ladd raised his eyebrows, surprised, and I said, "I want to tell my mother first." As if anyone at the party knew of my mother's existence, or she theirs.

"Of course," Paul said, pretending my request made sense. The three of us went outside to wait for Ladd's mother by the car.

I HAD BEEN TO one of Daniel Williams's Fourth of July parties before, last year, when Ladd brought me home to meet his family. This time I knew what to expect and wasn't taken aback by the valet parking, the full wait staff, the parquet dance floor installed on the lawn that overlooked the ocean. When we arrived, things were just getting underway. The band hadn't started playing, and Ladd's father went ahead and parked his own car, right beside the catering truck. Later on, there'd be professional fireworks, impressive enough to rival the town display down by the harbor. Ladd's parents stopped to talk to some other early arrivals, and I walked out toward the deck while Ladd went to get us drinks. Daniel emerged and waved at me in a kind of half salute, then reached out to take my hand and examine the ring. "That was my mother's," he said.

I waited for him to congratulate me, then realized he was too polite—too old-world—to ever congratulate the bride. Instead he said, "I hope you'll be very happy."

"Thank you," I said. Daniel didn't drop my hand. He lowered it carefully, back down to my side. Then he let go.

"May I ask you a question?" I said.

"Of course."

"Did your wife, Sylvia. Did she sign a prenuptial agreement?"

Daniel looked down at me. He had just cut his hair and it looked unexpectedly boyish. "No," he said. "No, she didn't."

"Did you ask her to sign one?"

"No," Daniel told me. He made his voice very careful. "No, Brett. I did not."

Ladd walked onto the deck holding two glasses of wine. He handed me my glass and Daniel shook his hand vigorously. "Congratulations," he said. His voice sounded very deep and very definite. "You have something good here, Ladd, and I'm happy for you."

"Thanks," Ladd said. The three of us turned to look out at the party. The guests all seemed to be arriving at once, and a swirl of navy blue and seersucker jackets blended with the wider, more colorful array of summer dresses.

"It's a beautiful night," I said. Daniel placed his hand on my bare shoulder, not squeezing but letting it rest heavily. If anyone else had done this—any of the other older men—it would have felt like a drunken gesture. But from Daniel it felt measured, even protective. When he excused himself to greet his guests, I sat down on the built-in bench, while Ladd stayed standing, his hand resting on the rail behind me.

"How come you didn't want to announce it?" he said.

I shrugged. "I don't know." And then, remembering my previous explanation, I said, "I want to tell my mother first. And anyway, it feels weird. All that attention."

Ladd nodded and sipped his wine, squinting out at the increasingly crowded lawn. "Look," he said. "Eli Moss is here. There's his mother, too."

I sat up for a better view. All I had to do to find Eli was let my eyes follow Daniel through the crowd. He shook Eli's hand and touched his shoulder, and then hugged the tall, blonde woman standing next to him—the curly-haired woman who'd picked Eli up from the ferry. Eli wore the same summer uniform as the other men. I guessed his mother had picked out his red tie and probably knotted it for him. Words he'd said years ago popped into my head: *We had this girl who used to take care of us during the summer, Sylvia, she was so great with animals.* Daniel's late wife had loved Eli, and Charlie, too. It made them and Ladd sort of cousins.

I looked back at Ladd. He said, "Daniel always invites them. I don't know why they weren't here last year. Funny, we would have found out then. That we both knew them."

"Funny," I echoed. "I think I'll go say hello."

We stepped down off the deck and partygoers closed in around us. One of them stopped Ladd as we made our way toward Eli, but I continued until another break in the crowd. The rainy day had morphed into a spectacular night. The temperature hovered a few degrees above cool. The wind blew just softly enough to seem romantic—the leaves on the trees fluttering, along with hems and stray wisps of hair. The grass felt slightly damp as I walked across it, toward Eli, who hadn't yet seen me. From this distance, I marveled at how *normal* he looked, and wondered if that impression would burst as I got closer. Whatever Eli's state, it made me happy to have someone there I knew, not because of Ladd or his family. I'd had a life before these people.

"Brett," a voice said as I approached the next section of crowd.

If I'd taken one more step I would have physically bumped into him. Him, Charlie, the only man at the party not wearing a coat and tie, grinning at me like I was something he'd misplaced, and nothing in the world could possibly be happier than at last, after all this time. Finding me.

I REMEMBER THIS MOMENT two different ways, depending on my mood. One way, I'm an immature and shortsighted girl who's mad at her boyfriend but not strong enough to say so, my fragile ego still not repaired from Charlie's rejection. I care so little for morals and responsibility that I ignore the diamond ring on my finger, the future I've accepted from the good man who sincerely loves me. And will-o'-the-wisp Charlie, thoughtless and charming, sizing me up because he hasn't seen any more interesting girls at the party.

AND THEN THERE'S THIS other way. The way, if I'm honest, I remember the moment most often, even now, knowing where it all led. I remember a single second where the sea of dark and pale blue, of summer paisley and Lilly Pulitzer pastels, fades away. It's as if every other person at the party suddenly transforms into a thin mist of smoke—leaving *him* standing there, not only without a tie but wearing blue jeans and a white-and-red-striped shirt with a Nehru collar. Charlie, with curly blond hair and eyes the precise color of the sky that frames him. But most important smiling—at me—in a way that contains every private joke I've ever wanted to have with him. If I see arrogance in that smile—a *how can you help loving me* kind of knowing—I also see something else, something that looks like very genuine fondness. That affliction—the beating plague in my chest—leaps without any directive from me. If it could, it would escape from my rib cage and tackle him on the spot, like a golden retriever welcoming its long-lost owner home.

"Hi," I say, hating the catch in my voice, the crackling octave rise.

All the little strands of smoke slowly resume their corporeal forms. Conversational noise—along with the surf and gulls—fills the air around us. A waiter comes by carrying a tray of Champagne flutes. Charlie reaches out and takes the wine glass out of my hand. He places it on the waiter's tray, takes two glasses of Champagne, hands one to me, then clinks his against mine.

"Do you remember me?" he asks.

"I do," I say. "You're the one who didn't read *The Sun Also Rises.*"

"But you read it."

"Of course I did. I was an English major. I'm named after Lady Brett Ashley."

"So why did you lie?"

Thump. Thump. Thump. Can he hear it? Can everyone? Can Ladd—somewhere in the crowd? Did he turned into a strand of smoke, too?

"Because," I say to Charlie. "Because I'm an idiot."

His smile widens, if that's possible. As if I'd just paid him the best compliment in the world. And I can't believe that he remembers as clearly as I do. I thought he had forgotten everything.

Charlie holds out his hand and says, "Present tense. Does that mean still? Still an idiot?"

"Apparently," I say, then take his hand, and we walk together across the lawn to the wooden steps that lead down to the beach. Ladd's grandmother's diamond presses into Charlie's palm.

When we reach the shore, I can't help saying, "I'm surprised you remember. About the book. About anything." I feel grateful that my voice sounds neutral, not wounded or accusing. Just honest.

Charlie says, "I remember all of it. The book. The bear. The snow. The whole night. I remember you, Brett."

For a moment, I can see it. He looks sad. He looks *sorry.* He's going to apologize, and might even explain. But Ladd must have seen Charlie and me emerging from the sea of people, walking hand in hand and disappearing behind the bluff. Not hard to catch up to us, our dreamy saunter, and he appears at just that moment, before Charlie can speak again. I remember turning—the sunlight so much flatter, in that direction, pixels from staring at the water still dancing in front of my eyes—and seeing Ladd coming toward us. To my surprise he doesn't look angry—as if anger, at this juncture, would be too risky. He just looks determined. And separate, as if the *us* naturally refers to Charlie and me. Ladd's face wears a poorly concealed woundedness, a question mark, whereas Charlie and I stand next to each other, no question mark at all. Owning this moment together, this reunion, but not the discomfort we have created for Ladd. And I know that when I think back on that moment it's obvious whom I should feel guilty on behalf of: Ladd.

But oh, Charlie. I'm so sorry. Because if only I had been truer, stronger, deeper. If I'd ever been able to control and squelch that frantic, girlish knocking inside myself. You would still be here today. Not with me, it's true. But here. Among the living.

6

What were you and Charlie talking about?" Ladd asked on the drive back to his parents' house, after five full minutes of loaded silence.

"Nothing. Just hello, how are you. That sort of thing."

"Why were you holding his hand?" He used a conversational tone that must have taken quite a bit of effort.

"I don't know." I tried to keep my voice equally neutral. "He just took my hand. It would have felt rude to yank it away. I think he was just being polite."

Ladd snorted. I didn't blame him. And I didn't have an answer for myself. Riding next to Ladd, it was like I'd just come out of a trance and couldn't account for my behavior while I'd been under.

He pulled the car into the driveway. His parents were still at the party, so we had the house to ourselves, but Ladd didn't go inside. Instead he walked around back and through the gate to the swimming pool. I stood on the lawn and watched him go, then went inside through the front door. In the kitchen, I poured two glasses of white wine and carried them through the hall and out the French doors. Rebecca's dog followed me. Ladd sat by the pool, still wearing his blazer, his pants rolled up and his feet dangling in the cool water.

I put the glasses of wine on the dry deck, then pulled up my skirt and sat down next to him. Ladd had his hands on his thighs, his fingers tense. The dog sat between us, staring out across the pool as if that were the activity of the moment. Which I guess in a way it was. I picked up my wineglass and sat there, waiting for Ladd to tell me how hurt he felt. Or else to tell me the various stories Eli had alluded to, about the girls Ladd and Charlie had warred over in their youth, in a tone that would warn me away from even thinking about Charlie. I imagined leggy debutantes on the tennis court, girls in bikinis. Blonde and blue-eyed girls who lived worlds apart from my own childhood summers of university day camp. I hate to admit I felt a little rush, a bit of unaccustomed ego. I had never been the kind of girl men fought over.

Ladd didn't say anything. I studied his face, which tended to flush pink around his cheeks and jawline, especially when he'd been drinking. Part of me wanted to reach out and touch him, reassure him. But I worried that might unlock whatever anger he was trying so hard to hold in. When he finally spoke, it was in that same tone, trying to sound calm but with an edge that threatened to break at any moment.

"Girls always loved Charlie," he said. Which I didn't want to hear, any more than I had years before, when Eli had tried to tell me.

Ladd went on, not looking at me. "Remember what Eli said? 'Another girlfriend in common with Charlie.' Like there had been a hundred. Really it was just one girl in particular. Her name was Robin. I met her my freshman year at Cornell and she came back here with me for the summer. Then she met Charlie. Need to hear more?"

If I said no, it might sound like *Of course she left you for him.* I brought my fingers to his cheek, very lightly. He kept his eyes on the artificial blue of the pool water, tensing as if he didn't want me to touch him. I lowered my hand to pet the dog instead.

"But before that," he said. "Summers when we were kids. Once we were thirteen or so. Any girl . . . the girls we met. On the beach. Yacht Club dances, that sort of thing. They mostly liked Charlie. They *all* liked Charlie. You asked why we stopped being friends. I guess that's mostly why. Robin was the final nail in the coffin. I had to see him, sometimes, because of our families. Obviously I still do. But I never really want to. You know?"

"What happened," I said, "with Charlie and Robin?"

"He broke her heart. She came running to me. I dropped out of school and went to Alaska instead of taking her back."

"Oh," I said. "That girl."

"Yeah. That girl."

"I'm sorry," I said. "I love you."

"Do you."

"Yes. I really do."

"You know what Robin said when she broke up with me? She said I was too intense. Charlie was playful, she said. He was fun."

Charlie is unattainable, I thought. Ethereal, beautiful, charming. Nothing I could say about Charlie would be in any way comforting, except the one word Eli had used, way back when.

"He's a womanizer," I said.

Finally Ladd turned to look at me. "Yeah," he said. "A fun and playful womanizer. You know what I think he would do? If he saw his fiancée walking down to the beach holding some other guy's hand?"

I waited for a moment, raising the wineglass to my lips. Before I could take a sip, Ladd put his hand at the small of my back and pushed me into the pool. The shove was a little too abrupt, too hard, to own the word *playful*. My glass went flying, erupting in a pale arc of Pinot Grigio until it landed, still a quarter full, to bob beneath the diving board. I treaded water in my red Calvin Klein dress, which had originally cost $400, but which I had bought on sale for $149—the most I'd ever spent on a single garment. I hadn't yet looked at the care label, but I had a good idea it said Dry Clean Only. The dog jumped in after me, paddling in noisy circles.

Ladd jumped in, too, without even taking off his jacket. He grabbed me by the waist. The water was too deep for me to stand in but not for Ladd; I wrapped my legs around him and he held me, kissing me too hard at first—kissing me angrily. Knowing I had caused this, I let him reclaim me. I didn't push him away. Until the kissing softened, and eventually we ended up in the shallow end, our wrecked clothes floating on top of the water along with the wineglass.

THE NEXT DAY LADD didn't say a word about Charlie. We drove north, to my mother's. She had a different way of operating than Ladd's family—not given over to loving people so quickly. At the news of our engagement, she smiled at me over the rim of her teacup, and I could see a kind of release in her face. Now I would be taken care of. All these years taking care of me, counseling me, worrying about me. And now her work was done, I would be happy. After dinner, outside in the overgrown garden, I told her about the prenuptial agreement.

"Well," she said, the old anxiety returning to her face. "You're going to sign it, aren't you?"

"Yes," I said. "I mean, why not. Right?"

Palpably her mood shifted back to happiness, all those years of single motherhood floating off into the summer air, which—after dark in Vermont—felt light and cool. She never understood how loyal I was, to her way of life, her poems and her gardens and just enough money to get by. In my mind I saw the house where we'd lived together sold, her things packed up, the garden weeded and mowed or even paved over for a patio. Life marching forward, the way it can, when people or responsibilities are shed.

NEARLY TWO MONTHS LATER, the day after I went ahead and signed the prenup, Eli showed up at school, out of nowhere, uninvited. Ladd and I had come home from Boston late the night before, after dinner at Sonsie on Newbury Street, and my brain had that particular cider-pressed feeling from too much wine and too little sleep. The law office had looked exactly as I'd pictured it, shining oak and Oriental rugs. Hundred-year-old portraits so thick with oil I thought that if I pressed my finger against one it would still feel wet. At some point, my mother had suggested I have a lawyer of my own look at the prenup, which seemed like a good idea, but I didn't know any lawyers, didn't know how to get one. I didn't know how much it would cost but felt sure it would be more than I could afford. It occurred to me to ask Ladd's uncle Daniel, but even that seemed too complicated, so much more difficult than just going to the appointment and signing with the Cross pen that was handed to me and then carefully reclaimed.

Of course as things turned out it didn't matter at all, that signature. What retained significance was Eli. I remember walking out of Bartlett Hall into shocking sunlight. Looking back, it surprises me that I recognized him through the glare, but I did, immediately. He sat on the steps, watching the door as students and professors and TAs streamed out, everyone blinking similarly into the brightness. Although he faced away from the light, and had been watching expectantly for me, I saw him first.

The Eli who waited for me looked much more like the boy I'd known in college than the one I'd seen on the ferry. His hair had grown out, and he'd lost a considerable amount of weight. His skin had lost that pasty pallor. Whereas before he'd looked puffy, lethargic, I could see even from this distance that he'd regained a certain amount of energy. Although I had no idea why he'd be there, the sight of him looking like his old self lifted my spirits. Then I paused for a moment on the steps, feeling exposed in my knee-length cotton skirt. He was your friend, said a voice inside my head, chastising myself for the hesitation. I didn't like the use of the past tense: Weren't friends as close as Eli and I had been friends forever after? No matter what strangeness transpired?

I walked over to him. He barely looked up, and for a second I thought he hadn't actually come to see me. He could have other friends at UMass or he could be taking classes himself, finishing his degree.

"Hey," I said, sitting down next to him, as if it were something I did every day, as of course it used to be.

"Oh," he said. Startled. "Brett."

For a moment, I felt like I'd intruded on something. Maybe I was wrong. From the way he looked ahead, still focused on the crowd, he really could have been waiting for someone else to emerge from the building. He had a pen in his hand, and he wrote something on his pants leg. I squinted, trying to read the tiny handwriting, and Eli put his left hand over it, hiding it from me.

We sat there for a moment, then I fished in my bag for sunglasses. I slid them onto the bridge of my nose, and once I was properly shielded I said, "What are you doing here?" I tried to make the question sound gentle. Along with the pounds, Eli seemed to have shed years. Except for him writing on his clothes, it felt almost normal sitting next to him, as if I had walked out of Bartlett Hall and into a geographical time warp, and now sat outside Hellems in Boulder, Colorado—which would explain the sunlight, way too bright for Massachusetts even in late summer.

"What am I doing here?" Eli said. He turned and looked at me, and I remembered his eyes from that night on the rooftop. It took considerable effort not to bring my fingertips to my forehead.

"Yes," I said. "Were you waiting for me?"

Something in his face softened. He reached out and closed his hand around mine. His grip felt gentle, and his fingertips chapped. Eli looked so sad. I took my other hand and placed it on top of the two of ours, and we sat there a while, me comforting him for a problem that hadn't yet been identified.

"I tried to go back to college," he finally said.

"You did?"

"Yeah. Tried a semester at Manhattanville after I got out of the hospital. But those fucking drugs they put you on, nobody can concentrate. You know how they used to lobotomize mental patients surgically? Now they do it with pharmaceuticals."

"Oh," I said, without thinking, almost laughing. "It can't be that bad."

"You want to try my Clozaril?" He turned his head toward me sharply, with such an air of rebuke that I drew my hands back.

"No," I said. "I'm sorry."

"And then community college. Remember how I was going to go to Harvard Med? How that was the plan? And I end up dissecting kitty cats at Westchester Community College. Not that I could handle that, even. Dropped out after six damn weeks."

"I'm sorry," I said. "But maybe you could still go back? Ladd did. People do all the time."

"Yeah, yeah," Eli said. "Once these drugs are out of my system, that's what I'll do." He spoke a little too loudly, a few people walking by turned their heads. He didn't notice, the decibels rising when he said, "Look. My mother's dying. I want you to come see her."

"Me?" I said. Then I absorbed the first part of his sentence.

"Eli," I said. "I'm so sorry. Are you sure?" I remembered seeing her just a few months ago. She'd looked fine.

"Am I sure? Is the fucking hospice turning our house into a death scene? Does she weigh like fifty-eight pounds?"

"I'm really sorry," I said again. It must have come on very fast. "That's terrible."

"Terrible," he echoed. "Terrible, terrible, terrible."

"But Eli, she doesn't know me. Why would she want me there?"

"I want you there," Eli said. "It's what I need. What I want. I can't explain everything."

The words came out too fast, too loud, running into each other. I felt a little afraid of him. Also afraid that if I went, Ladd would be furious.

"Is Charlie there?"

"His mother's dying. Where else would he be?"

I glanced down at Eli's hand, still covering whatever he'd written, more indecipherable words surrounding it.

"Please," Eli said. Sorrow strangled the word. "Please Brett."

I remembered that Colorado night, Eli carried away on a stretcher. *Do you want to ride with him?* And what had I done, that time, but nothing? So rare that life presents an opportunity, another chance, to do something better.

"Okay," I said. "I'll go."

ELI ASKED ME TO drive his car—or rather, his mother's car. He smoked cigarette after cigarette, and I would have asked him to stop except that it seemed to calm him. So I just buzzed down my window. We were driving south on I-495 before he spoke.

"So you're studying," he said. It was a pattern I would learn, an early sign, his concerted effort to punctuate moments with questions, expressions, that might seem normal. "What are you studying, Brett?"

"American literature," I said. "Mostly American Renaissance."

"Oh yeah? We had one of those, too?"

It sounded like something *he* would have said—the person I'd come to think of as the real Eli. So I smiled. I told him a little bit about what I'd just started to study at the time. How Emily Dickinson fell in love with Sue Gilbert, who broke her heart but stayed close by marrying her brother, Austin. Eli lit another cigarette and stared at the roadside trees. My words hung in the air with the smoke, and I stopped talking and rolled my window down a little farther.

When my phone rang, I said, "It's probably Ladd. Could you get it for me? But don't answer it." Eli fished through my purse, then handed me the phone.

"Where are you?" Ladd said, without any kind of a greeting. I had left him a message, telling him that I was going to spend the night with my mother.

"Didn't you get my message?" I glanced at Eli, who had his eyes closed, resting his head against the passenger's window. Hopefully he wouldn't speak. He took one last drag of his cigarette and lofted the butt out the window. Nicotine-stained fingers drummed restlessly on the dashboard. I wondered if he'd exhausted his supply.

"You're still driving?" Ladd said.

"Just taking the exit to Randall now," I said, measuring the words, testing for believability. I didn't have much practice as a liar.

"Well," he said, "tell her hi for me. You think you'll be back tomorrow?"

"Yes," I said. "Tomorrow. I'll call you in the morning. Okay?"

"Okay," Ladd said. "Drive safe."

"I will."

"You know, I can get in the car right now. I can meet you there."

"No, no," I said. "I mean, you don't have to."

He paused another second, then said good-bye and "I love you." I did the same, then tossed my phone into my purse at Eli's feet, slowing the car into the rotary before the Sagamore Bridge. I waited for Eli to comment on the way I'd lied to Ladd, but he didn't say anything, just stared out the window, looking—I finally realized—as if he were listening to something else entirely.

IS IT POSSIBLE, IN memory, to go back to a place that means so many different things? I know that on this particular day, the first time I saw the Moss house, it was dark by the time Eli and I arrived. But my mind provides floodlights with the strength of day, as if my first glimpse took place at noon rather than past sunset. It includes all the details that would have been invisible to me. As the two of us walked through the front door, the whole house smelled sour and antiseptic, like death and sorrow. Eli added the incongruous odor of sweat and cigarettes.

Hospice had been set up for their mother, and I felt not only like an interloper myself but for delivering Eli—his disturbed and disturbing energy—to a sick woman's bedside. I couldn't see the ocean view through the dark windows, and I didn't notice the brine scent off the ocean, overshadowed as it was by the one thing on earth that's more primal. We only had to take a few steps into the house to see through the open doorway of the downstairs guestroom, now converted to a stage for a last exit. Several people crowded into that room around a bed, but my eyes fell immediately on the back of a head with blond ringlets, the sort of blond ringlets you'd expect to see on a toddler—the sort I *would* see on a toddler, his toddler, not so far off in the future. And it suddenly felt awful, appearing at the most private scene imaginable.

At the same time I thought: Turn around, Charlie. Turn around and see me.

Charlie turned around. His face looked pale and stricken. For the first time, I noticed a small circle of colorless moles, just above his right jawline. His cheeks looked puffy, his eyes faintly swollen.

"Brett," Charlie said.

He stood up and walked out of the room, toward me. I could see his discombobulation, his grief, giving way to a moment of relief. Someone had arrived who could hold him. He must have noticed Eli, standing behind me. Clearly Eli was the reason I'd come, to support my friend, to bring him here (though of course he only needed to be brought because he'd come to get me). But Charlie, who seemed to think I'd come for him, gathered me up in his arms, pulling me in tight as humanly possible. He pressed his forehead into the crook of my neck. His hands tightened on my back, the fingers that already felt so familiar and familial, shaking there, taut and possessive and completely within their rights, asking me for everything.

• • •

HAD THIS BEEN ELI's plan? To bring me to Charlie? He'd always wanted to keep me away from Charlie. But maybe I was one small gift before their mother departed and Eli himself went completely off the rails. Or maybe that reasoning was just mine, trying to piece together logical motives where none ever existed.

All I know is this: Charlie needed someone. Eli, by design or coincidence, delivered someone to him in the form of me. And I played along. Did Eli disappear, or did I desert him? I barely remember him that evening, what he did or where he was. Instead I concentrated on his brother. When the time came to go to sleep—the guest room already given over to their mother—I went upstairs with Charlie, my phone buzzing away, unanswered, in the purse I'd left on the sunporch. And it wasn't that I didn't feel pangs of guilt and conscience toward Ladd. It was just that the pangs I felt toward Charlie were that much stronger.

In the morning, we came downstairs together, Charlie and I. Mr. Moss stood in the kitchen, pouring coffee for himself and a nurse. If he wondered about my presence or identity he didn't say anything. His wife was days away from dying, and he couldn't think about anything else.

"She wants to sit out by the water," Mr. Moss said to Charlie.

Charlie and I went outside through the dining room, across the back deck. He showed me where the lawn chairs were stacked underneath it, and as he went back inside I chose the most substantial, least frayed one and carried it down to the shoreline. High tide, the rocks were covered by water, leaving only a small, smooth expanse of sand. I placed the chair close enough that Charlie's mother would be able to rest her feet in the surf, if she wanted.

When I looked up at the beach stairs, Charlie stood there at the top, cresting the landing with his mother cradled in his arms. She wore a scarf around her head, its edges fluttered against his face, and an afghan wrapped around her shoulders. She couldn't have weighed more than seventy pounds. Charlie took each step so carefully, his arms grasping her firmly enough that I could see veins and sinews tighten. If ever a moment redeemed someone, this was it. Nobody had ever done anything as carefully, as intentionally, as Charlie carrying his mother down the stairs. For her, the morning fog had cleared, and the sky turned out a gorgeous blue. The day offered up exactly the right notes of summer and autumn—warming sun, cooling breeze. The kind that welcomes you gladly to the world, or sends you off with love.

At the bottom of the steps, Charlie's muscles relaxed the barest bit. Just a few steps more, toward me, and he lowered his mother into the chair. Her arms slid off his shoulders, their cheeks bumping in a way that would have been awkward if it hadn't been a mother and son. By now everyone else had arrived, except Eli—Charlie's father and a nurse and a plump woman in a Talbots cardigan. I was still standing between the chair and the water—Mrs. Moss's feet nearly touched mine, but if she noticed me or wondered who I was, she didn't give any indication. I wanted to kneel down and take off her slippers, or adjust the afghan that had slipped off her shoulders, but I worried the face of a stranger would startle her or that she would think I'd arrived from somewhere else, to take her away.

It was Charlie who knelt in front of her, pulling the blanket back over her shoulders and slipping off her moccasins. Her skin seemed so thin I worried it would slide off along with the shoes. Mrs. Moss sighed and edged her feet forward, dipping them into the salt water. "Thank you, sweetheart," she said. "Thank you, Charlie."

He edged around her, next to me, leaning into my shoulder, as if I had been planted in that exact spot for only one reason—to keep him standing.

AFTER CHARLIE CARRIED HIS mother back up to the house, I finally got around to calling Ladd. I found my purse on the sunporch, walked out to the back deck, and pressed the first number I had on speed dial. My fingers shook slightly as I brought the phone to my ear. Even I wasn't dishonest enough to tell myself I was comforting an old friend. Charlie and I hadn't made love, but we'd slept in the same bed, wrapped up together, arms around each other. When he woke, he had propped himself up on one elbow and stroked my head.

"Thank you, Brett," he'd said. He had ridiculously long eye-lashes. Later he would tell me that when he was a child, heavy snow would clump in those lashes, forcing his eyes shut. That morning I wondered—as I would many times over the coming years—how a man with so many girlish features managed to look not the slightest bit feminine. When Charlie kissed me, I kissed him back. Elated. Opportunistic. Despite everything that should have clamored in my head—the dying mother and the disturbed brother and the abandoned fiancé—elated.

Now, standing outside at the very edge of the deck, looking out toward the ocean, the day seemed too pretty for words. The gray shingles on the wall behind me were already chipping, fading.

"Brett," Ladd said, on the other end of the phone, his voice tinny through faulty cell phone service. "How's it going? How's your mom?"

"She's fine," I said. "She needs some help with a research project, they changed her deadline. So I might stay an extra day."

On the other end of the line, a pause, and I felt like he could see through the phone lines, all the way to Cape Cod, me here at the Moss house. I wondered if he could hear the change in my voice. Suddenly, already: I belonged to somebody else.

"Okay," Ladd said, stretching the word out carefully, over too many syllables.

Just then Eli banged out of the front door wearing nothing but a pair of maroon boxers, decorated with beagles and bugle horns. I turned my head toward him, sharply enough that any normal person would have read the signal. *Go away, please. I need to talk privately.* But Eli didn't seem to realize I was there. He swaggered to the edge of the deck, almost exactly where I stood—close enough that his bare elbow brushed my upper arm. Then he whipped out his penis and started to pee, a broad arc of morning urine gushing out in front of us. I took the phone away from my ear and stepped back. From across the lawn, Charlie emerged at the top of the beach stairs, carrying the chair I'd brought down for his mother. He strode across the grass, his steps slowing again as he got closer, taking in the scene, his face falling. It was an expression I would come to know well, the particular descent of his features when confronted with the change in his brother.

By now I held the phone down, by my side. "Brett? Brett?" Ladd's tinny voice called to me, useless, two million miles away.

"I'll call you back," I said, maybe not loud enough for him to hear, and turned off the phone.

From halfway across the lawn, from across all these fresh disasters, Charlie stared at me. Behind him, daylight widened over low tide, the expanse of beach now littered with wet rocks. Eli, finished, stood between us, swaying slightly, tucking himself back into his beagle-and-bugle boxers. I moved sideways across the deck, stepping off its opposite edge and onto the grass, toward Charlie.

A FEW HOURS LATER, Charlie walked ahead of me as we picked our way across the rocky bluff. I loved the way his back looked, his thin white T-shirt and Bermuda bathing trunks. When we stepped from the rocks onto the sand, he pulled off his T-shirt. I hadn't brought a bathing suit—I was still wearing the clothes I'd taught in the day before, the blouse and knee-length skirt, so I just stood there and watched as he trotted into the water. I didn't know yet about Charlie's strange faith in salt water. He believed it could cure anything from poison ivy to cancer.

All the words anyone could use to describe Charlie, my past experience with him—anybody's past experience—were steadily becoming eclipsed by the kindness and love he showed his mother. By his nearness. By the way he seemed to not just want but need me.

I stood there on the sand and watched him swim out, much farther than I ever would have dared. And Charlie stopped swimming a moment. I could see him, getting his bearings, scanning the shore, locating me. I waved and couldn't see—but imagined—him smiling. *She beckons, and the woods start.* Goose bumps formed on my arms and legs, and they felt like a swelling. Like my body could no longer contain everything that lived inside it, only wanting to burst outward, to join the ocean air.

A PERSON BETTER SKILLED at deception would have come up with a less verifiable alibi. When I stopped returning Ladd's calls, he phoned my mother, an even less practiced liar—she didn't think for a moment to cover for me. Ladd drove by my apartment and saw my car, parked in its usual spot. When I checked my phone again toward evening, the many messages left by him and my mother were fraught with increasing alarm.

I went outside to call Ladd, so I could shield Charlie from this fallout. If Charlie and I talked about Ladd at all during those few days, I can't remember it. So much else was happening. Instead of walking toward the ocean, I headed up the road, to the dirt path that lapped the cranberry bog.

"The Mosses'," Ladd said when I finally told him the truth. He erupted so loudly I had to hold the phone away from my ear for a moment. "How the fuck could you be at the Mosses'?"

"Eli came to get me." Telling him about Mrs. Moss's illness, I pitched my voice low, trying to inspire him to do the same. It didn't work.

"But you lied to me," Ladd said. "You flat-out lied to me. You stood in one place and told me you were in another."

"Because," I said, my voice almost a whisper now, "I knew you would react this way, exactly this way. I knew you would be angry."

"Angry," Ladd yelled. "Of course I'm angry. You lied! You're with Charlie fucking Moss!"

From a dead tree beside the bog, a red-tailed hawk swooped toward the road, landing on prey too small for me to see in this light, the gloaming.

"Not Charlie," I said. "Eli. Eli came to get me."

"Where are you staying? Whose room?"

"Nobody's room. It's not like that."

"It's not like people are sleeping in rooms?"

"Ladd," I said, admonishing. Years later I would see Charlie employ this same technique, responding to my justifiable rage and anguish as if they weren't caused by his actions, only beneath both our dignity.

"I'm coming to get you," Ladd said. Finally, with this pronouncement, his voice evened out.

"You can't."

"Oh, I think I can."

"She's dying," I hissed. "You can't storm in here and cause a scene when she's dying."

"Then you come home. Right now."

"Eli drove me. I don't have my car."

"I don't understand," Ladd said. It was his turn to whisper. His voice might have broken my heart had I not already steeled myself the way a person in my position—a person doing what I did—must. "Who are these people to you," Ladd went on, "that you have to be there at a time like this?"

It seemed to me that the question answered itself via the posing. So that all I could say was, "I'm sorry. I'll call you later." When I hung up, Charlie stood next to me, hands in the pocket of his Baja hoodie.

"Everything okay?" he said.

"Yes."

I didn't want to frighten him with how quickly my allegiance had shifted. Already I had removed my engagement ring and zipped it into the inside pocket of my purse. As far as the Mosses, apart from Charlie and Eli, my presence had scarcely been registered. Everything occurring in the house, from their mother's slow exit to Eli's disintegration, was so fraught and elemental that all social mores had evaporated. Tonight I would sleep in one of Charlie's T-shirts, folding the same clothes I'd been wearing two days straight, leaving them on a chair to put on again tomorrow.

"Let's not go back in just yet," Charlie said, closing the distance between us the phone call had imposed.

As he stood next to me, I slipped my phone into his back pocket. The two of us faced west. We could see the sun, setting, flooding the red bog with orange light. Steps to the east, the paved road extended upward, toward a hill, so quiet it felt hard to imagine any car had ever driven on it, though I myself had come this way, driving Eli in his mother's car, barely twenty-four hours ago. As I looped my arm through the crook of Charlie's elbow, I felt a shiver at the small of my back, not just because a chill descended with the night air but because exactly as the light dissipated a shadow appeared, up where the road started to curve downhill. A tall man, newly thin, walking with long-legged strides. Something wrong about his gait, just slightly lopsided, and carrying with him the noise of conversation, though no one accompanied him. Engaging his voices, a phrase I would learn before the day was over.

Charlie stepped sideways. My arm slipped out of its spot and slapped against my body. As he started to head up the road, toward his brother, I reached out to stop him. Charlie turned back toward me.

"Listen," he said. "This has to be done quickly. Because he can't be in there like that. Not now."

"Okay," I said. "What are you going to do?"

"I'm going to provoke him. I need you to come with me, all right? So you can be a witness."

"All right."

"He's got to be a threat," Charlie said. "To himself or others. That's the only way to get him into the hospital."

"Okay," I said again, not caring that Charlie didn't seem to be factoring my safety into the equation, let alone his own. Charlie was never afraid *of* his brother, only *for* him. As he walked forward, up the hill toward Eli, I followed him.

Something had come over Charlie. A new energy, like an actor who'd stepped into character. "Eli," he said. His voice was hard and loud enough to break through the monologue and cut it short. "What are you doing? Where are you going?"

"Home," Eli said. "To see Mom."

"You can't see Mom anymore."

By now I had stopped walking, standing back—close enough to see everything, but far enough to keep myself out of the way. Eli stood there, peering through the dark at Charlie. Silence for a moment, then a burst of laughter over something nobody had said.

"What's so funny?" Charlie said.

Eli sidestepped to get around him. Charlie blocked his way.

"I need to see Mom," Eli said. "You need to understand, it's very important that I be there."

The sentences sounded reasonable but not the tone, words bleeding together at first and then separate, staccato. Still, I saw Charlie falter, his demeanor slip just the barest bit toward normal. But when Eli started to walk forward, Charlie again gathered up his resolve.

"You can't be there," Charlie said. "No entrance for you, Eli. She doesn't want you there."

Eli didn't respond. He just stood there, his brow furrowed. I couldn't tell if the words had angered him, or he couldn't understand what they meant. Charlie stepped forward. He reached out and pushed Eli, first on one shoulder, then the next. Eli backed up a pace or two, then turned and started to walk away, back up the steep road.

Charlie ran after him, catching up easily. I stood there, not moving, watching as Charlie shoved him again, a sharp and instigating jab at the shoulder. Eli didn't respond, just kept walking, head down. Charlie stopped a moment, watching him go, then ran again. He jumped onto his back, placing his hands over Eli's eyes. For a moment, Eli concentrated on trying to take those hands away; then he shrugged Charlie off, a hard movement. Charlie fell backward—no attempt to brace his own fall, no tension in his body. He just let himself slam to the pavement. I could hear the thwack of his head hitting blacktop.

All the houses around us were dark, stars obscured by low-hanging clouds. I stepped forward, not nearly fast enough, as Eli turned to see Charlie, there on the ground. He sunk down over him, straddling his body, and for a moment I thought he would start pummeling him. But he didn't, he just sat there, with his arms outstretched, covering Charlie's face with his hands, his fingers spread out so that Charlie could breathe.

"Eli," I yelled, hoping somebody, somewhere, was close enough to hear. "Eli, get off him. Let him go."

He didn't say anything for a minute, didn't move. Then he withdrew one hand and with the other stroked Charlie's head, as if he could erase the damage. I knew Charlie was conscious because he lifted his hands and closed them around Eli's arms, but he didn't try to push him off. He didn't try to fight him. Eli started speaking again, muttering, indecipherable words running into each other. The only ones I could make out were "Charlie" and "Mom."

I wanted to step forward, push him off Charlie. But I was too scared. "Charlie," I finally said, because Eli seemed so unreachable. "Push him off you."

Eli's head snapped away, toward me. Then he stepped off Charlie and stood beside me, docile, hands resting at his side. Charlie sat up, one hand cradling the back of his skull. My eyes had adjusted well enough to see a warm pulse of blood snaking its way through his fingers. I walked around Eli and helped Charlie to his feet. Then I reached into his pocket for my phone. The fall had smashed it into four pieces.

"Go back to the house," Charlie told me. He pulled off his hoodie, bunched it up, held it to the back of his head. He draped his other arm over Eli's shoulders. "Call the police. We'll wait here."

WHEN I LOOK BACK now I hardly see Eli. I see Charlie. The different words people (including myself) could use to describe him, all of them true by varying degrees. I see all those qualities, the good and the bad. But in that moment I mostly see a kind of valor, and selflessness, that I was never able to find within myself when Eli needed me.

By now darkness had settled in for the night. I trotted through it, toward the only lit house in the neighborhood, the Mosses', incongruously cheerful, as if a celebration took place behind those bright windows, instead of all this urgent, if equally intoxicating, sorrow.

7

Charlie's mother died the next day. One son at her side, holding her hand. The other in a hospital lockdown ward. That afternoon I borrowed her station wagon to go to the Marshall's off Route 6 and buy clothes for a few more days, including a dress I could wear to her funeral.

A close encounter with someone in the throes of psychosis creates a very particular state of fragility. Even when the person is removed, the madness stays behind, inflicted. Moving through my errands, that twin sense of guilt and trauma pixelated at my core, making me feel not quite, entirely, flesh and bone. Across the street, the Verizon store stood as a rebuke, but I didn't replace my shattered phone. My body tensed imagining the messages Ladd must be leaving. Later at the funeral, I hovered beside Charlie as if I were already his wife; people who hadn't seen him in a long time assumed I *was* his wife. Charlie's face was drained, his bearing shaky. He needed me, a body, to lean into, and I had become mercenary to all other purposes. Not even Ladd's parents, filing into their pew and casting their uneasy, questioning glances, could drive me from his side. After the service, Charlie grabbed my hand and pulled me along with him to the receiving line. I stood there next to him, with his father and uncles and a cousin or two, Eli conspicuously absent, mourners too polite to ask my identity as they shook my hand and offered condolences. Charlie's father still didn't know my name.

Ladd's parents emerged from the chapel, starting toward the line and then stopping as they saw me there. Paul put his arm around his wife and pointedly led her in the other direction. "Brett," Rebecca called, over her shoulder, her face pained and confused. But I didn't go to her. I just stayed with Charlie.

Daniel Williams didn't run away from me. He walked straight to the line, shaking hands and expressing sympathy. If Charlie knew there should be some kind of discomfort between the two of them, he didn't show it. The four stitches in the back of his head were barely visible. He shook Daniel's hand.

"I'm very sorry for your loss," Daniel said, and then moved on to me. "Brett," he said. He took my hand in both of his and looked me straight in the eye. It was hard to interpret that look, exactly. Not forgiving, but not accusing either.

"Hi," I said. Probably I didn't remind him of Sylvia anymore. But maybe I reminded him of himself, the excessive love that both indicted and exonerated me. Daniel let go of my hand, and moved down the line. Ladd's parents skipped the reception, but Daniel didn't. As I shadowed Charlie throughout the wine-infused afternoon on his father's lawn, I would see him occasionally, deep in conversation, or else staring through the crowd at me.

THE MOSS HOUSE NEEDED to be closed up for the winter. I needed to get back to Amherst, to resume my classes and officially break Ladd's heart. Before his mother got sick, Charlie had been living in Maine, painting houses and doing odd jobs. I can't remember how we formulated a plan for what would happen next, I only remembered what happened: We drove to Amherst in his mother's car. He dropped me off and then headed north to collect his things. My apartment was on the top floor of an old Victorian house that had been divided into four units, across the street from the Homestead, the yellow brick house where Emily Dickinson lived almost her entire life. When I walked into my living room, the place smelled sourly of overused cat litter. I'd left Tab with several overflowing bowls of cat food. She chirruped furiously across the living room and jumped into my lap, alternating rubbing against me with grateful passion and scolding me for my desertion. I stroked her back and stared across the room, at the rickety side table and the telephone that perched on top of it. No longer reprieved by the broken cell phone, I had to face the process of disentanglement. I wanted it done before Charlie came back.

"Brett," Ladd said. His voice sounded flat and hard.

"Hi," I said.

"I hear condolences are in order." Dripping with sarcasm, none of the usual attempts to squelch emotion. I tapped my bare fingers on the table, noting the line where his ring had been worn all summer.

"I'm sorry," I said. "We need to talk."

"So I hear. Go ahead and talk."

By now, Tab had calmed down and lay in a large furry heap in my lap. She purred so loudly I guessed Ladd could hear on the other end of the line through his stubborn silence.

"Not over the phone," I said. "In person. I need to come get my things, and give you yours."

An intake of breath on the other end, like I'd just told him something he didn't already know.

"Seriously?" he said, no anger now, just incredulous hurt. "You're really doing this?"

"I am," I said. "I'm so sorry. But I really am."

"Because I can't believe it. I can't believe it at all."

I nodded at the phone. The reason Ladd couldn't believe it, I'd never told him about Charlie and the feelings I had for him. If I had, it would all make perfect sense.

Ladd said, "This is the stupidest thing you've ever done in your life."

"I realize that," I said, and then—not wanting to doom myself with the admission—I amended: "I realize that it might be."

"You know he's just going to break your heart."

I deserved that, so I didn't flinch away from the phone. In this type of situation, even the most contained person said cruel things, and of course all the worst ones would be true.

LADD HAD RENTED A house on Pleasant Street, not far from the one where Emily Dickinson lived for a time, on the other side of the graveyard. According to Richard Sewall's biography, as a child she would watch funerals from her bedroom window—knowing that she herself would likely be buried there and worrying about when. The Poet may have walked over this same path to Ladd's front door—what was supposed to be Ladd's and mine, starting in October. I balanced a cardboard box of his things in my arms. It was embarrassingly light. Usually I stayed with Ladd, not the other way around. The primary object the box held—along with a Red Sox sweatshirt, some T-shirts, and an electric razor—was a smaller box, blue velvet, which he had used to present his grandmother's engagement ring. I couldn't bear to hand it directly back to him.

It felt wrong to use my key. Instead I wound it off my key chain and dropped it into the box. I knocked on the screen door. After a minute with no answer, I rang the bell. Then I pulled open the screen door and knocked again. Ladd's car sat parked in the driveway. He could have walked somewhere, or ridden his bike, but I could see lights inside the house. I turned the knob, and the door swung open.

"Ladd," I called, from the threshold. "I know you're here."

"Then why not come on in," he called back. "Make yourself at home."

I paused for the barest second, then stepped obediently inside. It was a classic early-nineteenth-century house, the stairs presenting themselves immediately at the front door, each room contained unto itself, very few closets. Ladd's voice had come from the living room.

"Can I come in?" I said.

"I already told you. Come in."

When I rounded the corner, he sat in a wide-striped armchair, the matching ottoman pushed aside, his long legs splayed out in front of him. From his voice, I'd expected a half-drunk bottle of scotch somewhere in the vicinity, but I didn't see one. His hands gripped the edge of the armrests. Later that summer, Charlie would mix drinks in the evening, Captain Morgan rum and ginger beer. Dark and Stormys. The name of those drinks would always make me think of Ladd.

I sat down in the chair across from him—a stiff wingback—and put the box at my feet. A few moments passed like this, Ladd glowering, and me, sheepish, waiting for the barrage.

"Listen," I finally said. "Don't think I don't know this is the worst thing I've ever done."

"Then why are you doing it?"

"Because," I said. Something like tears had begun to gather in my throat, and I worked to control myself.

"Oh, because," Ladd repeated. "No better explanation than that, Professor?"

"I know," I said. "I know everything you're thinking about me and it's all true. So in the end it's best. Right? You're better off."

"You're doing me a favor." His voice wanted to be contemptuous but sounded more anguished. It brought me back, like a sense memory, to that winter after Charlie disappeared without a word. How much worse it must be for Ladd than my schoolgirl heartache over a man I'd barely known twenty-four hours. A man who'd done this very same thing to him already. The other girl, Robin: Ladd had refused to take her back. I'd assumed, coming over here, that he'd already be done with me.

"Ladd," I said. "Even if I came back now, why would you want me, after what I've done?"

Ladd moved forward in his chair, the storm clouds in his eyes breaking up just slightly, with this glimpse of opportunity. Before he could speak, I stood up. I knew I had to face him, and at the same time there was nothing to be said. By now Charlie had piled whatever belongings he had into his mother's car. He'd be heading back toward me by tomorrow at the latest. I wouldn't allow myself to think that he might evaporate again, unreachable. He would come back to me this time, and he would stay, because I had lucked into a window of opportunity, the one moment in time he really needed someone, and found himself possessable. Given my specialty in late-nineteenth-century literature, I should have known better than to think of it as fate, but that's exactly what I did. It seemed like proof that we were meant to be together.

"I'm sorry," I said to Ladd. "But I think I'd better go."

"But you know, I *would* take you back," Ladd said, his voice cracking. He stood up. "If you wanted me to."

The ceilings in the house were low and close. Trying to avoid eye contact, I noticed a water stain just above Ladd's head. Someone, years ago, had let a bathtub overflow, and no one had ever painted over the stain. He stepped forward, closing the distance between us. The only way to reimpose it would be to sit back down, which felt rude. So I stayed where I was, lifting my chin to look up, toward if not directly at him, granting him whatever came next as his due. The cruel things he had a right to say—about Charlie's breaking my heart or whatever aspersions he could cast on my character, so obviously lacking. My only excuse was being in love, and I couldn't tell Ladd that.

"Stay," Ladd said. His voice shocked me with its softness. He reached out and closed his hand around my wrist. The grip felt gentle, more plea than demand.

"I can't."

Anyone could have told me, and I knew even as I moved forward: This whole thing was a mistake. A disastrous mistake. Charlie had already rejected me once. And now I was leaving Ladd, breaking off my engagement, for a man who hadn't even said he loved me and maybe never would. Charlie was scattered, penniless, jobless. Who knew what he even aspired to, as far as character, as far as life? Whereas this man in front of me wanted to be great and good. Ladd loved me. Even after what I'd done to him, he was prepared to forgive me.

"I'm sorry," I said. "I have to go. Maybe one day we can talk about this, but not right now."

"Who decides that?" Ladd said. His grip became slightly less of a question. "Who decides all of this?"

"I'm sorry," I whispered. "I wish it were different. I wish I felt differently. But I don't. And I have to go." I tried to step sideways, but Ladd's fingers tightened. When I pulled my hand toward myself, away from him, he pulled it back.

"Ladd," I said. My voice sounded tinged with humor, it seemed so preposterous, that he would use force. "Let me go."

"Oh, I'm sorry," Ladd said, tightening his grip. "Is this not playful enough for you?"

The two of us stood there for a long time, me trying to step back, away from him. Ladd holding me there, his body rigid, his jaw set.

"You're hurting me," I said, but still he held on while I understood that the physical pain with its increasing sharpness was nothing compared to what I'd done to him.

Finally, Ladd must have seen himself and what he was doing—perhaps in the blood I could feel draining from my face. With a step backward he let go. I snatched my hand—myself—back. As I ran out the door without collecting any of my things, I could hear Ladd falling back into his chair. I knew him well enough to understand he would shift from anger at me to despair over what he'd done. I had come to his house to end things, and Ladd—ever the gentleman—had finished the job for me.

THE REST OF THE day, I tended to business. Replaced my cell phone. Renewed my lease. Replenished groceries, enough for two, remembering Charlie was a chef, buying things like fresh parsley and cilantro. Not just food, but ingredients. I didn't allow myself to consider the possibility that he wouldn't come back, not until night descended and I lay in bed holding an ice pack against my throbbing wrist, my landline and cell phone silent. Tab, grateful for my return, positioned herself on my chest, the weight and fluff keeping my heart firmly in place, perhaps the only reason I got to sleep that night at all.

She was still there when I woke, stubbornly unmoving. Sunbeams slanted through the plastic slats of the window blinds and I tried to stretch, my spine sore from having been pinned so long in the same position. The ice pack had fallen to the floor, and my wrist still throbbed. Tab let out an indignant "mep" as I pushed her off of me. For the first time since last April, the boards felt cold against my bare feet. When I peered through the blinds, I saw the car, the wood-paneled station wagon, one of the last of its kind, parked across the street, packed full to the brim.

It took a minute to fish my robe from the back of my closet and would have taken even longer to find slippers, so I just put on flip-flops. I had the presence of mind to brush my teeth and hair. When I got downstairs, there he was, sitting on the front stoop, wearing a khaki field coat with a dark corduroy collar, drinking coffee from a take-out Starbucks cup. As I opened the door, he turned and smiled, his face breaking open with pleasure at the sight of me. I hadn't yet seen him smile this way at anyone else. I smiled back, feeling overjoyed when I saw a second cup perched beside him. He handed it to me and I sat down next to him.

"You came back," I said, not caring what these words revealed.

"Sure," Charlie said. "I told you I would. Didn't I?"

I nodded, thinking that perhaps now everything had changed and he always would follow through on stated promises. Maybe it was just the unspoken ones that gave him trouble. Charlie kissed me, and I leaned forward to hug him, my arms around his neck, conscious that I not let my grip be alarmingly tight, or thankful. As I pulled away, he glanced at my left arm, then gently took hold of it for closer inspection. For a six-inch span, a pale brown bruise, punctuated by four ragged purple circles. Charlie held my arm in his lap, his curls falling forward as he inspected it.

"What happened here?" he finally asked. Ladd's voice would have been sharp, urgent. But Charlie sounded calm.

I shrugged, not wanting any controversy to interfere with his return. My idea of the day stood very clear in my mind. We would go upstairs and make love while more coffee brewed. Then we would carry his belongings from the car to my apartment, establishing him here, my residence now Charlie's, too.

He ran his fingers very lightly over my injury. "Looks like somebody grabbed you," he said.

I stared down at my arm, examining it closely for the first time. The sight of the bruises didn't make me angry. Ladd hadn't meant to hurt me. But I couldn't be sure Charlie would see it that way. "It was an accident," I said.

"Ladd? Did Ladd do this?"

"When I went to give him back his things. And the ring."

The closest we ever came to discussing my broken engagement. Charlie didn't look at my face. He kept his eyes firmly glued to my injury. It throbbed dully. I thought of a line from a James Wright poem, "delicate as the skin over a girl's wrist." How easy for Ladd to damage that expanse of skin, with just the slightest loss of attention to his own wounded interior.

"It's okay," I told Charlie.

He nodded, then lifted my arm to his lips and kissed it, as if that would make the bruises go away. As if he were apologizing for his own role in what had hurt me. Ladd would have risen to his feet and stormed away, to confront the perpetrator. But Charlie let it go. I didn't count this for or against him. Nothing mattered except the fact that he'd come back. I couldn't worry about Ladd, or my wrist, or my own guilty conscience. I was too busy breaking into blossom.

FOR THE FIRST COUPLE weeks, Charlie didn't look for work. I would go to class, and the library, and office hours. Charlie had a little money, the security deposit from his place in Maine, and he would shop for groceries and cook dinner. He went for walks. I told him the story of Emily Dickinson and her sister-in-law, the unrequited love, and how they lived next door to each other most of their lives. He showed an interest by touring the Homestead and the Evergreens. One day when he got home, there was a package from Ladd waiting on the doorstep, with all the thing I'd left behind at his house, and a short note apologizing for hurting my wrist. Charlie carried the box upstairs and never asked a single word about it.

Another day I came home to find a message from Eli on my answering machine. "Hey, Charlie," he said. No one in the world would have connected this voice with the one I'd heard weeks ago above the cranberry bog. It was clear and careful, a tiny bit slow, each word separate and precise. "It looks like I can get out of here on Wednesday. If you could get back here or find a way to call me before then . . ." and then the sound of a click. I could picture Charlie, running across the short expanse of my apartment, making sure to get the phone before his brother hung up.

"Is your dad coming?" I asked.

Charlie was in the kitchen, crumbling basil into the blender. Since his arrival, my kitchen had gone from bare bones to fully equipped, every kind of gadget and paring knife tumbled into the cupboards and drawers.

"He can't," Charlie said. "He's not . . . he doesn't do great with this, when Eli gets sick. My mom usually deals with it. Dealt with it."

"But," I said, as if what he'd said hadn't registered, "are you going to drive him down to your dad's?"

"Maybe after a couple days. We'll see." Our conversation halted for a moment as he turned the blender on to Puree, basil and garlic and olive oil and balsamic vinegar whipping into the vinaigrette that I would never be able to replicate, no matter how many times I followed the steps exactly as Charlie showed me.

"So where's he going to stay before then?"

Charlie looked up, one of his pointed moments of stillness, then took another moment to just look at me. Since he'd moved in, I'd found myself imitating his style in small ways, rope necklaces, Indian prints, whimsical flourishes. Today I wore a sundress that had been in the back of my closet for years, along with a thick wool sweater, my hair in a loose ponytail tied with a piece of his butcher twine. Charlie smiled and held his arms out. I stepped into them, my lips just even with the U of his clavicle.

"I thought he could stay here," Charlie said, his voice a little muffled against the top of my head. "If that's okay with you. Just for a couple days."

I wanted to turn and cast a glance at the tiny space, my one-bedroom partitioned from the living room by an open archway, no door. But that would have required moving away from the embrace and, worse than that, the possibility of displeasing him. "I guess he can sleep on the couch," I said, picturing Eli's long legs hanging over the armrest. I remembered a tapestry folded into the bottom of my sweater drawer, a dark-red-and-ivory print that Charlie would like. We could hang it in my doorway tonight. Refusing to have Eli here, in my house, would be like refusing to have Charlie.

"You're the best," Charlie said, winding his arms around me tighter. "I love you."

IF IT WEREN'T FOR Eli, Charlie and I never would have met. Still, over the years it was difficult not to imagine what we could have been without him, the specter of his inevitable comings and goings. "Only the mad will never, never come back," wrote W. H. Auden, and I found this to be true, although the two new versions of Eli—medicated (bloated, docile) and not medicated (wild, muttering)—did return again and again. But the original Eli, the real one—the boy I'd known in Colorado, the one who'd stayed resolutely beside me when his brother had not—seemed to be gone forever.

"My father's never been able to deal with it," Charlie told me again as we drove to pick up Eli in Pocasset. "It doesn't compute with him, he always just pushed it off to the side and let my mom handle it."

"Maybe now that she's gone he'll have to," I said. As little as I'd interacted with Mr. Moss so far, I still found it hard to believe he wouldn't take over his wife's job as primary caretaker of all things Eli.

Charlie nodded, his hands firm on the steering wheel. Over the years I would learn how it felt to visit or collect someone from a mental hospital; the way you brace yourself for profound and awkward unhappiness. It was especially sad seeing this in Charlie. The only time the weight of the world ever touched him was through Eli. And later, sometimes, me. Charlie talked a little more, telling me about the struggles they'd had with Eli since that night seven years ago when he'd jumped off the roof, jumped from one kind of life—normal and promising—into another.

"Well," I said, as if no one had come up with this solution yet, "he just has to stay on his meds."

"The meds suck," Charlie said. "They turn him into a zombie. A fat zombie. And they make him impotent."

An image came into my head, Wendy sitting in Eli's lap around a crowded table at the Rio. I'd run into her a few times after Eli left school. Once outside of Hellems, she'd broken down and cried. "It's so sad," she said when I told her I hadn't heard from Eli. "I always thought what a great dad he would be."

Back then, when he was dating Wendy, Eli had told me about the chemicals your body produces when you're in love. Pheromones and oxytocin. Those early days with Charlie, I was living on those chemicals, their fumes surrounding me every second, and I couldn't even consider the concept of impotence.

"If you could just talk to him," I said, "and really let him know what he's like when he's off his meds."

"That's the last thing he needs to hear right now." Charlie returned his attention to driving. "He'll already feel like shit about himself. His self-esteem will be at less than nowhere. It'll only make him feel like we're against him if we paint a picture of him at his worst."

I didn't say anything at all about how I worried Eli at his worst could be dangerous. My hands stayed firmly in my lap, resisting the urge to touch my forehead. Maybe all those years ago he hadn't meant to hurt me. And Charlie—he had meant to hurt himself more than Eli had done him any violence. I reached over and stroked the back of Charlie's head, the tiny bumps where his stitches had been ever so slightly detectable beneath my fingertips. And I remembered the way Eli had held his head in his hands, as if measuring the damage.

THE FIRST THING ELI wanted was a pack of cigarettes. The second was to see their mother's grave. She was buried in the Blue Creek cemetery, a bucolic piece of land despite its proximity to a busy street. Even the whoosh of constant cars took on a calming rhythm, like the wind soughing through the maple leaves and the crash of the waves from over the hill. The mound of earth over Sarah Moss's grave—swollen and fresh a few weeks ago—had already been tamped down by rains. Somebody had left a white plastic flowerpot, meant to look like a wicker basket, leaning against the stone, dried and wilted calla lilies poked into sodden Styrofoam. I picked it up and stood back. Charlie knelt and placed a little bottle filled with colored sea glass where the arrangement had been. He stood again, the two brothers shoulder to shoulder, staring at the grave as if the inscription were long and involved, not just a name and dates. Finally Eli broke the stillness by lighting a cigarette. He curved a tremoring hand around his lighter to block it from the wind. The smoke settled in around us, a defeated and outlaw scent. Eli's hair looked faded, almost brown, as if his time in the hospital had drained it of its brightness. It flopped across his forehead as he leaned into the cigarette, and I wondered if his mother had been the last person to cut it.

"It's crazy," Eli said, the emotionless voice I would come to find comforting. "It would be easier to believe she was there, down under my feet, if I'd seen it. You know? Seen her die. Seen her buried."

"I'm really sorry," Charlie said.

"Crazy," Eli said again. He flicked the ash from his cigarette. I waited for it to land on the grave, but it didn't, just blew toward the road, fading out to invisibility on its way.

"You want to walk down to the beach?" Charlie said.

"No. I think I'll sit here a while. You guys go ahead, I'll meet you."

Charlie took my hand and we headed toward the spot where the road turned into a brambled beach path. October now, with leaves and beach plums mulching into a cidery scent that mingled with the approaching ocean, both of us in sweaters and sneakers, I didn't think Charlie would swim. I didn't know yet, how he swam one day every month, and in order for it to count he had to dive under the waves at least three times.

"I want to say thank you," Charlie said, as he started taking off his clothes. "Because you've been right here whenever I need you. Loving me."

A kind of glow washed over me, as if I'd stumbled on a key so naturally. That was all I had to do—love him—and everything would be all right.

"You're my rock," Charlie said.

He kissed me and then ran off to dive into the frigid waves. By the time Eli lumbered down to join us—a shuffling, Frankenstein gait that had nothing to do with his old self—Charlie was bundled back into his clothing, his hair still wet, freezing Atlantic seawater beading at the base of his neck and dampening the collar of his sweater. I moved in closer when he put his arm around me, hoping I could transfer a little warmth. Eli walked down the shoreline wearing Charlie's field coat, smoking and looking out across the water. I kept waiting for the stream of voices to begin, to make their way across the rocks and sand to us; but whatever went on inside his head, for now it all stayed quiet.

BEHIND THE RED-AND-IVORY TAPESTRY in my bedroom with Charlie, the air persisted, still hanging thick with oxytocin and pheromones. On the other side lurked Eli, the cigarettes he wasn't supposed to smoke in the apartment, my lavender soap operating as a low base note after he showered, but beaten down within hours by the sour, sickly scent—a kind of ruined sweat—that clung to him in every temperature. Mostly Eli slept, shirtless in the living room, my mother's itchy nylon afghan sliding off over his belly—growing almost like a pregnancy, as if the enforced sanity were something that had to incubate. Despite promises from Mr. Moss to collect him, Eli stayed on my couch till the weather turned too cold for a throw, and it was an old down sleeping bag that failed to cover his nakedness when I crept out of my room in the morning. I could hear him snoring as I made coffee and showered, as I tried to be quiet as possible. He seemed less like an old friend than a convalescing stepchild. Meanwhile, Tab had abandoned me within days of his appearance, joining me in the kitchen only for her morning can of Fancy Feast and then immediately returning to her spot on his chest.

Was I afraid of Eli, during those days? Never once, never at all. Even in his heavily tranquilized sleep he would lift a hand to stroke the cat. I thought about his theory, human hands, as the cat's eyes glazed, her lids at ecstatic half-mast, and I felt sad that he couldn't ever be a vet, let alone a doctor. Then I would close the door quietly behind me with my hair damp, because I didn't want the blow-dryer to wake anyone, and return toward late afternoon with a bag full of groceries for Charlie to prepare our dinner.

• • •

"JUST PROMISE ME YOU won't marry him," my mother said.

We sat across from each other at the Black Sheep coffee shop, the rich chocolate cake she'd insisted on buying sitting untouched between us. I sipped my coffee to avoid answering, and she handed me her fork. "Eat," she said. "You look thin."

It was true. Despite Charlie's meals I was losing weight, the effort of loving him, of accommodating him, burning more calories than I could possibly take in. I picked up the fork and ate a small bite. My mother watched me, her brow furrowed. Fading freckles obscured whatever lines marred her forehead. She had blue eyes and fair skin. Her hair used to be red, and she'd let it fade to dark gray, still curly and abundant, pulled off her forehead with a silver barrette in a way that should have looked girlish but didn't. As one day few people would take Sarah and me for mother and daughter, so it had always been with the two of us.

Mom sat back, placing her broad, freckled hands flat on the table. "I don't understand what you're doing," she said. This was the posture she always assumed when posing questions to her class. Measured questions, meant to incite conversation and even argument. She would float them out and then sit back, waiting to observe and assess the reaction.

To stall, I took another bite. She wouldn't understand anything I told her. If my mother ever went on a single date after my father died, I couldn't remember it. I could only remember my serious, widowed, tenured mother. Two simple missions in life: raising me and teaching literature. Specializing in Yeats and Coleridge, all the romance in her life existing in the poems she studied. I couldn't say that Charlie was my Sue Dickinson, because she didn't agree with my theory. So instead I used Yeats's muse.

"He's my Maud Gonne," I said.

My mother removed her hands from the table and tilted her head with a loud and exasperated exhalation. "That," she said, "only works for poets. Not even for them. Just their work. And honestly I'm not sure it works for that post–nineteenth century."

A group of college girls banged noisily into the shop, laughing with each other and then with the baristas. My mother watched them find a table at the far side of the cafe. I took the opportunity to examine her face. She looked more worried than angry, but I also thought she looked the tiniest bit relieved that she hadn't found me in an even worse situation. In the stretch of time between Ladd's phone call to her and now, I'd avoided her, returning calls when I knew I'd get her voice mail. She had waited until fall break to make the ninety-minute drive from Randall and show up on my doorstep. Unfortunately, Eli had answered.

"Well," I said, when the girls' chatter was far enough away, and it looked like my mother wasn't going to break the relative silence. "No one's brought up marriage. So it's not a worry for right now."

"What about Ladd?"

"He hates me now."

Another deep intake of breath from her, this one more mournful than frustrated. I'd ruined everything.

"Listen," she said. She retrieved her fork and took a bite of the cake, then frowned at its sweetness. "I've been offered a teaching fellowship at University College Cork. It's a three-year position."

"That's great," I said. She'd always wanted to go to Ireland.

"I'm not sure I should take it now."

"Oh, Mom. Take it. I'll be fine."

"How long will his brother stay with you?"

"Not much longer," I said. "A few more days."

"Because I'm really not comfortable with this arrangement."

"It's not an arrangement," I promised. "It's just a visit."

Abruptly, as if we'd agreed on a specific time for this coffee date to end and she realized that time had arrived, she pushed back her chair and stood. As I followed her out of the cafe, a notice on the community bulletin board caught my eye, written on lined notebook paper. A kennel just outside town looking for a live-in employee. I ripped off one of the phone number tabs.

By the time I got outside my mother had already headed across the street to Sweetser Park. She sat on the edge of the fountain, staring at the tumbling water. I sat down next to her and said, "I'm sorry." She nodded as if apologizing were perfectly reasonable. She'd been so looking forward to the idea of me and Ladd, her daughter happy and rich and taken care of.

"I was thinking of selling the house," Mom said. "And moving in someplace smaller, an apartment maybe, when I get back. But now I'm thinking I'll just rent it. Maybe I can find someone on a month-to-month lease, so you'll have a place to go, if you need one."

Part of me wanted to protest, but I didn't. The loss of the house where I'd grown up—its book-lined walls and my mother's overgrown garden—would be great enough to want to forestall. Today, when Mom had arrived at my apartment, after Eli let her in, she'd spent less than five minutes talking to Charlie. Apparently that was enough time to convince her that one day I might need to run from him, or perhaps more accurately, that I would need a place to recover after he ran from me.

She said, needing me to urge her more than once, "Or maybe I shouldn't go at all."

"No," I said. "Don't be silly. I'm a grown woman. I'll be fine."

My mother frowned. "Just promise me you won't marry him," she said again, her voice so low she might have been speaking to herself more than me.

"Oh, Mom," I said, not wanting to say, *But I love him so much.* Instead I said, "You barely spoke to him five minutes."

"I know," she admitted. "But I've spent a lot of years with young people. I can read them. That one, Charlie, he's the kind of person who'd only come to every other class."

My lips twitched with the effort not to smile. Of course she was exactly right. Whereas Ladd would attend every single class, arriving on time, if not early.

"Okay," I said. "I promise I won't marry him."

On my left hand, the reverse tan line created by Ladd's ring had already become invisible. A few blocks away, at that very moment, he was packing up his house, probably making sure to discard any objects that held trace memories of me.

CHARLIE TOLD ME HE loved me in odd moments, not nearly as often as I wanted to tell him. If my life had become an effort not to complain—about Eli's remaining on my couch, about Charlie's running out of money and my TA stipend's feeding all three of us—the greater effort lay in not announcing my own feelings every time I saw him. I drank up every intimation of his possible love for me, the food he prepared, the broad hands he laid upon me so carefully, and—best of all—the smile that erupted at the sight of me. In all the world, I wanted one thing, to keep him with me. I had to prevent myself making any false moves, from frightening him away with the sheer degree of everything I felt.

As for Eli, he barely registered interest when I gave him the number of the kennel, but he did call. I helped him pick out what to wear for his interview. "Use lots of soap," I told him, before he showered, and he did, emerging damp, a towel wrapped around his growing midsection, the sour odor very nearly masked. I ironed a pair of khaki pants and a blue plaid shirt, clothes that took the interview seriously enough yet indicated a willingness to be muddied by dog paws. On the drive over I didn't say anything when Eli lit a cigarette, having already ceded victory in that particular battle. His hands shook, ever so slightly, as the flame caught the paper. It almost made me want to light it for him. He rolled down the window and sent the stream of smoke outside.

"Are you nervous?" I asked him.

He shrugged. "To tell you the truth, it's hard to feel much of anything these days." His brows did a funny little twitch, toward each other. It could have been anger or else an expression of nerves he didn't realize he felt. I wanted to reach out and touch him, close my hand around his forearm, or place it on his shoulder. Something. On the other side of the wall from where he slept, Charlie and I existed in a world of skin on skin. Whereas Eli's only physical contact was with the cat. Once again, his cat.

I pulled up in front of the kennel. It would be a noisy place to live, with dogs constantly barking. But there was a nice white clap-board office—I guessed the apartment was on its second floor. Its windows looked right out on the dogs. Probably the cats boarded inside and Eli would be able to sneak one out at night and take it to sleep with him if he got the job. I didn't consider letting him take Tab. My generosity always stopped just short of enough.

"Do you want me to come in with you?" I asked, as he stepped out of the car. Maybe they would take me for his girlfriend; I could confer the needed degree of normal.

"No, it's okay. I can do it."

"Break a leg," I said, and he smiled a little, a rare glimpse of the old Eli, the appreciative crinkle around his eyes.

While Eli interviewed, I sat in the car reading *Austin and Mabel*, the tangled account of Emily Dickinson's brother and the woman he became involved with after his marriage to Sue began to crumble. Every page I turned, every minute that ticked by, felt like a good sign. After about a half hour, Eli emerged with a plump gray-haired woman who appeared to be giving him a tour. Another good sign. I stepped out of the car to stretch my legs. A black-and-white collie took note and barked ferociously, a high-pitched warning. Eli reached through the wire and offered her a hand, and the dog quieted, trotting over to him.

"Hey," Eli said when he came back to the car. "I got the job."

I walked around to hug him. His fingers trembled at my back. "Good work, Eli," I said. "Congratulations."

By the time we returned to my apartment to collect his scant belongings, Charlie was there and came with us to install Eli in his new home.

"I love you," Charlie told me as the two of us drove away, the sound of barking dogs fading behind us. He reached out, covered my hand with his and added, "Thank you."

You know what happens next. After fall gave way to winter, and winter to spring. After Eli worked a few months at the kennel and then abandoned his meds and wandered the streets for weeks before landing back in the hospital. After my mother left the country. On an evening still cool enough for cardigans, Charlie and I carried a bottle of wine across the street and sat on the bench at the Homestead. He knew I liked to be there after dusk—not far from where the Poet herself used to garden, once the light had faded and she knew she wouldn't be seen.

"Tell me," he said, handing me a plastic cup, "what it was that Emily liked about Sue."

"We can't call her Emily," I told him. "We have to call her Dickinson. Or the Poet."

"Tell me what the Poet liked about Sue."

"Everyone liked Sue," I said. "She was very magnetic. Very charming. Beautiful. All that."

"Like you," Charlie said, touching a strand of my hair.

"No," I said. "Like you. Emily was like me. Studious. Infatuated."

"The Poet," Charlie corrected me, and I smiled. "Is that what you are?" he said. "Infatuated?"

"No. Not just that, anyway."

"You were going to marry Ladd."

"Yes."

"Do you want to marry me instead?"

A leap inside me. There was no ring. Only Charlie, sitting there, looking earnest. Spontaneous. Utterly believable. Still, for the first time since the Fourth of July party, I allowed myself to be suspicious of him. I was too afraid to let the gathering joy bubble to the surface.

"But Charlie," I said. "You can't commit."

He laughed. "I just did."

"Why?" I whispered. "Why me?"

"Because I can always tell what you're thinking."

This was the last answer I wanted, so I turned away from him, but he cupped my chin, gently bringing my gaze back to his face. Charlie's smiles never seemed like a reflex. They started slowly, his eyes on you. There was never any doubt—you were the one who inspired it.

"Look," Charlie said. "I could give you a list of qualities. Beautiful. Smart. Sexy. Right? But those are just words. They apply to a million women. But only this applies to you. I love you. Because I do. Okay? I just do. So let's get married."

He kissed me, not bothering to wait for my obvious yes. I let not only happiness boil over but triumph. *I knew it.* Even back in Colorado, even after I'd given up on him. Somewhere inside myself, I knew it. If only I could love him enough, he would come to me, and he would stay.

My mother traveled from Ireland for the wedding even though we scheduled it at the worst possible time for her, the fall, because we wanted to wait until Eli was well enough— medicated enough—not only to stand up with us but walk me down the makeshift aisle to the very edge of the lawn, overlooking the ocean. Me in a simple white dress, Charlie waiting for me in a white button-down and khakis. A string quartet played as I walked toward Charlie and the Unitarian minister, my arm looped through Eli's. I must have been beaming, because Charlie had the extremely fond and bemused look he generally wore in response to my adoration. I took the last few steps up to him, and Eli took his place beside his brother. We stood there, listening to the minister, and I kept my eyes mostly on Charlie, my hands closed around my sunflower bouquet. For one moment, I let my eyes leave his, to scan the crowd of a hundred or so people, many of whom I'd last seen at Mrs. Moss's funeral.

And when my eyes came back to meet Charlie's, he was gone. Vanished. I stood there alone, the minister still speaking, his voice strained with the effort of pretending nothing was wrong. It took me about ten seconds to locate Charlie, standing off to the side with his head in his hands. Eli stood next to him, talking quietly. I noticed a tangle of poison ivy in the brambles beside them and worried about Charlie's bare ankles in his Top-Siders. I didn't dare look at my mother.

It didn't last long. The whole episode took a total of two, maybe three, minutes. I stood alone at the altar while the minister politely continued to speak. Everything around me and within me froze, but I knew if I could only endure this short stretch of time (promising myself even in that moment that I would never so much as think about it again) my reward would be continuing on as Charlie's wife. And I was right: Eli brought him back to me, holding on to his elbow with purpose, Charlie looking pale and ever so slightly unlike himself. *Are you okay?* I mouthed, and he nodded, and reached over to fold his hands over the stems of my bouquet, weaving his fingers between mine. He said "I do," clearly and loudly, for everyone to hear.

Eli reached into his pocket and handed Charlie their mother's ring to slide onto my finger. We were pronounced husband and wife, and we kissed, and then Eli kissed me on the cheek—his hand tremoring at my shoulder—before Charlie and I walked back down the aisle together. Nobody ever said a word about that moment, at least not to me. And what did it matter? In the end, he said "I do." Of everything I'd ever wanted, this was what I'd wanted most.

8

In the American Renaissance class where I met Ladd, the professor was an eccentric and entertaining lecturer, given to innuendo and non sequiturs. But she was a tough grader. Or rather, she insisted that I, as her TA, be a tough grader, since she didn't read the papers herself. There were nearly a hundred students in the class, and I generally sat in the back row—sometimes grading while she lectured. So I might never even have come into contact with Ladd if Professor Keith hadn't told me to take five points off for every grammatical error on every paper. Midsemester Ladd walked into my office hours, holding the paper he'd written on *Sister Carrie*. It was folded back to the last page so the first thing I saw was the C+ I'd written in green ink because I'd lost my red pen. I didn't recognize Ladd when he walked into the huge office I shared with ten other TAs—our own little areas partitioned with filmy screens—but I recognized the apologetic note I'd written. It had been a good, sensitive paper on Carrie's theatrical ambitions and Hurstwood's lovelorn downfall. But Ladd had an unfortunate tendency toward subject-pronoun disagreement, and the mistake had cost him.

"I'm not a bad writer," he said, settling into the chair across from me. "Just trying to be gender-neutral."

"That excuse won't fly with Keith," I said, letting myself off the hook. "It's one of her pet peeves."

In the next cubicle, a girl was crying. Ladd and I could not only hear her, we could see her shadow, repeatedly laying her head on the desk, then lifting it up to speak.

"Don't worry," Ladd said. "I'm not going to start crying."

I laughed. Looking at Ladd, I also steeled myself. Professor Keith had an uncanny memory for every student, and if I changed his grade she'd suspect I'd either been intimidated or seduced. Before the semester started, she'd lectured me about favoring the white males in the class, a common pitfall, she said, for young teachers, especially young female teachers. I leafed through the paper, showing him the mistakes I'd circled and explaining Keith's grammar policy, my finger tapping the paragraph where I'd already written all this down. Ladd suggested that since it was the same mistake repeated I should only count it as one.

"It doesn't work that way," I told him.

He sat there, looking at me very intently. So intently I started to suspect he'd done this on purpose, thrown his grade so he could come in and complain to me about it. I wished I could remember his previous papers.

"You could go to the Writing Center next time," I said. "They'll read the paper over with you, catch these kinds of mistakes."

Ladd sat with one broad hand on each knee. He had a kind face, sincere and listening. I found myself not wanting him to leave just yet.

He said, "Maybe you could read it for me first. Next time."

I blinked at him, trying to think what I'd said that made him think such a request was appropriate. Maybe he felt like he could ask because he was older than me? Or maybe he could tell I liked him. I looked down at my stack of papers, hoping the warmth at the back of my neck didn't mean I was blushing.

"Or not," he said, sounding sincerely apologetic. "I'm sure you're really busy."

I paused, not wanting to be a pushover but also not wanting to disappoint him. Or embarrass him. So I said, "Maybe I could just once. Next time."

I looked up at him. His brows were raised, worried that he'd offended or compromised me.

"You sure?" he said. "It won't be too much trouble?"

"It'll be fine," I said, trying to sound definite, which I ruined by adding, "Don't spread it around, though." If Professor Keith found out she would kill me.

"No," he said. "I won't. Your secret is safe with me. Thank you, Brett. I really appreciate this."

"You're welcome," I said, and smiled.

IF LADD HAD NEVER grabbed me the day I left, if he had never hurt me, I would have been forever etched as the villain in our history. Anything good between us would have been erased by my treachery, so much so that we might never have communicated again.

But he felt so awful; it leveled something between us, and created a kind of matching regret, each of us with this knowledge—each having done something to the other we wouldn't have thought ourselves capable of. So that over the years when the chance summer meetings occurred in Saturday Cove—in restaurants or grocery stores or on the beach—they occurred with an awkward kind of carefulness, an examination of faces. How much we wished things had unfolded differently. I sometimes resisted going to Saturday Cove in the summer, with the inevitability of running into Ladd, or his parents, or his uncle Daniel. All that pageantry of decorum, with the memory of everything that had been so base, so uncivil, just below the surface.

We did go to Saturday Cove, though, because Charlie loved it. That's where we were when my mother died in Ireland, three summers after our wedding. Charlie and I had come down the week before his father arrived. Our second day there, I'd woken up around nine thirty to find Charlie gone. My phone rang while I was making coffee, still wearing Charlie's Herring Run T-shirt. The woman, a secretary from the University of Cork, was crying a little herself, and her Irish accent was so thick. It was very difficult to understand her.

"I'm sorry" was one of the few phrases I understood clearly. "I'm so terribly sorry to be telling you this."

I hung up and dialed Charlie's phone, which rang from upstairs, the whistling ring he'd programmed for me. I followed the sound of it in a daze and pulled on a pair of shorts. Then I headed out to the beach to try to find Charlie. Barefoot, I picked my way over the rockiest bluff, the direction of his most usual walk. He would alternate looking out toward the sea and collecting sea glass for his mother's grave. I passed the steps that led up to the Huber's beach house. Mr. Huber kept a kayak stashed beneath his deck. Sometimes in the winter Charlie snuck up and borrowed it; I hoped he wasn't so unreachable as out on the ocean. I didn't realize I was heading in the direction of Daniel Williams's house until I saw Daniel, out for a walk on the beach, coming toward me.

"Brett," Daniel said. "What's wrong?"

"I think my mother's dead." A very small voice, left over from childhood.

"What do you mean, you think?"

I told him about the phone call, the Irish accent, the way it made no sense.

"She hasn't been sick," I said. "I can't remember her ever being sick."

My mind went to Charlie's mother, the way we always described her illness and death as quick. Still time enough, though, to carry her out to the shoreline. Still time enough to say good-bye.

Daniel placed his hand at the small of my back and pushed me forward the slightest bit, enough to give me the head start, the power, to follow him back to his house.

THE LAST TIME I saw my mother was at my wedding. She had tried so hard to support me, even though I was breaking my promise marrying Charlie. Instead of complaining or pointing it out, she flew back from Ireland, interrupting her semester. She bought a mother-of-the-bride dress, split the bill with the Mosses, and never said a word about Charlie's disappearing act at the altar. She even gave Charlie my father's wedding ring.

But it had been a wedding, with a swirl of people, and no time to really sit down and talk. And the smiling facade made her seem not really like herself. My mother had always been such a serious person—or maybe she'd just become so after my father died. Maybe it was just being a single mom with a career that made her seem so stoic.

"I love you very much," she said to me the day after the wedding when I drove her to the bus stop in Barnstable. From there, she'd take a bus to Logan airport and a plane back to Ireland. Such a long trip to honor a marriage she didn't approve of.

"I love you, too," I said, hugging her good-bye.

What would I have done differently if I'd known that would be the last time I'd ever see her? Maybe breathed in the scent of her hair a little more fully. Maybe I would have thanked her again, for making the trip, stayed in her embrace a little longer. Mom.

At Daniel's beach house, I sat across from him as he made phone call after phone call at his beautiful oak desk. I ran my fingers over the carved inlay at the edges, wondering when I'd start crying, wondering how he knew all the right numbers to dial. By the time he walked around the desk and knelt in front of me, gathering up my hands, we both knew I'd figured out everything from listening to his side of the various conversations. But he told me anyway, in a careful and measured tone. That she hadn't shown up for a day's worth of classes. That the school secretary had found her at her apartment. It looked like an embolism.

"She can't have felt any pain," Daniel promised. "It would have been immediate."

"But she wasn't even sick," I repeated, the same dead, childlike voice I'd used before.

"That's how these things happen," Daniel said. "I'm so sorry."

I nodded. Still holding on to my hands, he offered to take care of things. "Make arrangements," he said. "To have her brought back here. For burial."

"What I need right now," I said, tears finally threatening at the thought of my mother, buried, "is Charlie."

Daniel let go of my hands and stood. "Of course," he said. "We'll find him for you." As if he had a security team at his disposal, waiting for just such a task. Which for all I knew, he did.

As we walked down the hall from his office, back to the living room, Ladd came in through the front door. He looked happy. A pretty girl edged in beside him, with wonderful copper curls and a sweet, open face.

"Brett," Ladd said. "What are you doing here?" And then, "What's wrong?"

"My mother died." This time I sounded more like myself, definite, and with the pronouncement the tears erupted. Ladd stepped forward and hugged me. I wept into his chest.

"She really loved you," I told him.

"I'm so sorry," he said, his hand rubbing my back in broad, concentric circles, while Daniel and the girl stood back, politely, forgiving the intimacy of this, a moment of grief. When he let go of me, I felt calm enough to gain the smallest presence of mind. Drumcliffe was several hours from Cork but so much closer than

Randall, Vermont. My mother was far too pragmatic to think such a thing could ever have happened for a reason. But she couldn't always have been, because look who she'd chosen to study.

"Don't bring her body back here," I said to Daniel, partially over my shoulder. Ladd still had one hand at my hip, his girlfriend the most patient woman in the world. "Yeats," I said. "He's buried in Drumcliffe cemetery. That's where she'd want to be."

Daniel nodded. "I'll take care of it," he said.

IF THE NUTS AND bolts of an emergency were Daniel Williams's specialty, Charlie excelled at navigating the emotional fallout. He drove me up to Randall for the university's memorial service and even wore a coat and tie. I watched him shake hands, that smile of his, held back slightly because of the somber circumstances, but still warm enough to comfort. Everyone who shook Charlie's hand remembered that life hadn't ended yet, not for the rest of us. I can't explain how he managed this. For the past year in Amherst, he'd been volunteering for a suicide hotline and had so much success they suggested he train as a 911 operator. But he didn't want to turn this gift into a stressful career; he only wanted to offer it for free. Charlie knew how to talk people off ledges. He also knew how to nurture a person suffering through grief. With tea and toast in the early stages. Meals and drinks of increasing richness. He always knew what to feed me.

It was Daniel who advised me not to let my mother's tenants renew their lease and to put her house on the market as soon as they moved. The timing was good, at the height of the housing market even in sleepy Randall, Vermont, and my mother had very

nearly paid off her mortgage. The rest of her estate was modest—
she had cashed in her life insurance policy to pay her share of my
wedding—but thanks to the sale of the house, I had a healthy
chunk of money for the first time in my life. It seemed like a cruel
substitute. I would much rather have had the house waiting for
me, the scent of vinegar Mom always cleaned with, her books
cramming the built-in shelves. And most of all her, sitting at the
kitchen, ready to brew a pot of coffee whenever I showed up. I
wanted her, and the house. Not the money. Maybe that explains
why I was so willing to throw it all away.

I GOT LADD'S LETTER in early September. *Dear Brett.*
Standing on the front stoop in Amherst, our mailbox still open
with the keys hanging from it, I read the whole rambling thing.
He told me that he and Sheila, the girl he'd been with the day I'd
seen him at his uncle's house, had broken up. *I should be mourning
the loss of Sheila. But I keep thinking of you.*

It was a sort of love letter, not a full-fledged one. There was no
praise in it, and no proclamation. Just a kind of intimate urgency.
How can I leave the country without telling you? By the time I'd
closed and locked the mailbox, I decided not to show it to Charlie.
But I didn't keep it, either. Good wife, good girl, I ripped it into
pieces and threw it away downstairs, not even bringing it up to
our apartment.

"I could help you start a restaurant," I said to Charlie, a few
hours later. We sat at the kitchen table, eating braised Brussels
sprouts and sole meunière. Charlie smiled as if I'd made a joke.

"No, really," I said, taking a bite of the rich fish, meltingly delicious and nourishing. Charlie refilled my wineglass, even though I'd only taken a few sips. I didn't want him to act this way, reluctant. I wanted him to be excited, grateful, at this gift I was offering.

"But won't we be leaving here," Charlie said. "Eventually. For you to teach somewhere?"

Something fluttered in my chest, irritation that he would resist, when here I was handing over my inheritance. Offering him something so huge. I wanted to ask him if he had any particular life's plans. If Charlie's mother's voice found its way into his head after she died, inspiring him to marry me, maybe this was how my mother's voice made its way into mine. I was suddenly frustrated by Charlie's lack of direction. A person didn't use talent like his just cooking for his wife. A person parlayed it into a career. The way I was parlaying my interests into a career.

"I won't be on the market for a few years, at least," I said. "And who knows, maybe we'll end up staying here. It's where my research is. There's plenty of time to work all that out."

Charlie hedged. He said that he'd never finished culinary school. He didn't know anything about business. Since we'd been together, he'd worked odd jobs, mostly painting, occasional handy work, his culinary abilities displayed only in our apartment. Like now, the only light the tapered candles he'd lit. A white tablecloth over the folding card table that composed its own tiny little dining room between the kitchen and living room.

"Well," he said, swirling the wine in his glass, the first sign of capitulation. "It *would* be fun to check out the competition. Go on dates."

So that's how we spent the money at first. We had to buy clothes, so we could arrive suitably dressed at all the best restaurants in Amherst. Trips to Boston and New York, too. On an October trip to New York, at La Grenouille, the waitress came to our table. Older than both of us, she was lean and almost professionally fit—I could see fine cords in her arm as she turned over our water glasses. She barely looked at me, but when Charlie ordered a bottle of wine, she complimented his choice, then reached over and righted his suit coat collar, which I hadn't even noticed was slightly turned up.

Charlie didn't act surprised at all. He leaned back a little in his chair and looked down toward the fixed collar, then back at her. "Well, thank you," he said.

"Helpful when I can be," she told him. Her face was still turned away from me, so I couldn't see her expression, but her white blouse was open at the collar and a blush sprouted, splotchy, at the base of her neck.

"Look at you," I said to Charlie when she walked away. "My Last Duchess."

"What's that?" Charlie, innocent, took a sip of water.

"'A heart too soon made glad,'" I said. "It's a poem. By Robert Browning." Though it was the waitress, and not Charlie, who had blushed, I added, "''Twas not his wife's presence only, called that spot of joy into his cheek.'"

"But it is," Charlie said, leaning toward me, eyes twinkly and intent, but most of all convincing. Any flutter of jealousy instantly tamped down. Then he said, "I remember that poem. He's looking at a painting, right? Of his wife? Didn't he kill her?"

"That's the most common interpretation," I said. "Did you read it?"

"I don't think so," he said. "But I remember the discussion in class."

"Charlie," I said. "I can understand not reading a whole novel. But a poem? You didn't even read a poem?"

"It's a long poem," Charlie said, with a blameless shrug.

I started to say something else, but the waitress returned with the wine. Charlie leaned back, that same motion, but this time was careful to keep his eyes, his smile, on me, even when she showed him the label, and poured the smallest bit for him to taste. After dinner, we went back to our hotel, and I think it may have been that night, careless on our travels, that Sarah was conceived.

IF I HADN'T PRESSED him, if I hadn't foisted the money on him, what would Charlie have done that year while I was pregnant and finishing my course work? In hindsight, cooking in someone else's restaurant would have made a lot more sense. Charlie was good at food, but neither of us had a head for business. When we were done splurging on research trips, we splurged on a space downtown on Main Street. We figured we'd get foot traffic first, word of mouth later. Sometimes I thought we were being adventurous and savvy. Other times I thought we might as well have loaded up my inheritance in his mother's old car and driven down the highway with the windows open, bills fluttering out into the wind.

It was Gift of the Magi. I thought I was giving Charlie this extraordinary opportunity, his own restaurant, while he went along with it only to please me. Both of us waited for the other to be grateful. When Charlie told me he wanted to call the restaurant the Sun Also Rises, I said, "You know that novel takes place in Pamplona. This is a literary town. People will expect Spanish food."

A warm night in April, we were sitting in the new, empty space at a table in front. Through the large front window, we could see people walking past, some still clinging to sweaters, some already in summer clothes. Charlie had a stack of résumés and was taking notes on a yellow pad. I reminded myself that I'd never seen him work so hard. He was trying.

He said, "It starts out in Paris, doesn't it? And doesn't everyone always think of Hemingway in Paris?"

I placed hands on my pregnant belly and cocked an eyebrow at Charlie. At this point he may have discovered Google, but I still hadn't seen him read a novel other than *Riddley Walker*. He put down his pencil and said, "I'll add some tapas to the menu." Obviously nothing I'd said would dissuade him from the name he'd chosen. His phone buzzed from underneath the sprawl of paperwork. Charlie had to shuffle through the mess to find it. As soon as the person on the other end started talking, his face went grim. I knew without asking the topic if not the speaker. Eli.

"Oh my God," I said when Charlie hung up before he could even fill me in—always a different version of the same disaster. "I can't handle this right now."

"Sorry," Charlie said, a new hard edge in his voice. "I'll tell my brother he has to have his psychotic breakdown when it's more convenient."

"You could call your father," I said. "Let him deal with it for once."

Charlie pushed his chair back and went toward the kitchen. Not quite ready to run after him, I pulled a résumé off the top of the pile. Deirdre Bennet. I scanned the page as if I'd have something to do with the hiring, then put it aside. I could see the restaurant was a mistake before it had even begun.

The baby did a startling kick, followed by a roll. I put my hand on my belly, trying to locate the foot, feeling protective and guilty at the same time.

CHARLIE CALLED HIS FATHER, who didn't offer to go up to Boston. "Keep me posted," Bob Moss told him. It was becoming clearer and clearer to me: for Eli, it was us or no one. Charlie and I went to visit him in the lockdown ward at Beth Israel. They had to buzz us through a series of glass doors. When we finally got inside, all the patients' eyes turned toward me, my swollen belly a lightning rod of possibility, normality, voodoo. I waited for someone to call out, predict the baby's sex or more, but no one came close, or spoke, except for Eli. His nicotine-stained fingers hovered just above my belly, not yet quivering from the meds and not quite willing to make contact, just testing the force field that emanated from his little niece—almost but not quite in the world with us.

We sat down with him at a table in one of the visiting rooms. Eli drummed his fingers on the tabletop.

"How are you doing?" Charlie asked.

Eli glanced at him angrily. "How am I supposed to be doing?"

I thought he was going to complain about his hospitalization—

his incarceration—but instead he launched into a theory about how Paul McCartney had died in a car crash in 1967 and Billy Shears had taken over his life. "It's the most successful case of identity theft in human history," Eli said. His voice sounded fast, lower pitched, each word spilling into the next.

"Oh, Eli," I said. Charlie looked at me, his face fallen the way it always did when faced with this version of his brother.

"What is this preoccupation," Eli said, "this obsession with orgasm?" He waved his hand at my belly as if it represented the entire problem. "Because that's not the thing, right? That's not the peak moment. It's the moment before that's the whole point. That's why I shouldn't be rushed along, when I'm the one who's paying, I shouldn't be forced to indulge in the cheapness, the ending. There's the reason they call it the little death, you know, it signifies the end of pleasure, the end of *feeling*."

"Can I get you anything?" Charlie said. "Do you want coffee or anything?" I wondered if they were allowed to have hot liquids, but Eli didn't seem to have heard him anyway.

"It would be a very different world," Eli said, "if the sexual revolution had gone the way it was supposed to. If Paul McCartney had lived. Or if they'd just left well enough alone and not brought in that asshole Billy Shears, with his fucking violins and trombones." He lifted his arms and pounded the air as if playing an invisible drum set. "Aw," Eli sang, in a sharp, angry voice. "'How do you sleep? How do you sleep at night?'"

We sat with him for a minute after that, none of us speaking, until Eli turned to me and said, in an almost normal tone, "They took my dog. Can you see if you can find her for me?"

That night, Charlie and I had an infant CPR class at the EMH. We drove back to Amherst and spent the evening practicing resuscitation on fake babies with open mouths and collapsible necks; a nurse walked us through the various situations of peril we might expect to encounter. By the time we finished, it was dark. We walked outside, the summer air heavy on our shoulders. Charlie placed his hands on my stomach, which had swollen well past the point of no return.

"I don't think we can do this," Charlie said. In another frame of mind, this statement might have worried me. But I just leaned my head into his chest. I felt exactly the same way.

First thing the next morning, I called shelters in the Boston area and found Eli's dog, Lightfoot, at the Animal Rescue League in Arlington. They said she had fleas and a mild case of heartworm but otherwise was in surprisingly good spirits and shape. She was a nice dog, a little Italian greyhound mix Eli had adopted from Angell. I brought her home with me until they let Eli out ten days later.

"It's not long enough," Charlie said, lying across our bed, hands covering his eyes. Lightfoot jumped up on the bed and peered worriedly into his face. Charlie had spent the past ten days giving interviews, finding suppliers, writing menus—and also traveling to Boston for commitment hearings and visits with Eli. It seemed like every time Eli was committed, they kept him for a shorter time, which translated into a shorter time before his next break. Charlie put one broad hand on the dog, half petting her, half pushing her away. He looked ragged.

"Eli will be back in the hospital in a matter of months," he said.

I sat down next to him and placed my hand on his forehead, as if he were a child home sick from school. Sometimes when Eli broke down I wished that he could stay in a hospital forever, sparing the rest of us. When he was better—medicated—the wish that he would stay that way was mitigated by our knowledge that that would never happen. The fog of complying with the meds would wear him down, he would quit taking them, and the voices would rise. The cycle would only continue, and no one but Charlie had the wherewithal to withstand it, and believe in him, one more time.

Eli reclaimed Lightfoot and went back to his job. I wrote him a check from our dwindling account so he could move into a new apartment. Meanwhile the restaurant started to look like a restaurant. Charlie hired his staff, among them an artist who helped him out with decorating before starting as hostess when the restaurant opened. In mid-May, we went to one of her openings. She was showing at the McCewan gallery with three other painters. She'd already worked with Charlie for a couple weeks, but I'd been too busy grading to come by the restaurant. At this point my one nice maternity dress was straining enough that I worried my popped belly button was visible through the stretchy black cotton. The space was brick-walled, one large and airy room, and everyone there held a plastic cup of wine.

"Go ahead," Charlie said as he poured a cup of red for himself. "What does it matter at this point?"

I shook my head, more from not wanting people to glare at me than worry it would do harm to the baby. Charlie glanced around the room and said, "We'll just say hi and look at her paintings. We don't have to stay long." Then he smiled at someone in the crowd, jutting his chin in her direction. I couldn't tell whether the gesture was meant as an additional greeting, to her, or for me—pointing her out.

A woman glided through the crowd, her arm outstretched to me way too early. I guessed she was a couple years younger than me, fair and elegant. Despite her jump-the-gun greeting, there was something preternaturally contained about her, and I thought Charlie had chosen just right. We'd learned from our travels the importance of having a coolly beautiful woman to greet customers, one who knew how to dress and carry herself.

"Brett," she said. "I'm Deirdre Bennet." I remembered her name from the résumés. Deirdre went on, "Charlie has told me so much about you. I'm so happy to meet you."

A broad, aggressively handsome man appeared and introduced himself as Deirdre's boyfriend. My fingers folded in on themselves when he gripped my hand.

"Come on," Deirdre said, closing her hand around my wrist. "I'll show you my work."

I let her lead me across the room. Watching her tiny waist, swathed in a shimmery Asian-style dress, I thought of F. Scott Fitzgerald's description of Rosemary Hoyt in *Tender Is the Night*: "When she walked she carried herself like a ballet-dancer, not slumped down on her hips but held up in the small of her back." By the time we got to the wall where her paintings hung, I felt tired and elephantine. Deirdre's work was all portraits. To me, the colors felt too garish, the brush strokes too visible. I leaned forward to read the cards that listed the price and title of each painting. The names sounded vaguely familiar: *Susan Smith, Céline Lesage, Andrea Yates.*

The boyfriend, seeing my mental struggle, piped up. "They're women who killed their kids," he said, enthusiastic, as if this were the happiest news in the world.

Deirdre let go of my wrist. "I'm obsessed with infanticide," she told me.

Putting my hands on my belly would have seemed defensive, so I resisted that impulse. When Deirdre and her boyfriend filtered back into the crowd of well-wishers, I slipped my arm through Charlie's.

"That," I said, "was a very odd thing to say to a pregnant women."

"I won't let her talk to customers," Charlie said.

"That will be great," I said. "A silent hostess."

We both laughed, but I pressed the issue. "Seriously. Wasn't that a little creepy?"

Charlie shrugged. "She's not so bad," he said. "It's mostly a put-on, I think. Trying to be shocking."

Charlie had one more glass of wine, and we snuck away from the party without saying good-bye to the artist.

WHEN SARAH WAS BORN a month later, Eli came to see us in the hospital. He was thickly medicated, the bloat just beginning to take its form. Still I let him hold her. Eli sat down in the chair next to my hospital bed, and Charlie lowered the swaddled, squirming miracle into his brother's cradled arms. The room filled with Eli's stale and acrid scent. His clothes looked disheveled, stained, and he hadn't combed his hair. Staring into the baby's face, his eyes were dull and glassy. He must have been registering some connection, though, peering close enough so that her newborn eyes could absorb his features. Sarah's little pink skull cap slid off her head against his elbow, revealing the vulnerable bald head, the soft spot at the crown. Eli petted her, gentle, as if she were a kitten.

A nurse swept into the room to deliver my lunch. She looked at Eli and then at me—shocked that I would let this man hold my baby. But I just smiled and looked back at Eli. He held Sarah so carefully. In his arms, she started, clenched fists jerking up above her head, the Moro reflex. It made Eli start, too. Then his face broke open into something like a smile, but awkward and unsure. Muted. I remembered the way his face used to look, how easily and naturally it moved into happiness, and felt the usual pang of loss. Still. I not only believed that Eli would never hurt Sarah. I couldn't imagine him hurting anybody.

9

Someone *must* have told us how much work a restaurant required. Not to mention a new baby. In that muggy, exhausted summer, I often wondered why we didn't listen. The Sun Also Rises opened in the throes of my sleepless nights and bleary days. Charlie would disappear midmorning and not come home till almost midnight. Every afternoon before service started, I walked downtown to eat dinner. Charlie would bring two plates of his favorite special to the table and sit down to eat with us, ignoring whatever crises arose in the kitchen until someone came to get him. When Sarah woke up and squalled, I had to walk her around the room while irritated waitresses set tables and polished glasses. Usually I ended up back at the table, trying to nurse Sarah and eat at the same time. Which made it kind of odd that Deirdre liked to join us for her shift meal.

"It's nice," she told me, "that Charlie lets us eat off the menu."

I nodded, but this was news to me, and I wondered how much it was costing. If I suggested to Charlie making a pot of pasta for his crew, he would just smile. Where would the fun be in that?

Deirdre picked at her food, usually wasting more than half. There was a gleam behind her pale eyes as if her thyroid function ran a little too high.

"He's so generous," she said. "Not like my boyfriend. You wouldn't believe how stingy he is."

"The same guy we met at the gallery? He seemed very nice."

"Oh, he's nice. Just don't ever try to get him to pay for anything. He got mad at me for drinking his beer. So I said I'd put a jar on the counter and put a dollar in it every time I drank one. I thought that would embarrass him. But he thought it was a great idea. Now every time I have a beer at my boyfriend's house, I have to put a dollar in the jar."

There was a pause, her fork in the air, her pale eyes focused intently on me. Deirdre owned the kind of good looks I recognized but did not appreciate. To me, she looked hard, too sculpted. I didn't know if I was supposed to exclaim over the awfulness of her boyfriend or offer a commiserating complaint about Charlie. Luckily he came out of the kitchen just then, a dishrag over his shoulder. He never wore an apron, so his T-shirt and jeans were splattered with food. Sarah had fallen asleep in my lap. When Charlie sat down, I transferred her to him very carefully and finished my dinner, wishing Deirdre would find something to do so that we could have this, just a little bit of family time out of the day.

"Can you say something to her?" I asked toward the end of

August, with the beginning of school looming and me fully versed in the pitfalls of Deirdre's relationship. Our downstairs neighbor, an undergrad named Maddie, had agreed to babysit for Sarah when I had class, but I wasn't sure how we were going to pay her. Business at the restaurant wasn't picking up the way we'd hoped, and we took out a new line of credit. Everything felt tinged with tension, and I wanted that time—one meal a day—to ourselves.

"Sure," Charlie said. "I'll mention it."

For a few months, it was just me, Charlie, and Sarah. Deirdre didn't eat at all, just moved around the restaurant getting things in order. Charlie must have phrased it in the most diplomatic way possible, because she never looked dejected, just coldly intent on her tasks. Watching her, I thought that a better plan would have been to hire an up-and-coming chef and put Charlie at the front of the house. I think I even smiled to myself as I thought it. All the hearts too soon made glad, returning time and time again just to see Charlie. It was a mistake to keep him hidden in the kitchen.

ONE NIGHT IN EARLY December I came in after an evening class to find Charlie and Deirdre alone in the restaurant, eating dinner together. The plates of food in front of them—duck for Charlie, some kind of prime rib for Deirdre—looked rustic, not plated for fine dining. It was only nine thirty, and the restaurant should still have been open. But the sign in the door had been turned to CLOSED, and judging from the swept and cleared state of the dining room, the absence of all other employees, they had stopped serving for at least an hour. The door jingled when I opened it, but neither of them looked up.

Deirdre saw me first. She waved, but the gesture seemed more

frustrated than welcoming, as if I'd interrupted something. Charlie
followed her gaze and stood, pushing back his chair. He looked so
genuinely pleased to see me that suspicion settled before it could
rise. I noticed that Deirdre's eyes were red.

"Brett," he said. "It was dead tonight. Do you want something
to eat?"

I followed him back to the kitchen where he put together a
plate of prime rib just like Deirdre's, laying a sprig of rosemary
and drizzling reduction sauce over the mashed potatoes. "Her boyfriend broke up with her," Charlie said.

Back at the table, I took my seat between them. Charlie poured
me a glass of red wine, though he knew I preferred white. Getting
another bottle would have meant leaving me alone with Deirdre,
but that didn't occur to me until much later, combing through
every possible detail.

She sat back in her chair a little, sipping her own glass of wine.
Right then I felt bad for her, and a little guilty for banishing her
from our table. Staring at me, her blue eyes glazed with tears.

"I'm really sorry about your boyfriend," I said. She probably
didn't need reminding about all the times she'd complained about
him. "How long were you together?"

"Three years," she said. "Didn't I tell you that?"

"You probably did. I'm sorry. That's so hard."

She turned away from me, looking down at her untouched
plate of food. Charlie rested his arm on the back of my chair, not
around me exactly. But still. Making a statement. I took a bite of
the meal and a sip of the wine. Complimented the food.

"Thanks," Charlie said. He lifted his arm from the back of
my chair and tucked a strand of hair behind my ear. I remember

thinking that it was a little mean of him, to be solicitous toward me while Deirdre nursed a broken heart.

"He's an idiot," I told her. "You're so beautiful."

She nodded, her eyes filling with tears, too choked up to answer.

Deirdre's face—strained and devastated—stayed with me all the next day. I thought about how she'd tried to be my friend and I'd shooed her away like a mere employee. After class, heading home, I passed the Amherst Day Spa. Out on the sidewalk they'd propped a green easel chalkboard, advertising a soothing peppermint pedicure for fifty dollars. The air felt crisp, a chill gathering. I had about a hundred dollars left on my last emergency credit card.

On my way to the restaurant, sun beat down on the back of my head, incongruously accompanied by a chilly wind. I felt lightheaded with my financially irresponsible good deed. It seemed like something Charlie would do. At home, I collected Sarah from Maddie and headed over to the restaurant early, around four thirty. Eventually Charlie planned on opening for lunch, but for now only did dinner service, which started at six. The dining room clanked peacefully with the sounds of silverware being laid, goblets being polished. Deirdre stood behind the hostess podium talking on the phone, wearing a black sheath dress, her long hair loose. She was one of those rare people made more beautiful by distress; clearly she'd been crying again, and it brought color to her cheeks, and darkened her eyes. I could see the sheet in front of her, empty, as she went ahead and penciled in the table for two. As she spoke, she glanced up at me and the sadness in her eyes became something blander, as if I were obstructing something she meant to look at, just behind me. I shifted slightly to the left, the gift certificate in my hand. Deirdre hung up and looked at me, waiting, as if she expected me to tell her how many people were in my party. I slipped the gift certificate onto the reservation book. She stared down at it, uncertain.

"It's a pedicure," I said. "I thought you could treat yourself."

Deirdre's brows knit together. She picked up the gift certificate, a pale mauve piece of cardboard wrapped in a beige piece of twine. "That's so nice," she said, not able to look me in the eye, just melting and breaking in front of me. She raised the gift certificate to her brow, as if shielding herself from too-bright light, and didn't start to cry until she'd turned around and headed toward the back of the restaurant, the kitchen.

Even looking back, I like her better in that moment than I ever had or would. It was a very human reaction. Someone she'd done a terrible wrong to was doing her a kindness. I saw that, even as I realized exactly what it meant. My gift broke through whatever rationalization she'd worked out for her relationship with Charlie and made her feel guilty enough to break down—though not guilty enough to keep from turning away from me and heading straight for my husband.

From where I stood, I could just see him, showing a sous-chef how he wanted something chopped. And as he raised his head, noting Deirdre coming toward him, his face rearranged itself into an apologetic kind of sympathy, not seeing the wife, standing back and watching—absorbing—it all.

And then he did see me. It wasn't so obviously visible, the fear that crossed over his face. Deirdre probably didn't register it, not knowing him—whatever she might think—the way I did. But the way he blinked and paused, that was Charlie, crestfallen, and it was the last shred of proof I needed.

WALKING AWAY FROM THE restaurant up Main Street, I couldn't get out of the commercial district fast enough, the wide plate windows serving my reflection back to me—in my boxy wool coat and flyaway hair. Unlike my mother and me, my father had specialized in twentieth-century literature. He would have appreciated my thinking of Rosemary Hoyt the first time I saw Deirdre. And he was the one who chose my name. Hemingway had modeled Lady Brett Ashley on Mary Duff Stirling, a glamorous British socialite. Trying to make it home, I couldn't have felt less like my namesake. Instead I felt like Hemingway's wife must have, the first time she'd read the book, realizing the romantic lead had been based on Duff and not her.

At Maddie's, Sarah lay asleep in her removable car seat. As I carried her down the hallway to our apartment, I could hear the phone ringing from inside. Sarah slept, a thin bubble on her lips, sparse blonde curls damp with sweat on her forehead. I waited till the ringing stopped before opening the door, then carefully lowered the carrier. Tab thumped off the couch and wound herself around my legs. I couldn't bend to pet her. My hand found its way to my heart, fingers curving into my chest as if I could actually cup it, squeeze it, measure it. But the beating didn't seem to be any faster than usual. Maybe it was a sign—that I hadn't seen what I thought I had, that I was wrong, that it was all just some weirdness of Deirdre's combined with some paranoia of mine.

Behind me, the door opened and in came Charlie, wearing an expression so similar to the one I'd seen—as Deirdre had walked toward him in the restaurant—that if I'd been holding something in my hands I would have thrown it at him. The door closed loudly behind him and Sarah woke, her infant's wail filling the apartment almost before her eyes were open. I bent down to unbuckle her.

"Look," Charlie said, his hands outstretched, his eyes unable to stop twinkling. Did I ever see Charlie without that light in his eyes, even when his mother was dying? No matter what was taking place, he always had that air, of being deeply amused by the world, even deeply moved by it. But never quite wholly, entirely, here.

Sometimes now I imagine him turning, with that expression, toward his killer. Whatever argument had arisen, Charlie would have been so certain he could soothe the other person—could elicit whatever response he wanted. Maybe he could. Maybe that's why the killer needed to wait for him to turn his back, before bringing the hammer down.

I sat down on the couch and unbuttoned my shirt to nurse the baby. Charlie took a step closer to us.

"It's over," he said. "I swear," he added, his tone supplicating enough that I understood he meant him and Deirdre rather than our marriage.

"Over," I said. "*Over*?" The worst word I'd ever heard. Absolute confirmation. There was something between Deirdre and Charlie, enough under way that now it could be declared *over*. While I had sunk all my inheritance into the restaurant that paid her salary. While I had, here in my arms, a baby, so that I couldn't even yell.

"Brett," he said. "I'm so sorry."

"Shut up." If I hadn't been holding Sarah, I would have put my hands over my ears. I would have screamed. As it was, my voice came out low and certain. "You need to leave."

"Leave? Brett. Come on. I love you."

"No," I said. "You don't. You never did."

"You know that's not true."

"Go," I said. "And don't come back. You can stay with her. You can move in with her."

"I can't," he said. "I don't want to. Even if you never talk to me again, that wouldn't happen."

"That's lovely," I said. "That's beautiful, Charlie."

"I love you," he said. "We're a family."

"How nice of you to remember."

I looked down at Sarah, Charlie's little replica. How could I even know which one of us he wanted to stay for? Charlie stood there, his face begging me to be reasonable. Reasonable! I could see the clock from where I sat. Dinner service would be starting. And what did it matter, anything he said? Despite every stupid thing I'd done since the day I'd met him, I was smart enough to know that someone who'd cheat on me would lie to me, too.

"Charlie," I said. "Just go. Go cook. And don't come back here. For once in your life, be a gentleman. Don't make me leave my home with a baby. Find another place to stay."

He paused for a moment, then shook his head. "No," he said. "I'm leaving now, but I'm coming back. We'll talk about this. It'll be okay."

I closed my eyes, felt his lips on my forehead. If I let myself cry he would stay, and I needed him to go. It didn't escape me how soon he must have followed me out of the restaurant, prioritizing my meltdown over Deirdre's, and I knew how pathetic it was to find comfort in that. Charlie would be coming back, and weak-minded, lovesick girl that I'd always been, I was in danger of listening to whatever he said.

THE HOUSE WHERE I'D grown up had been sold and was now inhabited by strangers, the locks changed, my mother's concerned face existing—watching—only from memory. So I drove to the only other place I owned a key for, the only other place I knew how to get to without a map. I didn't take anything with me other than a few days' worth of clothes and a bag of diapers. As I drove toward the shore, the autumn light and leaves bowing through the windshield, betrayal thrummed through my body like a drug. I wondered if Deirdre would stay at the restaurant to work her shift. How had my gift, the pedicure, rearranged itself in Deirdre's mind, during the walk between the podium and the kitchen? Maybe by the time she got to Charlie she had turned it into a calculated move, an attempt to flush them out. Maybe in the morning she would head over to the Amherst Day Spa and help herself to that peppermint pedicure, without remorse, even with a sense of deserving: the same way she'd helped herself to my husband.

When I got to the Moss house, Eli's car was parked in the driveway and Lightfoot sat on the lawn, panting. It was dark by then, but the front lights had all been left on. The dog sat just within the bright circle cast on the grass. She looked thin, even for her breed, and agitated. I checked the rearview mirror. Sarah was still tiny enough to need a backward car seat, but even if I hadn't had a baby mirror facing her, I would have known she was sleeping from the silence. I got out of the car and walked toward the dog, who stood up, very still, an intense look of assessment on her pointy little face, as if she'd been waiting for someone to help and couldn't decide if I were a likely prospect.

"Hey," I called. "Hey Lightfoot."

She ran toward me, full of relief. I knelt to pet her and her ribs felt sharp, alarming, under my fingers. I thought about loading the dog directly into my car and driving away. But where would I go? And could I really leave without checking on Eli? He was both my old friend and my family.

I glanced toward the backseat, where Sarah lay sleeping. A voice rose up in my head, battling the moment of uncertainty. *Come on. Do you think Eli would hurt a baby?* I was so used to Charlie's rebuttals they arose even in his absence, making me feel silly— selfish—for hesitating. Eli wasn't some bogeyman who would snatch my baby and swallow her whole. He was just Eli, my friend who suffered from a debilitating disease. Whatever state I found him in, he wouldn't hurt anyone. Quietly as possible, I clicked the infant seat out of its holder and carried Sarah into the house.

I'd barely crossed the threshold before realizing that talking myself out of my gut reaction had been a mistake if the house was any reflection of what was going on in Eli's mind. The living room looked ransacked, newspapers and garbage strewn everywhere, books tumbled from the shelves, clothes draped over every piece of furniture and all over the floor. A low-hanging odor of cigarettes and must, possibly urine and feces.

"Come on," I said to the dog, who had trotted to the middle of the room and stood there, expectant. "Let's get out of here." She hesitated, either waiting for me to find her bowl and fill it or else too loyal to desert Eli. "Come on," I said again, slapping my hip with my free hand. "I'll get you some food."

And then Eli appeared in the doorway from the kitchen, completely naked. A cigarette in one hand, his hair greasy and matted. I took another step backward, closer to the door, and moved the baby seat behind my knees, as if I could hide it.

"Eli," I said. I had to clear my throat to be audible. "Your dog is starving. I'm taking her to get some food."

He dropped his cigarette to the floor and ground it out with his bare foot. Then he went back into the kitchen. Still facing the kitchen doorway, I started to back toward the open front door, calculating how fast I could carry Sarah through the screened-in porch and to the driveway. Eli reemerged with an unopened bag of dog food. He ripped into the top and turned it over, the kibble pouring in a loud rush onto the floor. Lightfoot ran forward, her tail wagging, and ate while the two of us stood at opposite ends of the room, watching.

"There," Eli said. "There you go."

Standing on the other side of the room, staring at Eli and the ravenous little dog, I felt a rush of very serious anger. At Charlie and Deirdre, yes, but also at myself, and Ladd, and even my father and mother. All the little pieces, the unravelings, that had led me to this exact spot, again and again and again, the only place I had to go.

"Listen," I said to Eli. "I just have to get something out of the car."

He stood there, placid, as I left the house. Crossing the lawn, I gulped in the clean night air. Sarah woke up and started to wail, but I steeled myself against the sound, clicking the seat into its platform and climbing directly behind the wheel. I screeched out of the driveway and drove up the street, less than half a mile before I pulled over. Unsettling as the sight of Eli had been, I wasn't worried that he would follow me. It didn't take much distance, to stop being afraid of him. I climbed into the backseat and unbuckled Sarah. Once I had her nursing, I dialed Charlie.

"Brett," he said. "Where are you."

"I'm on the Cape. I just went to the house. Eli is there and he's in bad shape."

On the other end, an intake of breath, Charlie unsure which upheaval to address.

"I'm just calling to tell you," I said. "I'm not ready to talk."

"Are you coming home?"

"What does it matter? You're coming here."

"It matters," Charlie said. His voice sounded a little too devoid of worry, at least over what I would do. I could almost hear him saying, *You will always come back.* He would mean it as a compliment, a nod to my devotion. Maybe that was why he loved me.

But Charlie just said, as if he'd read my mind, "I love you."

Without thinking I said, "I love you, too," then hung up and tossed the phone aside.

I looked down at Sarah, her eyes half closed, long lashes like her dad's skimming the tops of chubby baby cheeks. How could they, I thought, my brain returning to its primary wound. Charlie and Deirdre (even as I thought it, my heart rebelled against the phrase, placing their names side by side like a couple), sneaking around, having an *affair*, while I was taking care of this little baby, maybe while I was pregnant, too.

For a moment, a rising and blinding anger blotted out my fear and sadness. I wanted to kill him. I really did.

"Your timing sucks," I said aloud. Maybe I was talking to Eli as well as Charlie. I'd come to the Moss house so I could figure out what to do next. If not for the imperative of my child, it would have felt wrong to leave Eli there. But I couldn't exactly unpack a diaper bag to stay with a naked madman. Find a comfortable spot to nurse my baby and wait for Eli to start monologuing about Billy Shears or whatever his latest delusion was. But I did wish I'd managed to take the dog with me. I thought about Eli's last dog, Manny, who'd been killed trying to follow Eli across Mass Avenue traffic. And then finally, I thought about Eli. All alone with the torturous workings of his mind.

I closed my eyes, trying not to give into thoughts of *if only*. Once, years before, I'd heard a recording of my father talking and been astonished to learn he had a Brooklyn accent. It wasn't the way I remembered him. *If only* my father hadn't gotten lymphoma, how familiar that voice would have been to me. Maybe he would be somewhere, right now, and I could run to him. *If only* Eli hadn't become schizophrenic, he would have graduated med school by now, be deciding on a specialty. Or maybe he would have changed his mind and become a vet instead. Maybe he'd have a family. *What a great dad he would be.* According to E. M. Forster it was the only tense we could never be sure about: what would have been.

I buckled Sarah back into her seat and climbed behind the wheel. On very dark nights, on deserted country roads, driving can feel like flying. The engine of my car hummed so quietly, the wheels moving imperceptibly over cool, invisible pavement.

Leaves, still dark, shimmered through shadows on either side of me. I drove past the long dirt driveway to Daniel Williams's compound. Ladd wouldn't be there—he was still in Honduras. And anyway, summer was long over. Daniel himself was probably back in Boston. Still, I found myself making the turn. Off the pavement onto the dirt, so I could feel the earth rumbling beneath the car, feel myself returning and connected to some sort of home. The house came into view sooner than I expected, because lights were on—in most of the downstairs and one upstairs window. A thin line of smoke spiraled up from the chimney. I stopped short of where they'd hear me approaching, wondering if it were just Daniel home or if he had guests.

Sitting there behind the steering wheel, I knew that if I knocked on the door, Daniel wouldn't treat me as if I were crazy to appear. He might not even ask me the reason. He'd just open the door wider and invite me in. Probably he'd be able to tell I had nowhere else to go and offer me one of his cottages or even a room upstairs.

But the thing was: I did have a place to go. Because whenever his brother needed him, Charlie would go. Immediately. No matter what. When I got back to our apartment, it would be empty because Charlie would already be on his way here. So I backed the whole long way out of Daniel's driveway, returning to paved roads and the sensation of flight. I arrived at our deserted apartment well past midnight, and instead of sleeping in our bed—too fraught with the scent of Charlie—I collapsed on the sofa. Sarah perched on the floor beside me, still in her car seat, my hand resting on the rise and fall of her little belly. In the morning, I called a locksmith to come and install a deadbolt.

• • •

THE NEXT DAY, WE woke to heavy snowfall. Everything was canceled. In the evening, Maddie watched Sarah while I pulled on my boots and trudged over to the Homestead. Next door was the house her brother, Austin, built for his wife—the object of E.D.'s unrequited affection living right next door.

I walked through the snow, toward the Evergreens, thinking that I would never entirely escape Charlie, even if I left him. For the rest of my life, we would share a child, and every time I saw his face—every time I handed her off, or met with a teacher, or went to a school event—my heart would fall, willing victim, the way it always had. He beckoned and the woods started. I would never, ever, get away.

My breath billowed out in front of me, glimmers of illumination moving through the air despite the hour, and I tried to imagine how very dark evenings must have been in the nineteenth century, with no electric lights from houses and no streetlamps. The world Emily Dickinson inhabited did not contain a glare from cities the world over, reflected back in the sky. Nights like this, the Poet would sit at her bedroom window, staring across the snowy lawn, toward Sue's, trying to believe her beloved pined back.

But her beloved married someone else, I reminded myself. Charlie married *me*.

My eyes blinked against the falling snow. If it hadn't been for Sarah, would Charlie have followed me back to our apartment and said that he wanted to be with me? Would I ever be enough, to fend off the revolving door of infatuated women? And how had my thinking already shifted, from determination to leave him—to wishing I could kill him—into the old worry, about how I could keep him?

The world stood dark and quiet. For a moment, I could believe that cars and headlights existed in the distant future. That electricity ran not through wires above my head and under the ground but in the current of possibility between these two modest and imperial plots of land. I lifted my hand and waved—a sad lover's gesture. Entirely appropriate to feel yearning, and hopeless, looking up through the snow at that west-facing window.

AFTER A DAY OF canceled classes, the roads were cleared and I went back to school. On the way home I drove down Main Street, slowly, trying to see if Deirdre manned her hostess podium, but I couldn't see through the window because of the glare. I thought about driving into the alley behind the restaurant to see if Charlie's car—his mother's old station wagon—was parked there, but didn't, because I knew it wouldn't be. He was on Cape Cod, trying to take care of Eli.

That night I made my own dinner for the first time since I could remember. I probably wouldn't have bothered if I'd been on my own—but I had to stay strong for Sarah, had to nourish my body so that it could nourish hers. As I cracked two eggs into the bowl, my phone rang. I knew it was Charlie. I drizzled milk into the eggs and picked up a fork, battling the urge to answer. Would he beg for forgiveness or launch into a report on Eli's well-being? *Let Deirdre worry about your crazy brother.* As those words formed in my head—filling me with regret and loss and self-loathing—I finally started to cry. I wept as I scrambled and cooked so that by the time the eggs were done all I could do was scrape them into the garbage. Still crying, I gave up and slept in our bed. With Sarah beside me, I breathed in the scent of Charlie all night long, thinking about what my life would be like if I never let him come home. A single mother, like mine had been, but relinquishing my baby for weekends and vacations. Watching Charlie walk away on a regular basis. The great love of my life—I had been so sure of it—now in the past.

The world is hardest on people who believe in the way it's supposed to be. *My basket holds—just—Firmaments,* the Poet wrote. *Those—dangle easy—on my arm. But smaller bundles—Cram.*

The bundle Charlie had left me with crammed so painfully, it felt impossible to continue. Still. When I got home from school the next afternoon, there was a letter in our mailbox, postmarked Saturday Cove.

I think about staying on the Cape, Charlie wrote, *and I think, I'd rather be with Brett. I think about going back to Amherst alone and I think, I'd rather be with Brett. I think about my life and I think, I'd rather be with Brett.*

Standing in the exact same spot where I'd read Ladd's letter, I looked up, across the street, to the Homestead. Charlie was my Sue Dickinson. He was my Maud Gonne. And the thing I kept forgetting about those two: they were unattainable, they weren't *meant* to be attained. I should have known that. I should have walked away.

But I couldn't. Beyond everything I felt, Charlie was the father of my child. We were married. The adult thing to do was tamp down the rising tide of anger and woundedness. It wasn't weakness, I told myself, to work on my marriage, instead of just letting it go.

The new dead bolt came off, my defenses went down, Charlie came home.

10

Winter continued in earnest, and Eli returned to the hospital in Pocasset. Lightfoot came to live with us. Charlie had already broken things off with Deirdre; now he had to fire her. He told me about the conversation in the office of our marriage counselor, looking at her instead of me.

"She says she won't go."

I turned to him, trying to keep my voice steady. "She won't go? How am I supposed to deal with that? You working with her every day, her still in our life?"

"She says she'll sue me. For sexual harassment." He shrugged. Helpless.

Later that day, at home, he told me he was letting his sous-chef take over for a few days while he figured out how to handle

Deirdre. "One thing we could do," Charlie said, "is just close it. The restaurant."

I sat down next to him on the couch. Sarah was napping in the other room, so we both talked in whispers. It seemed ridiculous, to shut down a business because of a jilted mistress. It also seemed like the only thing to do.

"It's losing money anyway," Charlie said, like nothing could matter less. "We've been getting four, five tables, even on weekends. The truth is, it's either close it now or close it in the spring. It's a failure. I'm sorry."

"It's okay," I said. Any sadness I felt over the restaurant's closing was eclipsed by relief that Deirdre would be ousted, that she couldn't stay in our lives with a lawsuit—claiming the truth, that we'd shut down the whole enterprise to get rid of her. I examined Charlie's face closely, for signs of mourning, and saw none. Maybe he felt relieved, too, or maybe this collapse was so closely associated with Deirdre's exit that he thought it would be tactless to let me see his disappointment. Or maybe it was just Charlie, of the slow smile and easy movements, glad to shelve the ambition that I had foisted upon him.

This way he didn't have to fire Deirdre face-to-face. He just called a meeting and told the whole staff that the restaurant was closing. I didn't ask much about it. I didn't want to talk about Deirdre, or think about her, or remember she existed at all. Because our counseling sessions amounted to one scheduled hour a week to talk about Deirdre, we stopped going. I guess it became our way of coping, to quit everything except each other. At random moments, Charlie would say, "I'm sorry," and I would reply with a silencing glance, wanting to continue with our plan, of none of this spoken out loud.

The thing about Charlie that I worked on remembering was that family was important to him. I clung to the image of him carrying his mother down to the beach. I thought of how he always came to Eli's rescue. Now I was his family, too. Whereas Deirdre was just a girl, whom he could abandon as easily as he'd abandoned me back in Colorado. For the first time, that memory gave me comfort.

The name Deirdre became like a ghost, hovering around our interactions, our conversations, but almost never materializing. The person appeared more frequently. I would see her in town, often enough that I learned to avoid the places she might be, the new restaurant where she worked, the coffee shop she liked. She did not take the same approach, and I would see her car, a blue Honda Civic, slowing down as it passed our house, her head turning up toward our window so directly I'd wonder if Charlie ever brought her here. She ran by our house, too, white pony tail whipping behind her, snapping back as she turned her head away from the sight of me on the front porch or as I carried groceries up the sidewalk, parsley spilling out the top of the brown paper bags. As she picked up her pace, I could see her imagining the meal Charlie would be cooking later. Occasionally I would spot her at the university, which was odd because as far as I knew she wasn't a student. Maybe she had a new boyfriend—a professor or grad student. Whatever the reason, there she would be—spectral as she was in the air between Charlie and me. Hard to believe someone who appeared so insubstantial had managed to do so much harm.

Every time I saw her something gathered inside of me, a piece of the anger I fought to subdue, rising and burgeoning, forming a nagging pile of resentment.

"I think we need to get away for a while," I told Charlie, as the school year spooled to its end. We were both in the tiny bathroom, me perched on the edge of the tub while Charlie showered. He'd gone back to his odd jobs, and his legs and arms were caked with white paint. When he pulled the curtain aside, I could tell from his face that he had also seen the way she watched us. Charlie's comings and goings were less regular than mine. To find him, she would have had to skulk in produce aisles. I thought about asking if he'd heard from her but worried it would sound too much like an accusation. And anyway, I had stopped counting on him to tell me the truth.

"Maybe we can go to the Cape," he said. "My father was talking about staying in Florida this summer. We can have the place to ourselves. We can even stay on if we wanted. You can work on your dissertation."

"What will you do? For work?"

Charlie paused, then pulled the curtain back. The stream of water shut off with a heaving sigh. Sometimes I thought his affair with Deirdre was a way of showing me what would happen if I pushed him in directions he didn't want to go. For so long, there had been a sacrosanct element to my love for Charlie, and it almost seemed like I was the one who'd muddied it, by trying to turn him into a married worker bee.

Just when I thought he wouldn't answer he said, "You know. This and that."

From the next room, Sarah began to cry. I went to pick her up, and carried her into the kitchen to make some rice cereal. She was on my hip, hand closed into my hair, when Charlie emerged, wearing nothing but khaki shorts, still dripping. I noticed a splotch of paint he'd missed on his forearm.

"We'd have to give up this apartment," I said.

He shrugged. "We could always find another one. If we wanted to come back."

I stared into the filmy white baby food, stirring it unnecessarily. It felt sad to give up this place, where I could stare out the window toward the home of the Poet, where I could walk across the street and stand in her garden. This was the first place I'd lived with Charlie, the first place we'd brought Sarah home. For so many days, she'd retained that newborn scent, of someone who had been living in the most primal, underwater world. Were Charlie and Deirdre having their affair then? Did he leave me that very night we brought Sarah home, on some fake errand, to meet her? It seemed like I would never, ever stop thinking about it. I poured rice cereal into a bowl to cool, holding the pot at a distance so Sarah couldn't reach out and grab it.

Charlie stepped closer and eased Sarah out of my arms, calmly stating his case. My coursework was finished. I had a little fellowship money. We wouldn't have to pay rent.

"There's Eli," I said.

"He's okay now," Charlie said. "He has his own place to live." Released from Pocasset, Eli had reclaimed Lightfoot and was back in Boston working at Angell.

"For now," I said.

"Look," Charlie said. "We won't live there forever. Just for a little while."

He sat down at the kitchen table with Sarah on his knee. I sat down across from them, blowing on every spoonful before offering it to my baby, who waved her hands excitedly between each bite, oblivious to everything that went on between Charlie and me.

AFTER PEOPLE DIE, YOU'RE expected to speak for them. What would your mother do? What would Charlie say? As if I had ever been able to predict the thoughts and actions of those people while they were living. Sometimes I try to imagine my mother coming to Amherst after Sarah was born, to help, which would have given her a front row seat to everything that happened with Deirdre. But it was hard to reconcile this projection with the mother I remembered. Maybe she would have come for a visit, and then gone back to Ireland. I would send her pictures over email, making our life seem perfect. She would check in once or twice a week by phone.

And what about Charlie and me? Would my forgiveness have succeeded? We moved to Cape Cod as Sarah turned one. I worried over when she would take her first step while Charlie shrugged and said she would do it on her own time. In July Tab was killed at the top of the road by a too-fast driver, and Charlie tended me carefully. I tried to be grateful, and then I tried to focus on mundane annoyances—discrepancy in child care, the debt the restaurant had left behind, Charlie's lack of a job. My car broke down, and we junked it instead of fixing it. "Do you love me?" I asked him too often, and Charlie always said yes. Looking back,

I'm not sure I ever said "I love you" to Charlie in the time between finding out about his affair and finding him dead. I only said, "I love you, too."

What would that period of time have become if Charlie had lived? Would it have led to the end eventually, a failed attempt at holding our family together? Or would it have just been a period of time we needed to get through, to be solid again, for Deirdre to become a little blip in our history. Would Charlie have learned his lesson, or would he have proved himself to be incorrigible, and years later I'd find myself in just the same spot? Emily Dickinson had decades to become disillusioned with Sue, to forgive her and love her again, and finally turn away. How many times would I have needed to repeat the same process until I'd finally settled into permanent anger? Or would it have been different, with Charlie and me?

The summer after Deirdre, I kept asking myself these questions in the future tense: Will my anger ever go away? Will Charlie ever do this again? It was such a difficult time. No matter how hard I tried, how definitely I decided, there was still this strain of uncertainty and of injuries that refused to disappear. All that conspired against us, churning into the day I walked into Ladd's cottage, the same day Charlie's heart stopped beating.

If it hadn't stopped beating. If Charlie had lived. The answers and the memories would have unfolded together into discovery. *What would have been*: it's the only tense we can never know.

TO OTHERS, IT MAY have seemed clear that Eli's life led up to Charlie's death. But in my mind it didn't seem that way. Clear. It seemed instead like *my* life, arriving there, in that first part of September. The time of year technically called summer but which everyone in New England knows is really fall. On that day, the last day of Charlie's life, I drove over to see Ladd at his uncle's compound. He'd said he had some books for me. I parked my car—the old station wagon that once belonged to Charlie and Eli's mother—in the empty space beside the shed.

Ladd could have stayed in the main house. Or he could have used his parents' house—which was better suited to winter habitation, situated away from the shore's buffeting winds. But his postcard had said he was staying in the cottage. In fact, there were three cottages on Daniel's property—two of them oceanfront, built years ago from old Sears kits. But I knew exactly the one Ladd meant. It sat back in the scrub oak woods, out of sight. It was the same one in which, years ago, we had showered and changed, and made love, before going to tell his parents about our short-lived wedding plans.

The path behind the house was overgrown. I wore my long Indian skirt, a pale blue tank top, and leather flip-flops. The soles slapped against my heels, and I stared down at the chipping nail polish on my toes. By now I could see the cottage—in my head it had already become *Ladd's cottage*—settled in among the trees. You had to know about this little house to find it—hunched under the taller scrub oak, small and unassuming, like something for children scattering bread crumbs to stumble upon. I saw Ladd through the large window, sitting at a wooden table and staring at a laptop screen. I wondered if the cabin, for all its rustic isolation, had Wi-Fi.

Even though it felt like a creepy thing to do, I stood there for a while, staring through the window, watching Ladd. Seven years had passed since I left him for Charlie. More than two since I last saw him. But he looked exactly the way I always remembered him: tall and ordinary, with a kind, craggy face. After a minute he sensed me there, staring at him. He turned and started, pushing back his chair. I lifted one hand and curled my fingers down one at a time, an overly girlish wave. By the time he'd walked to the front door—only a few paces worth—I was there to meet him.

"Brett," he said at the same time the door slid open with a rasp.

"Hi Ladd," I said.

We stood there for a moment, wondering if we should hug and sharing an awkward decision not to. He cleared his throat and said, "Come to see those volumes?"

"You bet."

Ladd stepped away from his door and held out his hand, gesturing to the threshold. I thought of the brief exchange I'd had with Charlie earlier, about the joking, fantasy make-out session with Ladd. In my mind, I had pictured a rusty teakettle and piles of dusty books, maybe dirty socks in the corner. But Ladd's cottage was neat—if his bed was unmade, it was politely hidden overhead in the loft. And the teakettle that he immediately turned on was brand-new or recently polished. I'd forgotten that about Ladd, the way he kept order. In one corner of the cottage sat a small pine table surrounded by mismatched chairs. I knew the books the moment I saw them, from across the room, stacked there, waiting for me. *The Years and Hours of Emily Dickinson*, by Jay Leyda, both volumes. I crossed the room as he fiddled with boxes of tea bags. Before he could ask me which kind I wanted I brushed my hand over the top cover.

"Look at these. Were you expecting me?"

He poured steaming water into large green mugs. "I thought I might bring them by later," he said. "That way I could say hi to Charlie, too."

Since when did Ladd ever want to say hi to Charlie? The books looked ancient, musty, sacred. Funny to see something—solid and right there—that I had been wanting for so long.

I said, "It was really good of you to remember. Thank you."

"They're Uncle Daniel's," Ladd said. "They belonged to his wife." He dropped tea bags into the mugs and handed me mine. I closed my hands around its lovely warmth, the steam rising up around my face.

"You know, Brett," he said. "I'm glad you came by, before I saw you and Charlie. I don't even know if you ever told him about that letter I wrote."

It surprised me that he would bring this up so quickly. I shook my head. All of a sudden it became very apparent, this close space hidden in a thicket of trees, the intimacy of the two of us, here together. Would Charlie mind? Or was his trust in my adoration so complete that he wouldn't give it a second thought?

"I've been embarrassed for two years and counting," Ladd said.

It would have been appropriate to take time and weigh my response. I wondered, again, if anyone had told Ladd about Sarah. Probably this would be a good time to tell him myself. But at that moment, for whatever reason, my field of vision had narrowed to these four wooden walls and the crooked floorboards. And I felt like just me, a person, instead of a mother and wife.

"Don't be embarrassed," I said, remembering how I'd ripped it into pieces. "I love that letter. It meant a lot to me. It still does."

Ladd tilted his head to one side. I noticed gray at his temples. On the other side of the room, my corporeal lines blurred a little bit, and while I didn't exactly step out of body I became acutely aware of a sort of dreamlike quality, a sudden out-of-timeness. Who could have known, when I woke up that morning, that the two of us would be standing here together, in this small enclosed room, with nobody watching. I thought of Eli, heading toward Cape Cod, and Charlie, nailing in shingles as if I hadn't even left. Then I thought of that Fourth of July seven years before and wondered what my life would have been like if I hadn't agreed to sign on the dotted line or followed Charlie through the crowded party.

"So," Ladd said. "How's the dissertation coming?"

"Slowly." I didn't want to talk about my dissertation. What I wanted to do was tell Ladd something I hadn't told anybody aside from Maxine and our marriage counselor; I wanted to tell him about Deirdre. *You were right,* I wanted to say. *Charlie broke my heart.*

"A lot's happened since you went away," I said. It occurred to me that he was just back from an adventure, a life-changing experience. I should have asked him about that. But I was too full of my own life-changing experience. So I said something else, something for which I must never be forgiven: "Charlie had an affair with the hostess at his restaurant. So we had to come here for a while to get away from all that."

Ladd leaned against the sink, his fists behind him closed around the edge of the counter. I remembered those same fists closing around my wrists and guessed that he did, too. That same flush of anger came over his face. At first I thought it was directed at Charlie. Then I realized it was at me, for confiding in him.

"Why are you telling me this?" he said.

"I don't know. Why did you write me that letter?"

Ladd pushed away from the sink and walked toward me, but he didn't make it all the way across the room. Instead he took a seat in an ancient armchair. This cottage had been built in 1920, and the chair—with its unraveling weave and tired springs—looked like it had been there from the beginning. Everything as old and worn as the pain that Charlie had caused me, and the echoes I had stirred here with Ladd. I felt like I should step back a little, retreating from what I might have just set in motion. But I couldn't get any closer to the table without moving around it, toward the far wall, which I felt would call too much attention to myself. As it was, Ladd hadn't taken his eyes off me. He watched me like something he was studying, and when he spoke, his voice was careful, considered.

"What am I supposed to say now?" he asked. "Something about how I thought of you while I was in the jungle?"

"I guess you could say I told you so."

Ladd blinked, letting up his gaze the tiniest bit. "I always wanted to ask," he said, "if you left because I made you sign that thing. Because if that was the reason, you could have told me. Christ, you could have done anything in the world except run off with Charlie."

So long ago and far away, that day in the Boston lawyer's office. Clearly the point of that day was not to expect anything as a gift. It would all be on loan—the man, the marriage, the family fortune, the good pen. Dependent on my good behavior.

"Charlie Moss," Ladd said. "Of all people in the world."

That name, even or especially then, like a fist closing around my heart. And I was so tired of feeling that way. As usual, I thought of Deirdre, her wounded, icy-blonde face.

"So you're not going to say it?"

"What?" Ladd said. "I told you so? Would it make a difference now?"

"I doubt it."

"You know," Ladd went on, "that day you left my house, when I didn't come after you, I thought I was doing what I had to, what I was supposed to do. Respecting your wishes. I felt so horrible. Charlie never did one thing to deserve you and you married him anyway. Lately I've been thinking about it, all the time I've spent doing what I'm supposed to do. Every second and minute when I've been obedient and responsible and considerate. What would be so bad about taking one minute to myself, to just do what I want?"

The last time I'd broken a rule—really, seriously misbehaved— was when I left Ladd for Charlie. I thought of all the time I'd spent since then being faithful, and the work I had done trying to forgive him, to stay with him. And before and after that, just the simple wifeliness of my days. Even in the end, the failure of the restaurant, and Deirdre—the way we'd gone back to what life would have been if it had all never happened. Day after day, for as long as I could remember, just being faithful and devoted. The great good wife, standing by while Charlie did what Ladd said he would do, what he had always done: broken my heart.

I stared back at Ladd and recognized him as full of something, in regard to me, that Charlie had always lacked. Not love, ex- actly. Because Charlie did love me. I knew that. Maybe what I saw instead was simple longing. Why would Charlie ever have had to long for me when I'd always been so immediately there?

"Ladd," I said. "Do you know what I'd do? If I could take one single minute of my life? To just do what I wanted?"

His face lost the smallest amount of color. I crossed the room to where he sat in the ancient armchair. Somewhere in those few strides my feet lost their flip-flops as I walked my way over to Ladd and crawled onto the chair, my knees on either side of him, pressing into the worn springs. I placed my hands against his face and cradled it there for a moment, taking in his features, the face I used to know—not beautiful to everyone but even now beautiful to me. I pressed my lips to his forehead and then his cheek. My hands moved down to rest on his shoulders as I made my way, in a circle, kissing his face.

It took up the whole minute I had granted us. A long and very pregnant minute, during which Ladd sat frozen, his eyes closed. When it ended, they fluttered open. I sat back a little. Ladd studied me with an expression almost like sternness, and I thought he was about to accuse me of something.

"Just one minute," I said, "out of all these days and hours."

"Let's make it thirty," Ladd said. And then kissed me on the lips.

After another few minutes, I amended. "Let's make it an hour."

It didn't last an hour, not quite, and it could have been worse. Our clothes stayed on. Our hands didn't wander, not much, and even when Ladd reached beneath my skirt he only let his hand rest above my knee, holding me there, while we kissed and kissed. Perhaps the worst thing was the way Ladd looked when we said good-bye, a kind of expectation that this would continue, whereas by the time I got to my car, I had already returned to thinking about Charlie.

Driving back to Maxine's, an overhead cloud obscured and flattened the sunlight. My hands shook on the steering wheel. I knew how this would all play out, the same way it had hundreds of times before. My anger with Charlie would fill to capacity and then burst, its remnants floating away on the ocean air, leaving me with the simple fact that I adored him. My husband was an elusive, inscrutable will-o'-the-wisp, which was why he drove me crazy and why I never could manage to walk away. I blinked back tears, thinking that the secret to marriage did not lie in compatibility, or even commitment, but the willingness to endure heartbreak. I, for example, had loved Charlie well enough to paste my heart back together a hundred times or more since the day I first met him.

Retreating from Ladd's, I had no confidence at all in Charlie's willingness to repair his heart on my behalf. My chest filled with fears that would soon be rendered entirely irrelevant.

And I know what you're thinking. How I used up my husband's last heartbeats in so unforgivable a way. And I do relive those moments with excruciating guilt, but the truth is, not so much more than anything else. Because I relive every moment of all those years with the same emotion—the same overwhelming regret. In my head, it plays over and over again, and it plays like a death march.

For example, the real and true beginning. The day I met Eli. We were trying out for a play, a musical. In the dance portion—

downstairs in the studio, the far wall lined with mirrors—we had to pair up and imitate each other's movements. The crowd paired off before I had a chance to turn around, and there stood Eli. He was wiry and blond—straight hair that hung to his shoulders. Round blue eyes that I didn't yet know were just like Charlie's. We stood facing each other, and I let him take the lead. He spiraled his arms in wide strokes. Everything he did was broad, the expression on his face mock serious, so that I kept breaking down in laughter. Neither of us got a part in the play. But we became friends. As Eli told Ladd on the ferry that day: best friends.

THE DAY AFTER I found Charlie dead—once his body had been removed to the coroner's—a female police officer escorted me back to the house so I could collect enough of Sarah's and my things to last a few days, a week. The two of us tromped in and out, carrying suitcases and bags of diapers. As I rolled the stroller over the wood floor of the sunporch, from below my feet I heard something jump and skitter.

Maybe if death hadn't felt so close, hovering all around the house, I wouldn't have reacted to the sound. But when I heard it, I thought so immediately of Tab. Maybe the portal through which Charlie had left still gaped open, giving Tab the opportunity to return. I let go of the stroller and walked outside, kneeling in the same spot I always did, to coax her out before sunset, and keep her safe from the coyotes that sometimes crossed the distance between salt marsh and shore.

"Tab," I said, squatting down and peering under the porch. That skittering sound again, and along with the scent of dusty mold—the underneath of things—an even more distinct odor, the kind that can only rise off skin and fur. My eyes adjusted to see a small black form pressed against the cement foundation of the house, her shivering so contained that the small metal tags on her collar didn't make a sound. Lightfoot.

I called to her and called to her, but she wouldn't come toward me, not even when the police officer brought sliced turkey from the refrigerator. Finally I had to slither under the porch on my belly and drag her taut, quivering form across the pebbly dirt, her nails dragging in protest, wanting to remain pressed against the far wall.

Outside in the sunlight, I gathered the dog in my lap and brushed the dust away. Defeated, she went ahead and ate a slice of turkey. She weighed twelve pounds, composed of bone and tremble under short, coarse fur. Once I'd pushed away the thickest layer of dust, I found myself searching for any sign, any splatters, of blood. But of that her coat was clean.

Yet each man kills the thing he loves. It's not a poem I've studied seriously. The right part of the right century, but I specialize in American poetry. Still, from time to time, Wilde's lines will leap into my head. They leapt into my head that day, as I studied the dog, her quivering ears flat back against her head. Because I knew myself to be a coward. Because I'd supplied the kiss and let someone else wield the sword.

PART THREE

I had a terror since September, I could tell to none; and so I sing, as the boy does of the burying ground, because I am afraid.

—EMILY DICKINSON

11

There had not been a murder in Saturday Cove since 1980, when a summer resident killed his wife and two children, and then himself. It shook people up, of course, but the suicide let the police off the hook. It didn't give them any practice. For such a long time, law enforcement only dealt with the occasional winter break-in, shoplifters, drunk drivers. There was no homicide department. To investigate Charlie's murder, they borrowed detectives from Hyannis, scarcely better practiced, who arrived to interview me. They took my computer. They searched my car, collecting the messy depths of our station wagon into zip-top plastic bags of various sizes, even the empty coffee cups and candy wrappers. They cataloged pacifiers and teething rings. The postcard from Ladd, its corner bent and crinkled where Sarah had chewed on it. They searched for blood, DNA.

If they had asked me to retrace my steps of the day before, to tell them everything I'd done and everywhere I'd been, I would have. The hour I spent with Ladd sat heavy on my brain, every molecule of my body protesting against it. But they didn't ask. Because I wasn't a suspect, they accepted the bare bones of my movements: I'd brought my baby to my friend's house because Eli was coming. In the morning, I'd gone to check on Charlie and found him dead and Eli bloody. They wanted to know everything about that morning, what Eli had done and said. I told them how I'd leaned over Charlie and tried to pick him up. How I'd run away.

I told them about Deirdre, too, about her affair with Charlie, and the way she used to watch us. They nodded and took notes, asked a couple questions about the timing, and the last time I'd seen her. Just going through the motions, not particularly interested. As far as I could tell, in this killing there was only one suspect.

But they couldn't find him. Eli seemed to have evaporated into the late-summer air or flown away with the migrating bank swallows. Maybe if I'd been able to dial 911 as soon as I'd left the house, the police would have been there in time to catch him. One thing we knew, Eli hadn't driven away, at least not in his own car, which still sat in the driveway when the police arrived. But he didn't leave any small personal items behind, not an overnight bag, not even a toothbrush.

Maybe Eli had swum out to sea, shoes and all, and drowned himself. But then: wouldn't his body have washed up on shore? The police scoured the tide line, the cranberry bogs, the lakes, the scrub oak woods. According to all evidence Eli had come to Saturday Cove, killed his brother—and then vanished.

That didn't stop me from expecting him to return at any moment. The evening of the day I found Charlie dead—when uniformed police officers and swirling lights and sirens had finally dispersed—Ladd showed up on Maxine's doorstep. When he rang the bell, Maxine and I both jumped, grabbing on to each other. Sarah looked up from the floor where she sat stacking red plastic cups, her hand stalling in midair, staring at us.

"It can't be him," Maxine said, meaning Eli. There was a patrol car stationed in her driveway. Anyone who made it to the front door would have been vetted by those officers. Still, Maxine wouldn't step forward, and I wondered if she'd ever be able to open her door again, to anyone. She hadn't even seen Charlie dead, and she was wrecked by it all, the proximity to so much violence. I started to move and she pulled me back.

"It's okay," I said, twisting my arm from her grip. As I headed toward the door, she walked to the counter to grab her phone, and stood there, watching me—her fingers poised, even though the nearest officers sat just a couple yards from her front door, and we could probably call them faster just by screaming.

I looked through the peephole. It was Ladd, his dark head bent, his shoulders tense. I turned toward Maxine and told her, "It's only Ladd." The bell rang once more, and I looked through the peephole again. In the triangulated glare of the motion-detected porch light, Ladd looked determined, like a man running to his lover in her time of need. When I opened the door, he stepped forward toward me, ready to gather me up in his arms. The movement I made—stepping back, my hands rising the barest bit—stopped him just short of the threshold.

The police officers had gotten out of the car. They stood there, watching us, the sound of their radio crackling into the evening. They must have spoken to Ladd, cleared him for visiting, but still they kept careful eyes on us. It made me wonder if I was a suspect. Shouldn't I be a suspect? Wasn't the spouse, always? Sarah toddled over to my side, gripping my pants leg and staring up at Ladd. He started at the sight of her, this indelible bit of proof—of my real life.

"Brett," he said, recovering. He made a motion with his hands, almost but not quite opening his arms, still expecting me to fall into them. "I have to know if you're all right." Realizing the ridiculousness of this statement, he amended. "Tell me what I can do."

Tell me what I can do. Charlie had only just died. I had found him that morning. And I had not touched my phone all day. My mother no longer existed for me to call. Yet here Ladd stood, frantic with knowing. For a moment, the air radiated with the news, spreading in its small town way. *Charlie Moss murdered. Can you believe it? I just saw him yesterday.* The words from every house in town gathered around our heads, buzzing. I didn't want to stand out here, exposed.

"You can go away," I said. "Please. Go away and leave me alone."

And I closed the door, turning the dead bolt as soon as the latch clicked. Then I scooped up our baby—Charlie's and mine—and held her close, breathing in her skin, her scent, as if it might erase everything that had happened these past forty-eight hours.

BOB MOSS CAME UP from Florida with his second wife, to arrange the funeral. They stayed in a hotel and managed everything with barely a word to me. All I had to do was show up.

Maxine loaned me a dress and found a babysitter to stay with Sarah. The church was already packed when we arrived. As I walked down the aisle, I felt an illogical longing for Eli. After all these years, I still barely knew Charlie's dad. Both my parents were gone, and now my husband. I remembered the way Eli had brought Charlie back to the altar on our wedding day.

I let my eyes roam up each aisle. I saw family friends and friends of mine from grad school; even a couple of professors had made the trip. But I didn't see Ladd. Daniel Williams was there—he nodded at me as my eyes fell upon him—and so were Ladd's parents. Why wasn't Ladd sitting with them? When I had told him to leave me alone, I certainly hadn't meant that he shouldn't come to the funeral. He must have realized that. After all. He and Charlie had grown up together, summers here in Saturday Cove. They were practically cousins. Ladd lived just down the road from this church, close enough to ride his bicycle or even walk. Of course he shouldn't be banging on my door, wanting to see me alone. But if he didn't come to Charlie's funeral, everyone would know the only possible reason: he had been with me the day before, the two of us betraying Charlie with only hours left of his life. Before the funeral even began, everyone would know.

And then my eyes stopped cold on a familiar figure in the second row, precisely behind the spot they'd saved for me. Deirdre Bennet, sandwiched between the Saturday Cove librarian and Charlie's aunt Marian—not as she should have been (if she had to come at all) with the rest of the crew from the Sun Also Rises, who were sitting in the back. My feet halted, and I stared at her, and she stared back with her pale, watery eyes, as if she'd been crying nonstop for days. Her dress was yellow, too cheerful, with long sleeves. The color and weight were wrong for the day; she should have been sweating. Around her neck she wore an owl pendant. At first I thought it was on a leather string, and I pictured her, spattered with blood, leaning over Charlie, removing it from his neck and tying it onto hers. After a second, I realized it wasn't leather but a slim black ribbon. The way she brought her fingers to her neck, just short of touching it, made me wonder if it had been a gift from Charlie. Or maybe it was just because of the way I was staring.

"Come on," Maxine said gently. She still didn't touch my arm. "Let's sit."

The two of us sidled down the row, squeezing into the one spot reserved for me next to Bob. I could feel Deirdre's eyes, intent on the back of my head, and I sat still as possible, not wanting to give her even the slightest movement. As the service began, I found myself wishing again for Eli. In fact as the minutes ticked by I became more and more convinced that he would show up. Because how could he miss it? His own brother's funeral?

I barely listened to the verses that were read or the people who spoke. Charlie never cared about things like that, about ceremonies. About poems. But he would have wanted his brother to be there. The past few days I had cowered in Maxine's house when what I should have been doing was searching for Eli. Not so he could face any kind of justice. But so he could be here, with us, attending Charlie's funeral as he had not been able to attend their mother's. As I sat in the front pew, what I saw in my mind was not the pastor—a stranger—but Eli rushing down the aisle in a coat and tie, late for the seat we should have saved for him.

I could hear the sound of people trying to muffle their crying. I could hear Deirdre, behind me, and Maxine, next to me. But Bob and I, neither of us cried, we just sat there, carved from stone, waiting for the service to end. Which it finally did. People stood, began shuffling out. I stood. The back of the pew separated Deirdre and me. She reached forward and I flinched, but she was only returning the hymnal.

Outside, afternoon sun had shifted to its widest, most unflattering filter; it sifted into the church even through the stained glass, and I could see the places in Deirdre's translucent skin where small veins had broken and pores had muddied. I thought of our twin griefs—having been left by Charlie once when he rejected us. And now. How could he be gone? Standing there between Bob Moss and Maxine, staring rudely and unstoppingly at Deirdre while she refused to look back at me, I could feel the realization like something hovering, a hand raised to hit me full force, as it had not yet, not even when I'd knelt beside his body and tried to lift it. Charlie dead. Gone. Never coming back.

I sat back down in the pew. Was it possible that once upon a time, Deirdre's face represented the most pain I had ever experienced? Was it possible to feel the weight of this loss and ever stand again? A hand came down on top of my head, its palm flat. Thinking that it was Deirdre, I jerked away, then looked up to see Bob, staring down.

"I'm sorry," I said, my voice gnarled as the scrub oaks that lined his property. He nodded and then turned away. I looked up to where Deirdre had been standing. The row was empty.

"Do you know that girl?" Maxine asked.

"That's Deirdre," I said. Maxine sat down, and I added, "I

wonder if she'll go to the reception." Bob had hired a private room at a local restaurant. Obviously he couldn't have it at the house.

"If she does," Maxine said, "I can tell her to leave."

"Or I could just not go. Do you think I have to go?"

"No," she said. "I think people will understand. But you know. If you want to go. You should."

"The only thing in the world," I said, "that would make me strong enough to go to that reception would be if Charlie were there, too."

"Because of her?"

"Because of Charlie," I said.

Sitting next to me, equipped with hat and handkerchief, Maxine did what I couldn't. She cried. I put my hand on her knee, my eyes still facing forward. All the noise had shifted to the back, a receiving line, where I was expected to be, shaking hands, accepting condolences. A pair of soft soled footsteps approached, polite steps.

"Brett," Daniel Williams said, stepping into and blocking out that intrusive shaft of light, placing us in his shade. "I just wanted to tell you how sorry I am."

"Thank you," I said.

For some reason, it was easier to meet his eyes. He kept his hands in his coat pockets, his straight shoulders at ease. Unlike everyone else—even Maxine—he didn't seem to be braced for my hysteria. I wondered if he was still staying on the Cape, his summer spilling into the fall, or if he'd come down from Boston especially for the funeral.

"If there's anything I can do," Daniel said. He removed one

hand from his pocket and gestured outward, a graceful and elbow-driven movement, indicating the church, the neighborhood, the wide world. "Anything at all."

"Thank you." I hoped I sounded sincere enough to convey that I knew: while other people said this, Daniel meant it.

He nodded, and then turned to walk back down the aisle. With his having paved the way, other people moved from the back to offer their hands and their sympathies. Until finally the church emptied out, and Maxine and I sat there, alone, the only mourners left.

THE NEXT MORNING SARAH stirred, as always, with first light. She sat up, delighted to find Lightfoot lying between us once again, and set immediately to examining the dog's ears, prodding her fingers into the exposed cartilage. Lightfoot woke and must have remembered everything she'd seen, because she set immediately to trembling.

"Gentle," I told Sarah as she pitched forward to press her face against Lightfoot's, one hand still clutching a pointy ear. Sarah scrunched up her brow and looked at me reproachfully. Then she slid off the bed and marched to the window. Maybe if I'd remembered to close the blinds, she would have slept later. Sun poured in with increasing speed. Outside, it reflected off the lake in small explosions, gathering itself for the day. It would be hot, another stretch of Indian summer.

"Pool," Sarah said. "Pool."

I dressed us both in our bathing suits and we headed downstairs. Maxine had set the coffeepot to brew automatically, so I poured a cup and hoisted Sarah to my hip, not quite ready to let her practice walking on the steep slate steps to the water. I put her down where pebbly dirt met sand, and dumped our towels. Lightfoot rushed forward, touching the top of the water with one delicate paw. A pink plastic shovel rested near the bottom of the steps, making up for my absentmindedness in forgetting to bring toys, and I handed it to Sarah. She knelt in the inch or two of water, scooping up the silt and watching it plop back through the wavelets. She babbled to herself, some words recognizable and some not. It felt so strange that something so devastating could have occurred without her knowing.

From up above, I heard a car pull into Maxine's driveway, and turned, putting one hand over my heart. I didn't know where Eli's car was now—impounded in Hyannis, it would have become evidence. A door slammed, and in a moment Ladd appeared at the top of the steps. He must have seen us from the road. With Sarah so close to the water, I couldn't keep my eyes on him as he walked toward us.

"Brett," Ladd said. He stopped several feet short of me.

I didn't feel like small talk. "Why didn't you go?" I asked, still not looking at him.

"What do you mean?" Ladd said. "Go where?" I glanced over as his face shifted, confused.

"To the funeral," I said, turning my eyes back toward Sarah. "You should have been there."

"I was. I was there. I promise. I got there just after you, I saw you go to the front with Maxine. I had to stand in the back, it was crowded. You didn't go to the receiving line. I thought I would see you at the reception."

A fat cloud blew overhead, white and empty of rain, but for a moment blocking the gathering sun. I stepped back toward Sarah, noticing for the first time that Lightfoot was gone. I lifted my hand to shade my eyes as the cloud wisped away, looking out toward the lake to see if a little black dog was struggling in the water.

"They read the Twenty-Third Psalm," Ladd said, as if he needed to prove it to me. But don't they read the Twenty-Third Psalm at every funeral?

"Charlie wouldn't have cared about that," I said.

"No," Ladd agreed.

I knelt down next to Sarah, digging my hand through the little trough she'd made where the water met the soaking sand. "No," she said, pushing my hand away. "No, Mommy."

I looked up. A red-tailed hawk swooped in lazy circles, and I wondered if it was the same one that nested in the cranberry bog by the Moss house, less than two miles away. Maybe it was heading back there right now. What sort of activity would it find below if it executed the same meandering wing flutters it did now? Did the house stand empty, yellow crime-scene tape rustling under heavy sun and vague wind? Or did the police have more business there? Was someone stationed, waiting for Eli, in case he came back? Was Bob there, collecting whatever last items he wanted to take with him?

"I told you not to come back here," I said, keeping my eyes fixed on Sarah's shovel, not wanting to see any kind of expression on Ladd's face. "I told you to leave me alone."

"I know," he said, very quietly. "I know you did. I'm sorry."

"Did you think I was joking?"

Ladd's shadow, elongated on the sand, quivered. I spoke to it, refusing to be moved by the way it had brought one hand to rest on top of its head, a characteristic gesture of helplessness.

"I wasn't joking," I said. "There's nothing you can do to help. You are not my *boyfriend*."

The shadow's hand came down, its body spilling wider as another cloud moved overhead. Sarah still sat beyond its reaches, concentrating, her hat falling nearly over her eyes. And I finally stated the most obvious thing, which I'd never had the courage to say aloud, to Ladd, not even when I'd left him.

"I don't love you. I love Charlie."

The shadow shifted, uncomfortable. Several sharp retorts floated down from Maxine's house. Ladd, Sarah, and I all turned our heads toward the noise. We saw Maxine, standing at a back window. She held Lightfoot under one arm and lifted her hand to rap on the window again, frantic. Unimpressed, Sarah went back to her digging, but Ladd and I both looked around, obediently, trying to locate whatever had alarmed her so. It took us almost a minute to realize it was just us, out here and vulnerable in the open air.

"I THOUGHT I WOULD die," Maxine said.

We were back inside the house, Sarah and I—Ladd having driven away before we gathered ourselves from the lake. I put Sarah down on the floor and an impressive hunk of sand dropped from her bathing suit. Maxine grabbed a broom and started sweeping furiously, still wearing her nightgown, her hair disarranged from sleep. Her salient trait had always been a cool put-togetherness; it was disconcerting, this new impression of utter disarray.

"I woke up," she went on, "and your bedroom door was open

and both of you were gone. Then the little dog is scratching at the door, all frantic. I was almost too scared to open it."

I could imagine Maxine, mustering up her courage to open the door just narrowly enough to let the dog shoot through. Lightfoot, recovered from whatever fright Ladd had given her, jumped up on a broad leather armchair. With the broom, Maxine reached out and gently shoved her off. "Then I look out the window," she said, "and there's this *man* . . ."

"It was just Ladd," I said, conscious that my voice should sound soothing and not defensive. As far as Maxine knew, Ladd was not upsetting.

"I know that now," Maxine said. "But for that one second . . . I thought I would die." She looked briefly remorseful at repeating that most extreme of expressions, but then, reconsidering, wanting to affect me, she said it again. "I thought I would die."

"Well, you didn't," I said. "Right? Here we are. Alive, still."

She stopped sweeping and closed her eyes. A buzzing sounded from my purse. At any other moment, I would have ignored it, but grateful for the interruption I hustled across the room. Probably it annoyed Maxine, the way I tossed my purse on the nearest available surface and forgot about it until it was time to leave again. She always hung hers on the coat stand by the front door. Fishing for my phone, I made a mental note to start doing the same.

"It's Charlie's father," I told Maxine before I answered.

"Listen, Brett," Bob said. Sometimes family can be most evident in a person's voice. Traces of Charlie and Eli, like living molecules, came wafting in. He said, "I'm heading back to Florida tomorrow and I need to get the keys from you."

"The keys?"

"The keys to the house. Don't you have keys?"

"I do."

"Meet me at the Olde Pub," he said. "It opens at eleven."

"He wants his keys back," I told Maxine when I hung up. Her eyes widened, and I could tell that for a moment she wanted to exclaim over this, the nerve, how could he. But then something shifted, and she kept quiet. I realized that although I'd been staying here in this house for over a week—with no particular plans to go anywhere else—I didn't have a key. A year ago, my key chain had rattled with our apartment key, and the one to our building, the ones for my office at school. Now, once I handed Bob Moss back his house key, the only key I'd own would be the one to our old car, Charlie's mother's car. And quite possibly I'd have no place to drive it.

FOR SO LONG, CARRYING Sarah everywhere, I'd thought life would be easier once she learned to walk. In the parking lot of the Olde Pub, she squirmed in my arms with much more strength than someone her age and size should possess. The second I put her down she didn't walk but ran, in the direction opposite the restaurant, toward a patch of grass and a couple Canada geese. The larger one spread its wings in warning, and I sprinted after her.

"Oh no you don't," I said, in a singsong voice, scooping her up and biting her cheek. She laughed, a burbly giggle, and a small piece of joy rose up inside me. It shocked me, that joy was still a possibility.

"Hey," I said, holding her fast. My voice sounded so normal. "I know you just learned to walk. When did you learn to run?"

"Run," she yelled, a primal yawp.

"We'll get you some fries," I said. She nodded and put one finger in her mouth.

Bob was already there, sitting at one of the booths. I put Sarah on the bench opposite him; she walked across it, her feet sticking slightly on the beer-scented vinyl. "You brought the baby," Bob said. His voice was flat, surprised.

"I thought you'd want to see her," I said.

When the waitress came to deliver his beer, I ordered fries. Bob leaned forward as Sarah examined the deep grooves in the table. She picked up the butter knife and pressed it into a blackened pair of initials.

"Sarah," Bob said. "It's me. It's your grandpa."

Knife still in hand, she looked up at him. Bob's face looked jowly and drained of color. The veins on his hands protruded, and they trembled slightly as he looked at Sarah, Charlie's face in miniature staring back at him. I waited for him to remark on the resemblance, but he didn't. His eyes look watery and red.

"Do you have the keys?" he said.

The waitress arrived with Sarah's fries. She slid them in front of her and I pulled them back. "Hot," I said as Sarah protested. I reached into my purse and grabbed the keys, which I'd already separated from my key chain. Bob didn't reach out as I handed them across the table, so after a few seconds I just put them down. Sarah picked them up and I started breaking her fries in half so they'd cool off faster.

"I'm going to sell it," Bob said, staring at the keys in Sarah's hands. "Put it on the market right away."

"Okay," I said, wondering who in the world would buy it now. Bob looked braced for some kind of response, maybe an objection. As if I'd want to go back and live there, ever again.

I watched him take another sip of beer. He reached out and took a fry from Sarah's plate. He bit into it, then returned it to the edge of her plate. I slid it off and hid it under my unused napkin. And although I didn't want my daughter to eat his half-gnawed food, I couldn't be mad at him. I recognized the expression on his face, the one staring back at myself from the mirror. He was here, breathing the oxygen, making stabs at eating, for one reason only: he had a living child. So he had to stay in this world, because sooner or later Eli would return. As far as I'd witnessed, Bob had never been much of a parent. He wasn't enough of a parent now to stay here, on Cape Cod, and look for Eli, or even wait for him to show up. But still a parent. As I stared at him across the knotty pine table, the smell of beer and fried food thick around us, all I could think of was everything he'd lost. His first wife. Both his sons. Any kind of peace of mind, or happiness, ever.

What can a person do when one child murders the other? Murders the other and then disappears—not only into the vast, unknown world but the more unknowable recesses of his mind? I guess you do what Bob Moss did that day at the Olde Pub, right before my very eyes. You turn pale, and frail, and very old. You wring your hands and forget your grandchild. You don't think to reach out to the daughter-in-law, almost equally ruined, sitting there across the table, except to take the keys from her and say good-bye.

• • •

SARAH FELL ASLEEP IN the car. When we got there, a police cruiser was parked in front of the house. I parked beside it and got out, leaving the door open so the sound of it slamming wouldn't wake Sarah. Inside, the same police officer who'd escorted me back to the Moss house, a young woman, stood in the front hall talking to Maxine. The sight of her back, rigid and official, made me tense. When she turned, I almost expected her to draw her gun, or cuff me.

Maxine nodded toward the counter. "She brought your computer back."

"Thank you," I said.

I felt deflated, as if they were making a mistake, and felt another rush of insult at being so easily dismissed as a suspect. They had taken my laptop because Charlie used it, too, and it now sat on Maxine's counter with the cord wrapped around it. Beside it sat a gallon zip-top plastic bag, filled with everything they'd collected from our station wagon. I could see Ladd's postcard, the bright toucan's bill, pressed against the clear plastic. Apparently that wasn't worth keeping as evidence. I walked across the room and picked up the bag, then threw it away in the garbage bin under Maxine's sink. Lightfoot clicked across the room to greet me, and I knelt to pet her, then stood to get the computer.

"I can walk you out," I told the officer. "I'm just going to sit outside a while, my daughter's asleep in the car."

On Maxine's stoop, after the officer had driven away, I turned on my computer. I hadn't checked email in over a week. My account was clogged with messages from Lands' End and Old Navy, Planned Parenthood, and the NRDC. Notices from the university, and colleagues checking in. I went down the page, marking them all for deletion. And then I saw it, several pages back, already opened and read by the police. Charlie Moss. *Your Dinner* was the subject heading. The time next to it, 7:30. An hour or two left for him to live.

Hey, Charlie wrote. *I guess I'll have to feed Eli your coq au vin. Then I'll tell him he needs to leave in the morning. Please give Sarah a kiss for me. Love, Charlie.*

A few feet away, Sarah stirred in her car seat. She lifted her hands off her knees and let out a great sigh, as if she had read the message, too. Then she returned to stillness. *Your coq au vin.* All the tastes Charlie created, now gone forever. I remembered that pot of food, still sitting on the stove when I went back to get my things. If only I had stopped, to spoon it into my mouth, no matter how spoiled it was, the last thing Charlie ever cooked.

I brought my eyes back to the screen for a long minute, then hit the Reply button.

Dear Charlie, I wrote, *It's okay. Eli can stay as long as he likes. Just please don't wait for him. Come over to Maxine's right away. Spend the night with Sarah and me. We miss you so much.*

Up above, a great flutter as a flock of gulls rose into the air and headed out across the lake. For a moment, the sound could almost convince me I had turned back time and even now Charlie was walking across all the miles and endless days that stretched out over this past week. Headed home to us.

"Listen," Maxine said after Sarah had gone to bed. "I have to get out of here."

I sat in the leather armchair, holding a wineglass as Maxine filled it. She marched the bottle back into the kitchen, filled a glass for herself, and started to return the bottle to the refrigerator. Instead she closed the refrigerator door, filled her glass a little fuller, and left the bottle on the counter.

"I'm not sleeping," she said. "It's hard to eat." She let her voice trail off as her eyes roamed around the house, falling on the spot where I'd entered after finding Charlie.

"When I didn't know where you were this morning," Maxine said, "it just all came washing over me. I can barely stand to leave the house. I'm so scared, Brett. I'm so scared that he'll show up."

"Who?" I asked.

Maxine put her glass down. Lightfoot jumped into my lap. I knew Maxine didn't want the dog on the furniture, but maybe she wouldn't mind if I was operating as a buffer. Against my body, the dog quivered.

"Who?" Maxine said, her face incredulous. "Who do you think? Charlie's brother."

She knew Eli's name. But it had become too heinous to speak. Someone out there lurking, waiting to appear, to pounce. I remembered Eli flying off the roof of the fraternity house, arms outstretched, a superbeing with heightened powers. Until he hit the ground and became mortal. I remembered another dusky night, the way Charlie had let his own head smash to the pavement to save his brother.

"Eli wouldn't hurt us," I said. "I'm not even sure he hurt Charlie."

I recognized the look on Maxine's face. It was the same way Charlie and I used to look at Eli. The moment someone said something so off the wall that you knew logic had left the building, so you had no idea what to do or say next. Maxine took a sip of wine and then a deep breath, visibly composing herself.

"Brett," she said. "Who else? Who else in the world? And how?"

"I don't know. But someone else. And Eli saw it. Or else he showed up just after and found Charlie that way."

"He was covered in blood."

"So was I. I was covered in blood, but nobody suspects me."

Maxine frowned, as if what I'd said was worrisome on some level that made it more necessary than she'd thought, to stay with me. Lightfoot's ears twitched. The house ticked a bit in the silence between us. Water whooshed as the automatic sprinklers outside turned on. I ran my hand over Lightfoot's tiny spine. She sat taut, alert and listening.

"I'm so sorry, Brett," Maxine said, moving past whatever guilt she was grappling with. "For everything. But I have to go away for a while. I have to close the house and go home. I would have by now, you know, anyway, if not for all this."

I nodded, mostly because I couldn't think of anything else to do. Either now or later, when Maxine left. If only I could disappear, like Eli. But I had a small child. The money in my bank account would only carry me through these next months if I didn't have expenses like rent. *What would your mother say?* For the first time, I knew. She would tell me to get out of Saturday Cove as fast as possible. But even if I'd been able to come up with a destination and the means to get there, Charlie lay buried in the Blue Creek cemetery. *I'd rather be with Brett.* How could I leave him?

"I'm sorry," Maxine said again. "I wanted to help."

"You have," I said. "You really have. So much." I took a sip of wine, less because I wanted it and more because I wanted her to see me accepting something she'd given me. Being helped. Maxine could have offered to let Sarah and me stay here, in her empty house, after she'd gone. She could have invited us to come with her to Newton. But if we stayed or followed, the fear of Eli would remain with us and therefore with her. She had already done as much as she possibly could, and a person can never do any more than that.

"Do you have somewhere to go?" she asked. "Someone who can help you?"

I looked up at the ceiling, toward the room where Sarah lay, breathing quietly. She had no way of knowing that in the whole world, there was only one broken person to look after her. And there remained the possibility—what all reasonable people would call a very strong possibility—that Maxine was right to be afraid. Maybe at this very moment Eli stood out by the lake, watching the house, keeping tabs on my movements, waiting to make a movement of his own. Even if Eli hadn't killed Charlie, someone else had. A murderer still moved freely about the world, our world, his whereabouts a mystery.

"Yes," I told Maxine. "I have someone who can help me."

ON THE DAY CHARLIE died, when I moved to get out of the chair, Ladd held me closer. "Don't go," he said. "Stay."

I let him kiss me a little longer.

"What is there to go back to?" he said when I pulled away and started to get up. He tightened his grip in protest but then—remembering—let me go.

"What are you going to do?" he asked. I was standing now. One motion to smooth my skirt down, another few to comb my hair back into its ponytail, as if these simple movements could erase what just happened.

"I don't know," I said. "I can't think yet."

"Is that what you said to him?" Ladd asked. The hardness in his voice told me we'd traveled back in time, a full seven years.

"It wasn't like that," I said. "It wasn't like this." I sank into one of the small wooden chairs at his table. Our mugs of tea sat there, gone cold.

"What was it like, then," Ladd said, with that same angry edge.

"His mother was dying. His brother was nuts. It was hectic. And complicated."

"Right."

"We didn't have sex. I swear we didn't."

The bizarreness wasn't lost on either of us, but I didn't know what else to say. The best defense I had for myself—that I had always loved Charlie—would have been the most damning. Ladd held his arms out to me. I stayed where I was, already separating, worrying, giving my brain back to my husband.

"I'm sorry," I said for what felt like the hundredth time, though I hadn't said it—for that particular wrongdoing—in years.

"Well," Ladd pressed, "what now?"

My mind tangled up with everything I still had to deal with, Sarah at Maxine's, Charlie back at home, Eli on his way. I remembered the way Ladd had grabbed my wrist years before. Would he repeat that assault, holding me there with him? Would Charlie recognize the injury when I finally showed up?

And what if I didn't end things with Ladd, right then and there. If I let the summer unfold, carving out moments like this for the two of us. Would it be any different from what Charlie had done with Deirdre? And another thing: I could leave Charlie for Ladd. I thought that. I admit it, I did. Worries about Eli, money, fidelity—all gone.

"Look," I said to Ladd. "I don't know. I just don't know anything right now. But I'll call you. I promise."

When I drove away, leaving the house behind me, my life stretched ahead. And the emotion that took over was fear: somehow Charlie would find out, and I would lose him forever.

JUST OVER A WEEK later, on a sunny morning, Maxine hugged me good-bye and apologized again. I drove away from the lake, across Route 6A and over to Eldredge Lane. The Moss house was a little more than a mile down the road. I turned, down a longer and more private driveway, the wheels of my ancient car rumbling over dirt and roots.

I parked in front of the garage. The ocean stood below the lawn, a wide patch of grass to traverse, a steep drop of beach steps, so I could let Sarah walk, her lurching steps with Lightfoot trotting beside her, up toward the house. Even older than the Moss house—built in 1720—a mixture of white clapboard and gray cedar shingles, the original front door now standing open. Sarah reached it first, slamming her little body into the rattly metal of the screen door, so Daniel got there before I did and was holding it open when I reached the short brick steps. Something about his face, the way he held it as he watched our approach—too calm or maybe concealing—made me feel he'd been expecting us.

"You said if there was anything you could do," I told him.

Sarah and Lightfoot had already disappeared around his legs into the house. Daniel held the door open wider and moved aside so that I could come in.

12

Daniel's bedroom must have been downstairs; the upstairs was nothing but guest rooms. He led me to the largest room, past the crawl space, at the end of the long hallway. There was a crib in the corner with a fat teddy bear that looked brand new. It had a lemon-yellow bow around its neck. Sarah marched over and reached through the bars, trying to pull it out toward her. She'd never slept in a crib in her life. Curtains swayed in the open window, a perfect view of Cape Cod Bay. I turned toward Daniel.

"Sometimes guests have children," he said.

We walked back to the stairs. Sarah protested as I insisted on holding her hand going down the steep eighteenth-century staircase. At the foot of the stairs, she broke away and pulled open the drawer to the occasional table, the one Daniel had led me to all those years ago. There it still sat, the little leather envelope. Sarah opened it and examined Sylvia's picture solemnly.

"Lady," she said. Then she snapped it shut and held it over her head to show us. "Lady," she said again.

"Sarah," I said weakly. "Don't open drawers."

"It's quite all right," Daniel said. He smiled at her, and it didn't look like an obligatory smile. It looked genuine. Sarah returned the picture to the drawer and slid it closed with intense concentration. Daniel asked me, "Does Ladd know you're here? Did you tell him you were coming?"

"No," I said.

"I'd better go ahead and do that, then. I think he's in his cottage. Why don't you take Sarah down to the beach?"

Sarah and I left the house through the sliding glass door that led to the back deck. The morning sunlight had given way to thick gray clouds, bringing with them a salty, autumnal scent, the slightest chill. Lightfoot skittered out ahead of us, then paused to wait for Sarah. The two of them had adopted a funny way of moving in concert, Sarah swaying back and forth, Lightfoot running in little circles around her. To avoid holding my hand, Sarah descended the beach steps by sliding on her butt from one to the other, one at a time, all the way down.

On the sand, Sarah and the dog both broke into a run toward the water. It was low tide, the tide pools swept away, the beach strewn with gray foam and pebbles and seaweed. I ran after them but they stopped at the shoreline, Sarah kneeling down to inspect water that ran over her little white sneakers, soaking them.

Lightfoot let out three short, sharp yaps of protest, and I started. The dog, I realized, had barely made a sound since I'd found her huddled under the sunporch.

I knelt down. Lightfoot turned and battered her little body—cold and soaked from the waves—against my chest, leaving a damp blotch on my shirt. The dog knew what had happened to Charlie. If only I could ask her, reach the information stored in her little head. As obvious a suspect as Eli might have been, there should have been other obvious suspects. Like me, or Ladd, or Deirdre. And of course there could be others, people I didn't know about, people Charlie kept secret. Some man, some husband, whose wife had fallen madly in love like the rest of us. Maybe it was Deirdre's boyfriend, back in the picture and wildly jealous. Or maybe just some crazy person, happening by the neck and stumbling upon Charlie, killing him, leaving him for Eli to find, and me.

Some crazy person. A different one, not our own. That new headache of mine, sharp but malleable, like a squiggly piece of mercury, rattled behind my eyes. If I let my brain work hard enough, I could turn this into a murder mystery. I could be the plucky wife, taking on my own detective work, finding the real murderer, saving Eli. Or else, finding Eli, and turning him over.

From down on the beach, a figure approached as mist gathered. A tall man in a blue rain slicker, with a mop of unruly curls. Sarah sprang to her knees, her gaze serious and intent, looking out toward the bluff.

"Arooo!" Sarah called, at the top of her voice. Who knew a false elephant trumpet could sound so musical? Up above the skies broke open, dumping rain as if a faucet had been turned on. Lightfoot jumped off my lap and I stood. The rain tried its best, without luck, to tamp down both Sarah's curls and those of the man who approached us. Sarah lifted up her arm, her hand rolled into a fist, and waved it through the air, a fluid motion from her shoulder through the elbow.

"Arooo!" she called, "aroo!" and ran down the beach, toward the man.

If it had been Charlie, how surprised he would have been—seeing her move so quickly and nimbly, just over a week since that very first step. Or maybe he wouldn't have been surprised at all, believing, as he did, in biding his time, waiting until he could do a thing well before attempting it. As the man approached, he proved himself to be a gangly teenager, smiling perplexedly at Sarah, his curls not yellow but a gingery brown. Sarah halted in disappointment, her face scrunching into an angry expression that was both confusion and realization. The soaking rain fell. Passing us, the young man pulled the hood of his raincoat over his head. I caught up with Sarah and scooped her into my arms. The dog's ears flattened back against her head. From up above, the top of the beach steps, another man appeared, holding a huge, polka-dotted umbrella.

"Brett," Daniel called. "Come up, it's pouring."

I looked down at Lightfoot to see if she would cower or run the other way. But she didn't, just trotted on ahead, up toward the steps, as if she had seen an umbrella before and knew it meant cover from all this rain.

Inside I met Daniel's housekeeper, Mrs. Duffy. She was warm and round, with silver curls and a faint Irish accent. She told me that during the winter she lived in her own place in

Boston and went to Daniel's house to clean and make dinner. In the summer, she came with him to Saturday Cove and lived in one of the old Sears kit cottages overlooking the ocean. "It was ordered right from the catalog in the 1930s," she said as she whipped together a toddler supper for Sarah, homemade chicken nuggets and cooked carrots. "The first year I lived there I found an old shipping label under the staircase."

I leaned in the doorway, nodding. I imagined her cottage as rustic, disposable, nothing but tin silverware and old board games inside, because you never knew when a hurricane might sweep through and take everything away. Just what all seaside homes should be.

"Usually we'd be back in Boston by now," Mrs. Duffy said. "It's your good luck he decided to stay a bit longer." She patted my cheek. "Why don't you go into the living room and have a drink with Daniel before dinner? I'll take care of this one."

To my surprise, Sarah didn't protest when Mrs. Duffy hoisted her from my side into a waiting high chair—another inexplicable piece of baby equipment. Maybe very wealthy people just owned everything anybody might ever need. Mrs. Duffy handed Sarah a spatula, which she immediately began pounding on the tray. Lightfoot sat stock still right beside it, knowing that food would soon begin tumbling to the ground. I headed into the living room at the same time Daniel emerged from the Butler's pantry with a tumbler of scotch and a glass of white wine.

"Thanks," I said. I sat down on the sofa and he took one of the matching wing-backed armchairs, wondering if Ladd would show up and what he would think about my coming here.

"How are you?" Daniel asked, crossing his long legs.

"I don't know. It's like I'm traveling from panicked to broken to numb and back again. You know? Did you feel this way when Sylvia died?" It didn't feel insensitive asking this question. Maybe at another time it would have. But just then I felt a strong sense of kinship with Daniel, who couldn't stand to come around corners and be taken surprise by his wife's face.

"When Sylvia died," he said, "I was broken and confused. But she had been sick. I knew it was coming. *Prepared* isn't the word I'd use, because really you can never prepare for something like that. Still, if it had just come out of nowhere, and so violently. I can't imagine what you must be feeling now."

"I can't imagine, either."

"It's too soon," he said.

"Yes. Too soon."

"We'll wait," he said.

I nodded, and at the same time wondered for what, exactly. What would it look like, when all this became permanent. Sarah rounded the corner with Lightfoot click-clacking beside her. I thought she was headed toward me, but instead she stopped at the side table next to the couch and opened the drawer.

"Sarah," I said, more for Daniel's sake than hers. If there was a verbal way to stop a toddler from doing something, I hadn't yet discovered it.

"It's okay," Daniel said as Sarah found what she wanted—another small leather envelope. She held it over her head in triumph, then brought it over to me. I looked at Daniel, asking permission. He nodded.

This picture was different from the other I'd seen. Still by the water, but wearing shorts and a T-shirt, and holding a smiling blond toddler around Sarah's age.

"That's Eli," Daniel said. He leaned forward, peering at the picture. "I used to look at her with him and think: that's what she'll be like with our children."

"Charlie, too?" I said.

Daniel nodded. "Charlie, too," he said, but I could tell from a note of apology in his voice, Eli had been her favorite.

My eyes lowered, back to the picture, but before I had a chance to examine it more closely, Sarah snatched the envelope back and returned it to its drawer. Then she toddled past the coffee table—priding herself, I noticed, in not touching it for balance—in search of more drawers.

As her chubby hand closed around the knob to the matching end table, Daniel said, "I'm afraid she'll find one there, too. One for nearly every drawer. My own morbid scavenger hunt."

"I don't think it's morbid," I said, having very recently sent an email to my murdered husband. Charlie always kept a clean inbox, deleting email after he read it. Now mine would sit there unopened, forever.

Mrs. Duffy came into the room and told us dinner was ready. She scooped up Sarah and said, "I'll bring this one outside so you can eat in peace."

In the dining room, our meal was a grown-up version of the meal that Mrs. Duffy had fed Sarah—breaded chicken cutlets with wild rice and a salad of mixed field greens. When we sat down, Daniel continued the conversation about Sylvia.

"Ladd must have told you," he said, "that's how we met. My sister-in-law Rebecca and Charlie's mother were good friends. The boys had a standing invitation to use this beach, and Sylvia used to bring them here to play with Ladd."

I pictured it, Daniel—young uncle and gentleman—hosting the children and their pretty au pair. He would have stood back, not overtly interested, just watching her very carefully, sometimes offering to help with the boys.

"It turned out we were both at Harvard," Daniel said. "I was going to business school. She was getting her PhD in English. Her dissertation was on *The Faerie Queen*." He looked at me, waiting for a professional response, maybe even hoping I shared the same specialty.

"Nineteenth-century American poetry," I said, pointing to myself, apologetic for the distance from Spenser. "Late nineteenth century."

Daniel speared a piece of arugula, too polite to express disappointment. "It would have broken her heart, what happened to Eli. And now Charlie."

Years ago, when Ladd told me that Daniel had paid for Eli's hospitalization at McLean, I'd assumed this was the reason—his late wife's attachment. Sitting across from him, now myself the beneficiary of his impulse to help, I thought there was something more to it. Most of us think of ourselves—our true selves—in terms of intention, the person we're trying to be. Whereas everyone else sees the failure, the flailing, between the intention and the attempt, Daniel seemed wholly contained of these two spaces, with no bridge in between.

"I'm sorry," I said, not sure if I was expressing sympathy for Sylvia's death or her would-be broken heart.

Daniel didn't seem to mind the lack of clarity. He just said, "Thank you."

"And now," I said. "Don't you have to go back? To Boston, and your job?"

I had no idea what he did for work. Something to do with banks. All the men's work in Ladd's family had something to do with banks. Probably one day soon, after he was finished with English degrees and travels, Ladd would give up and go to work in a bank. I wondered where he was now, what he was having for dinner. If he was angry with me for showing up here, when I had told him so firmly to stay away.

"I can work from here," Daniel said. "Often I stay late into the fall, through the end of October."

I knew from what Mrs. Duffy had said this wasn't true, but I didn't say anything. Maybe he was doing this for Charlie and, by association, Sylvia. Maybe he was doing it for Ladd. It didn't matter, I just clung to the offered harbor, calculating in my mind the time this would buy me, if Daniel let me stay. Time to do what, I still wasn't sure. Figure out what to do next. Go back to Amherst? I couldn't see how I could possibly leave before Eli was found. Charlie wouldn't have left before Eli was found.

"It's the best time here," Daniel said. "The fall."

"That's what Charlie always says. Said."

Daniel nodded. For a moment I waited for tears to come to my eyes. It would be a good time, here in the safety of Daniel's gaze, with such a sympathetic audience. A torrent of tears, a good session of sobbing. The way I had in this very house when my mother died. The way I had when I thought my marriage was over. The way Deirdre had been crying at the funeral and—from the looks of her—for days before. A few years ago, here in Saturday Cove, Charlie and I had visited an old friend of his after her sister had died unexpectedly in a boating accident. *Keening*, that would have been the only way to describe how his friend had wept, bereft and shaking. The way I should have been, this past week, more than a week now, since I found Charlie. I should have been shaking and sobbing and keening to the rafters. But so far, I only moved in circles. Expecting tears was like expecting Charlie to walk through the door. It always seemed like it might happen at any moment, but it never did.

OUR ROOM WAS JUST above Daniel's. When I lay down, stroking Sarah's curly head, I could hear him through the old floorboards, moving around, water turning on and off, drawers opening and closing. He sounded fastidious and graceful, a routine that had been performed a thousand times in exactly the same order. Lying awake, staring at the beams above the bed, I listened to Sarah's soft breath, my hand resting on the rise and fall of her chest. And I imagined I could hear Daniel's breath, too, from the room below.

At about 5 a.m. I slipped out of bed, placing a pillow beside Sarah. In addition to the crib, there was a simple table and chair in the room, pressed against the far wall. Yesterday I'd slid my computer onto the table, and now I opened it and turned it on. For a long time, I sat staring at the email Charlie had written.

He didn't have a computer, just borrowed mine once a day to go online. His fingers would have moved over these very keys, in his surprisingly fast hunt-and-peck. I could picture him, sitting in the chair in my makeshift study, maybe with a beer in one hand. He always drank from a glass, never a bottle, and would have perched the glass right next to the laptop, the way he always did, the way that drove me crazy. Maybe, remembering this and conscious that he was trying to make amends, he would have stopped for a moment and pushed it away toward the stack of books I'd left there, one of them still open, the words I'd underlined so angrily, "Sue, you can go or stay."

My books. The day I'd gone back to collect my things, I'd only thought about what we'd need to get us through a few days or a week. Clothes and baby equipment. But I'd left all my books behind. Although my old life hovered so close in the past, it was impossible to imagine I'd ever return to any part of it. It only hit me now: I needed my books. Once today began—the sun rising in earnest—I would have to go and get them. Bob Moss may have taken back my keys, but I knew where Charlie had hidden a spare.

Sarah kicked her feet out of the covers, the first sign of approaching wakefulness. I turned back to the computer, like I was a machine myself, programmed to respond one way. *Dear Charlie,* I wrote again, the same words, the only ones I could think of. *It's okay. Eli can stay as long as he likes. Just please don't wait for him. Come over to Maxine's right away. Spend the night with Sarah and me. We miss you so much.*

BY EARLY AFTERNOON, DANIEL was working in his office, the door shut. When I asked Mrs. Duffy to watch Sarah, she accepted the vague word *errands*. As I walked out to the car, Light-foot trotted after me and hopped in. But when we arrived at our destination, wheels crunching over the seashell driveway, I realized it had been insensitive, thoughtless, to let the dog come along. At the sight of the Moss house, she started trembling and crawled in the back to cower underneath the seats. I rolled down the windows and left her there. Hopefully the cross breeze would keep her from overheating; if not, she could gather up her courage and jump out.

No birds except gulls, flying above. I walked around the house, across the lawn. The swallows must have started their journey south this past week. I wondered if the police officers and detectives had stopped to appreciate the staging, tiny birds practicing their formations, wonderful swoops and swells. From around the rails of the deck, the police tape had been removed, but I could see that the boards where Charlie's body had lain were gone, either collected as evidence or simply removed for replacement. I knelt down and looked under the deck. Even the dirt looked new, its top layer swept away.

I sat down and lay back. The grass felt wrong, sharp, too groomed. My eyelids fluttered closed, and I stretched out my legs. The sounds I could hear included the waves, the wind, a cardinal's trill. A car drove by, too fast. The sound of a squirrel's tiny feet skittered across the rail, then stopped. I lifted my head to confirm: one-eyed Wally, already thinner and more scraggly, as if we'd been grooming as well as feeding him.

"Hey, Wally," I said.

He twitched his tail, waiting for a nut or bread crust. I wished I had something for him. It felt right, somehow, returning to this, the seminal moment and place, around which everything would always revolve, and around which everything always *had* revolved, whether or not I'd known it. It felt wrong—that I wasn't cowering, trembling, like Lightfoot.

He's not dangerous, Charlie always said. It was just that the only way to get him the help he needed was to provoke him into danger.

According to the coroner, Charlie had been killed by the hammer. A blow to the back of his head. Why would he have turned his back on Eli in the midst of trying to provoke him? Charlie would turn his back on me, on Ladd, even on Deirdre. But on Eli he would have remained focused, watching him, registering his every move. I remembered the way Eli's hands had come down on Charlie's head, regretful, after knocking him down. Whoever had killed Charlie with the hammer had also slit his throat, still vengeful.

I stood up and walked around to the garage to retrieve the hidden key, then let myself into the house through the side door. Upstairs, the books I'd left out on the desk had been moved back to the shelf. *Rowing in Eden. Open Me Carefully. Master Letters. The Life of Emily Dickinson. Austin and Mabel.* There were too many to carry at once, so I made a couple trips to the car. Then I went into the kitchen and started collecting all of Charlie's good pots and pans. His wood knife block, minus the one the killer had used. I couldn't shake the feeling that I was trespassing. And stealing. But I wanted Charlie's copper pots. Never mind that I couldn't remember the last time I'd cooked anything more complicated than instant oatmeal or scrambled eggs. I carried them to the car a few armloads at a time, the metal conducting particles of Charlie into my bare skin.

But before I left, I went back to the house and walked through each room, looked under every bed, and opened every closet door. Just in case Eli was there hiding. When I got back into the car, Lightfoot had moved to the floor of the front passenger's seat, rolled into a little black pile like a roly-poly, quivering. I leaned forward and stroked her back.

"It's okay, baby," I said. "It's okay."

She unzipped herself in one quick motion and jumped into my lap. I backed out of the driveway. The dog's trembling slowly subsided as we made our way past the cranberry bog, away from the house. And I couldn't believe the dog would feel so afraid—still so afraid—if she'd only arrived late at night with Eli to find Charlie already dead. I felt sure that she had seen it happen, that she had been there. Which meant that one way or another, Eli had been there, too.

BY THE TIME DANIEL knocked quietly on the door of my bedroom, I had stacked the books on the desk in the corner. Sarah sat on the floor, surrounded by her father's pots and pans. Daniel stood on the threshold, staring at her, his brow furrowed, and for a moment I worried he thought I'd stolen them from his kitchen.

"I went over to the Moss house," I said, hoping my voice sounded calm and not defensive. "The pots belong to Charlie."

Daniel nodded. "Of course," he said, as if nothing could make more sense than a pile of good copper cookware in an upstairs bedroom. "Would you like a box for them? You can store them in the garage if you like. Or in the hall closet, I don't think there's much of anything in there."

He turned to walk down the hall and I followed him. The wide closet was almost as big as my study at the Moss house had been.

There were rolls and rolls of toilet paper and paper towels, and a carton filled with cleaning supplies, along with miles of empty floorboards.

"See?" Daniel said. "Plenty of space in here. Unless . . . you'd rather keep them in your room?"

He seemed not only poised and ready but forgiving in advance for any grief inspired lunacy. Perhaps he pictured me sleeping with the pots, the smallest sauce pan clutched to my chest like a teddy bear.

"No," I told him. "The closet would be fine." And then I added, more to myself than Daniel, "I need to get his clothes, too. At some point."

We walked outside to the garage, where he thought there was a collection of boxes. Sarah toddled after us. Daniel leaned over to pull up the door with a graceful and effortless arc of his back. As soon as the door disappeared overhead, Sarah darted underneath it. A small red wheelbarrow sat toward the front, filled with plastic beach toys, but Sarah bypassed it in favor of a yellow flyswatter, which she picked up and began swishing at the air.

"Do you want me to take that from her?" Daniel asked as I stepped around a lawn mower.

I waved my hand, dismissing the germs from decades of smashed flies. "She's fine," I said. "It's keeping her busy."

He nodded in the way of nonparents, disapproving but ceding to my greater involvement. Sarah waved the flyswatter, laughing at its plastic springiness as if it were a miracle of modern invention.

"Here," Daniel said, bending over a stack of boxes in a corner. "I think some of these might be empty."

I walked over to the wheelbarrow and tested its weight. Maybe if Sarah saw me carrying it, she could be tempted out of the garage. It felt light enough to carry, so I balanced it carefully—hoisting it over the lawn mower and rakes and lobster pots—and deposited it on the driveway. Sarah bopped over, still clutching the flyswatter but willing to investigate the new loot. As she sifted through the toys, one-handed, I heard a car turn in from the road. It was Ladd, driving the old dented blue truck.

"Crab," Sarah said, holding up a plastic mold.

"Ladd," Daniel called, from the back of the garage. "Dinner's at seven."

"Thanks," Ladd said. He slammed the car door shut and ran a hand through his hair, looking at me and then at Sarah. She picked up the crab and held it up in the air, showing it to Ladd—the newcomer—and toddled toward him.

"Crab," she said, proud of the word, announcing the correctness of it. Ladd stood, frozen, as if it were Godzilla coming toward him instead of a toddler. He looked pained. He looked guilty.

Sarah's little head bopped on toward Ladd—her head that still smelled like a baby's, with her father's curls. In my mind an image formed, those same curls stained and matted by blood.

I could kill him. Had Ladd said that when I told him about Deirdre? Or had I? An amalgam of memories burst at the same time, like a water balloon or something squeezed too tight.

"Sarah," I called. I pitched forward with quick steps and scooped her up, then stepped back, away from Ladd. Finally he had to look at me, a startled glance. *Are you crazy.*

Sarah dropped the crab and closed one hand into my hair. The flyswatter bobbed, grazing my nose, but I didn't move to push it away. I gave up on speaking and headed toward the house. It took a great amount of effort to walk quickly, Sarah bouncing awkwardly on my hip rather than breaking into a flat-out run. Lightfoot wasn't running behind me. She must already have gone into the house when I wasn't looking.

"Brett," Daniel called. I didn't turn back to see him but could tell from the sound of his voice he'd returned to the open air. "Are you all right?"

My voice wouldn't answer. I lifted one hand as I walked, hoping it looked nonchalant, fine, *Yes, I am all right.* But I had one target, the front door.

Time did a funny sort of leap. It's not exactly that I couldn't remember reaching the house and going up the stairs. Just that it happened in very thick fog, my vision dull and murky, as if I swam to the house, and through it, rather than walking. Sarah and I hit the bed the same moment the bedroom door slammed shut. My breath returned only at that moment, sucking through my lungs in great, insistent relief, like an asthmatic reunited with her inhaler.

WHEN EMILY DICKINSON WAS a girl—when she first fell in love with Sue—she lived out in the world with the rest of Amherst. She went to parties, she worked in her garden. She loved to take long walks in the hills above town—so much so that her father bought her a Newfoundland for protection. "My shaggy ally," she called him. His name was Carlo, after a dog in *Jane Eyre*, her favorite novel.

After Carlo died in 1866, Dickinson's real reclusiveness began. "I do not cross my father's ground to go to any house or town," she wrote. She still gardened but only at night. During the day, she would interact with her family, and sometimes with Sue, but to other visitors, even close friends, she would pass letters from the other side of her bedroom door.

How much safer, and easier, to hide like that. I found myself practicing this position when Daniel came upstairs to check on me, behind the partially open door, sitting at the little desk he'd set up for me in the corner of the room. What I had meant to do was pick up Richard Sewall's biography and scan the index for Carlo. But I only got as far as resting my hand on the thick paperback before I heard a tentative knock.

"Yes," I said. "I'm in here." As Daniel pushed the door open, Lightfoot darted in and jumped up on the bed with Sarah. I had finally taken the flyswatter away from her, trading it for a plastic ring of keys. She lay on the bed, holding them over her head in a prenap stupor, examining their contours and colors one at a time. The dog settled in beside her.

"Brett?" Daniel said, his careful formality just slightly amplified. The door stood between us. I could just see his outline through the crack by the doorframe.

"Hi," I said. And then, even though he hadn't asked how I was, I said, "I'm all right." I turned halfway in my seat and could see Sarah's eyes starting to droop, preceding her hands, which still sat resolutely in the air above her.

"Good," he said. "I left a couple boxes for you out here in the hall."

"Okay," I said. "Thank you."

He paused a moment, held back by a gentleman's force field

that didn't allow him to cross the threshold of my room. Then he slowly closed the door. Sarah's arms flopped to the bed, as if commanded by a hypnotist. I stood up and opened the Richard Sewall book to the index, running my finger down the page for mention of Carlo. When I tried to flip the book back to the correct page, instead it opened itself, to somewhere in the middle. A piece of yellow lined paper fluttered to the floor. It had been folded carefully in half, but the flight to the ground turned it open, facing me, lying across my feet so that I could only make out the salutation, in Eli's slanted handwriting.

13

*D*ear Charlie.

That's not how Eli's letter began. Eli's letter was for me. I should have taken it directly downstairs. I could hear Daniel and Ladd through the floorboards, talking quietly, probably discussing my behavior. Discussing the problem of me in general, how I had ended up here, and where I would eventually go. Right away, I should have left my sleeping child, carried the letter down to these two men, and handed it over. One of them would have called the police. The detective work would unfold from there. When had he left it? When had he placed it in the book? Where was he now? *Where was he now?*

Before I had a chance to think any of that, Eli's letter fluttered from the pages of my book. I bent to the ground, picked it up, read it. The paper felt damply wrinkled, as if an entire season's worth of seaboard air had seeped into its fibers. I listened to the sound of Sarah's breathing, the little dog curled up beside her.

I did take the letter downstairs eventually. I hadn't gone completely insane, only enough to sit down at the desk and start to write a letter of my own. *Dear Charlie*, I wrote. Then I brought the pen to my lips. It was a good pen, a uni-ball, the kind I used—back when I worked—to underline passages in books (I'd never liked highlighters) and to make notes on pages of my dissertation.

Dear Charlie.

Apparently Daniel liked uni-balls, too. He had outfitted my desk with four. I held the pen to my lip and thought of all the things I wanted to say. For instance, how to describe the weirdness of where I was, in the home of Ladd's uncle, with Charlie's copper pots waiting to be piled into a box and stored in an upstairs closet. Things. The people they belong to, and whether they survive. Where they end up. At the Moss house, I had grabbed the most obvious possessions of Charlie's, but what else remained there? Whisks and slotted spoons. His ancient paperback of *Riddley Walker*, dampened and wrinkled by the same air as Eli's letter. Photographs. Tennis trophies. I thought, if I can write this letter, I can ask him what else he wants me to retrieve, what he wants Sarah to have. I pressed the pen to the page, but the words I scribbled—as if my hand were guided by some Ouija spirit—had nothing to do with my intentions.

Dear Charlie. It's okay. Eli can stay as long as he likes. Just please don't wait for him. Come over to Maxine's right away. Right now. Spend the night with Sarah and me. We miss you so much.

I imagined opening my bedroom door the barest crack. Passing the letter to the other side. Where Charlie would be standing, not pressing the door open, but respecting my wishes to stay hidden. He might carry the letter halfway down the hall before unfolding it. At the top of the steps he could read, nodding quietly. Heeding my words for once in his life, strolling back into the past, and returning to us all.

I MUST HAVE BEEN very quiet, coming down the stairs. Ladd used to complain about it, my lack of audible footfall. He didn't like being sneaked up on. *I wasn't sneaking*, I'd say. *Just walking.*

Daniel and Ladd sat in the living room, Ladd on the couch—his back to the doorway—and Daniel on the wide leather chair, leaning forward, a tumbler of scotch in his hand. Already cocktail hour. I waited for the same alarm to overtake me, but it didn't, the continued and unreasonable swings of my reactions. The two of them were talking intently, quietly, the lights dim. I felt like a little girl in a nightgown, padding downstairs after bedtime.

Then Daniel noticed me. He put his tumbler on the coffee table and stood up. I walked forward, out of the doorway and into the heart of the room. The letter sat steady in my hands, and both men looked down at it. I guess I could have just explained, to both of them, but my feeling in that moment was that I had to hand it to one. I had to choose. Both faces stared, concerned in the proprietary way of a certain kind of man—the kind who considers himself in charge. And I don't recall making a conscious choice. I just gave the letter to Daniel. As he started to read, I realized he'd first expected that I had written the letter. The two of them both thinking I had reached a point where I would go upstairs, write a letter, and then come down to give it to them.

The reality did not provide any relief. I watched Daniel's face as he began to understand what the letter was, what it said, who had written it.

Dear Brett.

I hesitate calling you dear because you should know that I can see you wherever you are. A hundred years ago you would have been chattel. Before 1967 you would have been a prostitute. Charlie's slave and he never even knew. You were my discovery and I saw exactly what happened. Society isn't crumbled yet, we still have rules. You and I need to talk.

I love you. Eli

Daniel looked up at me, a tense sort of preaction expression tightening his features. "Where did you find this?" he said.

Ladd stood and took it from Daniel's hands. I didn't want to look at him as he read what Eli had written, so I kept my eyes on Daniel as I explained about the book. I could see, peripherally, that Ladd had finished. He dropped his hands to his sides, his grip crumpling the edges of the letter. I suppressed the urge to snatch it back from him. Despite its salutation, the letter didn't belong to me anymore. Unlike the postcard Ladd had written to me, this letter now belonged to the State of Massachusetts. Evidence.

NONE OF THE LETTERS Emily Dickinson received survived, not a single one. Her sister burned them shortly after her death. It was a common enough practice, in those days, burning the correspondence of the deceased. So it is our good fortune to have so many of the letters Dickinson wrote. The day Charlie died I was reading from a book of those letters, half a correspondence: *Open Me Carefully*, the ones she wrote to Sue.

Two weeks ago, the Richard Sewall book where Eli hid my letter would not have been at the top of my stack when he walked into my study. I was working almost exclusively with the letters. The biography would have been on the shelf beside the table. I remembered what happened very clearly. Sarah took a step, I pushed the book aside. I didn't deposit it on top of a pile of other books. I recalled the motion exactly—closing the book and then sliding it across the table before standing and walking over to embrace my family, the clock ticking. Late morning. Charlie with less than twelve hours to live.

How and when had Eli delivered the letter? Had he arrived at the house and gone upstairs while Charlie puttered in the kitchen? Had he sat down and written to me, with my own pen, then pulled out the fat biography and tucked it into its pages? Unlikely that he could have written it any time in the hours after Charlie died. Eli had been covered in blood. There was no residue of blood on the letter, or anywhere upstairs.

My fingerprints, Daniel's, Ladd's. All sullying the letter now. The detective dropped it into a zip-top plastic bag, frowning.

"Maybe he came back," Ladd said. "Maybe he's somewhere close."

I imagined Eli living in the scrub oak woods, perhaps in the dunes by Crowes Pasture, or somewhere beneath the bluff, in a cave, like the bank swallows. Or maybe he was camping out in one of the hundreds of homes, abandoned till next summer. How many empty houses, September on Cape Cod? Even if they could search all of them, Eli would only need to move from one to the other, making his way from Saturday Cove to Provincetown and all the way back to Sandwich. He could live all winter that way.

As the detective left, I stayed in my chair, imagining Eli walking up the rickety beach stairs to his house, walking across the lawn, unseen. Making his way upstairs, he might have let his hand rest on the railing. Then in my study—his old childhood room, summers, though according to Charlie he'd rarely used it, the two brothers instead staying together—he would have sat down at the desk, flipped through my yellow notepad for an unused sheet, taken the pen that had rolled from my fingers, and written to me. There was no question that Eli had written the letter in the house. The page was from my yellow pad—faint indents were visible, of notes I'd jotted on the page above it. He used one of my pens. Reaching for the Sewall book, the fattest choice, inserting the letter, and then sliding it back onto the shelf.

THE NEXT DAY SARAH continued her search for photographs. I followed her groggily from room to room as she opened and discovered the little leather frames. "Lady," she would say, while searching and upon discovery. She would slide a drawer open, reach her hand in to fish inside it. If there was not a photograph she would say in a distinct tone that sounded almost British: "No lady." When she did find one, she would hold it above her head and declare "Lady!" before dropping it back into the drawer.

In the midst of her scavenger hunt, someone knocked gently, just loud enough for me to hear, on the front door. Since my arrival, it no longer stood open as it had for years. When Daniel had left an hour before on some unnamed errand, he had shut and locked it behind him, as propriety would dictate, when a killer was on the loose. Still, I didn't peer through the glass at the side of the door, but just swung it open, while Sarah and Lightfoot stood a foot or two back.

It was Rebecca, Ladd's mother, looking pale, her eyes full of water and sympathy. She wore a bathing suit and cover-up, and a wide-brimmed straw hat.

"Brett," she said. "Darling. I'm here to take the baby."

"Excuse me?"

"Didn't Ladd say? Take the baby, your little girl. To our house for a swim. So you can rest."

I stepped back from the door so she could enter. As soon as she was in the hall, she put her arms around me.

"Poor Brett," she said. "You poor thing."

She smelled of sunscreen and expensive shampoo. I had seen Rebecca many times since Ladd and I broke up, and she'd always been understandably cool toward me. It took this, my husband's murder, to remember her old fondness. I found myself patting her back until she released me and turned her attention to Sarah, who had inched closer, and was now reaching up toward the hat that had been knocked slightly askew during our embrace. Rebecca immediately handed it to her, then knelt down, her long and elegant limbs folding themselves up with ease. She squinted at Sarah, examining her very closely.

"She looks like her grandmother," Rebecca said. "Let me take her so you can get some rest."

She didn't have a car seat so I gave her the keys to my station wagon, then walked back through the empty house. Mrs. Duffy was back at her cottage resting, so I was alone there for the first time. And I found myself doing what Sarah had, opening drawers, looking for pictures of Sylvia. Each one was different, a new image of her strong-boned face, brilliant in addition to beautiful. I had applied to Harvard as both an undergrad and graduate student and been rejected both times. It seemed odd to feel jealous of a woman who cut such a tragic figure.

If I had died instead of Charlie, how would people be taking care of him? Probably they would be bringing him casseroles, la-sagnas wrapped in aluminum foil for the freezer, never mind that the main thing he knew how to do was cook. Charlie, it struck me, would have stayed in his father's house. He would not have pictures of me tucked away in drawers forty years in the future. I opened an envelope, a close-up of Sylvia with her hair brushed off her forehead. Not smiling, she looked almost stern. *Why are you thinking of what Charlie would do? What about what you will do? Charlie is the one who died.*

Charlie was the one who died. He was gone. And still I found myself thinking that he didn't love me enough, not as much as I loved him—instead of thinking about the pictures I had. Would they be scattered in drawers throughout my home decades from now? I thought of the framed wedding picture back at the Moss house, which I had walked right past, even while gathering the things that were most important to me.

Sometimes in the morning I would wake, and emotion would grip me before the details descended. In my fog, I would feel an-guish and loss for a split second before recalling the reason. The same thing had happened in the weeks following my discovery of Deirdre.

I wondered where Daniel kept his wedding photos and imagined what that day would have been like: here at the beach house, Sylvia looking like a photo out of *Town & Country*, Daniel looking wholly adoring. Somewhere, there must have been a picture. I strode past the many drawers where Sarah had already made her discoveries and went into his study, opening the door very carefully, even though I knew he wasn't home. I found three different pictures of Sylvia in his desk, but none of them were wedding photos.

I headed down the hall, the part of the house I'd never visited. His bedroom smelled of expensive soap, and old wood, and the musty scent that clung to all Cape houses, especially the ones by the water. On the floor lay a worn blue rug with swirly white flowers. I imagined Sylvia picking out the furniture—good oak dresser and nightstands, a blue bureau that looked so heavy you might have to chop it into firewood before ever trying to move it again. My eyes searched all the surfaces as I walked into the bathroom. I should have known there wouldn't be a picture in plain view. Hadn't he told me that he didn't like her face to take him by surprise? He needed to prepare himself before seeing her again. He needed to take a deep breath, decide which image of her he most wanted to see, and deliberately go to the place he'd stashed it.

I went back to the bedroom and started opening drawers. Both bureaus—I slid open drawer after drawer, each one relinquishing itself without so much as a squeak or whoosh, each one containing neatly stacked and folded clothing. Between the two windows that looked out onto the ocean sat a beautiful antique secretary. It had the good manners to protest with age as I opened the front, but everything was as neatly arranged as the drawers had been. Letter openers and rolls of stamps. Envelopes and stationery plus a small pile of yellow legal pads. I closed the front and knelt, opening the drawers to the desk, finding nothing but files and papers.

Who knows how long Daniel stood in the doorway, watching me root through his things? He hadn't made a sound entering the house or coming down the hall. And he didn't make a sound now, not even when I finally closed the last drawer and got to my feet. It was me who made noise, when I saw him, an intake of breath so sharp it sounded like a little shriek.

Daniel wore khakis and a polo shirt. Maybe he had gone for a haircut, it looked particularly neat and boyish. His face, watching me gravely, looked impassive enough that the only thing I could do was tell him the truth.

"I'm sorry," I said, feeling my face turn bright red. "I was looking for a wedding picture."

He stood silent a moment, then walked over to the heavy blue dresser. The drawer he chose was cracked just the tiniest bit open from my earlier invasion. It bulged with polo shirts, different colors. Daniel reached under the clothes and pulled out an eight-by-ten-inch silver frame. Then he stood, holding it to his chest. I walked over to the bed and perched on the edge. He sat next to me and lowered the photo into my hands.

"Thank you," I said.

"You're welcome."

"This is the first picture I've seen of you two together."

"Well. She was the main attraction." Daniel reached across my lap. He let his fingers graze Sylvia's face, which smiled underneath an antique veil. On my wedding day, I hadn't worn a veil, just a white sheath dress, my hair down. Casual compared to these two—despite their youth, with a formality that belonged to another age, a hundred years ago instead of forty. Daniel's hair was fairer than I would have thought, less like Ladd's. In his twenties, he hadn't looked like his nephew but insistently like himself. Handsome, I thought. He drew his hand away from the photo, as if he'd heard the word in my head.

"I'm sorry," I said again. "You've been so kind to me, and this is what I do."

"No," Daniel said. "It's all right. You can't be expected to behave normally. I understand. We've both lost something, you and I."

Outside, a car rumbled up over the driveway. We heard a door slam shut, and I stood. Too early for Rebecca to be coming back with Sarah. It could be Ladd, and he could be coming into the house, and I didn't want him to find me sitting here on the bed with his uncle.

"I know it doesn't seem like it," Daniel said. "And it may take a long while. But it will be better one day. I promise."

"Thank you," I said.

I left the door open as I walked out of the room, feeling his eyes on my back—watching me leave.

SATURDAY COVE WAS NOT brimming with hotels and resorts. There was one bed-and-breakfast, and one small motel—ten or twelve rooms—abutting the post office. The summer population owned homes or rented them. There were two public beaches that required town stickers to park in their sandy lots. From down on Daniel's beach, I could see one of those beaches, deserted since Labor Day. There was only one couple, walking close enough to the shoreline that they held their shoes in their hands; I watched them until they rounded the far bluff, and once again I had the world to myself. A lone woman, easy to spot, perhaps the first thing an eye would fall to when surveying the view.

Lightfoot ran out with the waves, then turned and ran back toward me as they swept back in. Low tide stretched far down the beach, and I walked with her out toward the water. She stopped well short of the tide this time, stopping beside a high, flat rock. At the moment, the rock had a wide berth from the ocean, but once the tide came in it would be submerged. When I placed my hand on top of it, it felt damp, mossy. Periwinkles itched the inside of my palm. I knelt down and filled both fists with sand, then let it drip onto the rocks, like frosting from a pastry bag, forming small, swirling turrets.

Those turrets had multiplied by the time Ladd came down to the beach, holding Sarah's hand. Water had started to approach the rock but hadn't quite arrived yet. I'd been working as intently as I had on anything in a long while, and by now the castle rose impressively, covering the rock, its towers of different heights and styles.

"Mommy," Sarah said, pointing.

"It's a sand castle," Ladd told her. She looked up at him, dubious, not ready to test drive the word.

"Hi baby," I said. "Did you have fun swimming?"

She nodded and let go of Ladd, then walked toward me, stopping short to examine a small tide pool that had formed as the tide came in.

"Hey," Ladd said.

I stopped working and looked over at him. His face looked strained and pale. I waited for Lightfoot to run away, as she had the last two times he'd appeared, but she just kept running along the tide line, prancing through the mild waves.

Ladd said, "I don't know what's going on here."

"I'm building a sand castle."

"Brett," he said, an old and familiar sharpness. "You told me to stay away from you. And then you show up here. Where I happen to live."

I let the too-wet sand dribble through my fist, the globules piling onto themselves in a mutant tower. "Your uncle offered to help me," I said simply. "And I needed help. From someone who isn't you."

"He's pretty goddamn close to me."

I looked over at him, my gaze skimming the top of Sarah's head as she scooped up a handful of periwinkles. Ladd's brows reached toward the bridge of his nose in an expression that might have been anger or anguish. Then he knelt to gather up the drier sand at his feet. In a minute he stood next to me, packing it around the bottom where the sand I'd just placed dripped down, staining the rock.

"It's a good castle," he told me, his voice returning to its newer, dealing-with-a-crazy-person tone. "When all the other castles are washed away, this one will still be standing."

It was a funny thing to say, especially considering there were no other castles on the beach. I took my hands off the rock and watched Ladd work. Whereas my sneakers were getting soaked, he had the prescience to go barefoot with his cuffs rolled up. I took off my sneakers and threw them up onto the sand past the tide line. Then I rolled up my jeans and set to constructing a new tower.

We worked for what felt like a long time, Sarah playing in the sand above the tide line, until the water surrounded us, lapping at our cuffed jeans, deep enough for Lightfoot to swim around us in little circles. We sloshed back toward shore and sat, not saying anything to each other but occasionally speaking to Sarah, now the only one of us at work, still digging through the tide pools. By now the water swarmed all around the castle—just like Eli had said, it looked like medieval ruins. The day, in its early-autumn morph toward evening, had turned overcast, that otherworldly flat light. I wished I had a sweater. The water was black beyond the jetty and green closer to shore. Sarah chattered away while she dug, her diaper getting soaked by the salt water, while low gray clouds formed on the faintly pink horizon. The fantastic castle floated amid it all.

"I should go get a camera," Ladd said.

It would have been lovely to photograph. At the same time, I didn't think a camera could capture the precise magic. And I didn't want to be left alone. I couldn't decide—I didn't seem to know—who or what to be afraid of.

"Don't," I said. And then, startled by the urgency in my voice, added, "Let's just save it for this one moment."

Ladd nodded, his gaze fixed on the rising castle. A part of me hoped that Eli *was* close, even watching, appreciating—with the pieces of his old mind—this tribute. The thing of beauty that he would recognize, just like the ones he used to make, out on the rocks. If he ever remembered a time, those summers, when his mind belonged to himself, no other voice but his own.

14

That evening Ladd, Daniel, and I stood on the back deck staring out at the water where the sand castle still rose. Sarah dropped a tennis ball for Lightfoot, who chased it for several bounces, then caught it and brought it back to her. She shrieked with astounded hilarity—the discovery of fetch. From inside the house, Mrs. Duffy called to us. I picked up Sarah and followed the two men inside. On top of the sideboard sat a white bakery box. When I peered through the plastic, I saw the swirling yellow script, *Happy Birthday Brett!* Sarah pressed her hand on top of the plastic, smudging the letters. I put her on the floor.

"Did you forget?" Ladd said. His voice sounded so gentle. It made me want to turn and shove him against the table. "Of course you would forget," he said in that same careful voice. "With everything that's going on."

Of course I would forget, with no wish for time to move any direction but backward. I lifted up my hands to cover my face. My shoulders shook but still no tears. I could sense both men, standing back, not sure if embracing me would be wrong in some way. Sarah's hand closed around the hem of my skirt, just above my knee. The room felt weighted heavily with the two of them, not willing to hug me, so I picked up Sarah and wrapped my arms around her. She hugged me back, tightly, and I realized that between swimming and playing on the sand she hadn't napped. I could put her to bed early. I could escape.

Mrs. Duffy marched out of the kitchen and put her arms around both me and Sarah.

"There, there," she said. "It's too much, it's all too much. It's more than a person can be expected to bear."

"Thank you," I said, not looking at any of them, Mrs. Duffy's arm still protective across my shoulders. The cake sat there, its writing smeared, its festiveness awful. "But I'm just so tired. I think I'll go upstairs."

"Brett," Ladd called after me. His voice sounded impatient, maybe even angry. I didn't turn around, just kept climbing the steps, and he called out again.

"Leave her alone," Daniel said. By now I was in the upstairs hall, but his voice was sharp enough that I could hear it. "You can't know what she's going through."

I closed the door behind me, wishing it had a lock. Ladd was going through something, too. I'd seen it on his face, beyond what had happened, beyond concern for me. Regret, washing over his every movement. But I couldn't worry about that, only about what had happened, and who remained out there, in the world, waiting to be caught.

CHARLIE WOULDN'T HAVE BEEN working on the back deck anymore when Eli arrived. Probably he was in the kitchen, stirring. He had this ability to stand over the stove, endlessly tending, steam rising up around him. It might have been where he felt happiest. What did he think about, staring into the pot? Lost in dreams of spices and temperature? Or was the concentration less complete than it sometimes seemed? Was there room, perhaps, for thoughts of me?

Eli will be here any minute. Maybe when Eli showed up, Charlie was upstairs, composing his email. Maybe he meant to write more but heard Eli's tires in the driveway and hastily typed *Love, Charlie.* Then walked downstairs to tell Eli he had to leave in the morning.

Once at a dinner party I heard Charlie trying to explain unmedicated Eli to a friend. "It's not that the logic doesn't add up," Charlie said. "It's that logic doesn't exist at all. Two plus two doesn't equal five. Two plus two equals motorcycle."

If I pictured anybody else killing Charlie, the thought seemed crazy. But I was familiar enough with crazy to go ahead and think it anyway.

THE DAY AFTER MY birthday, I let myself into the Moss house. A home that's been uninhabited for days and then weeks: the silence piles up on itself from one hour to the next.

"Eli?" I called, and then stopped to listen for footsteps, or a returning voice. I stepped as quietly as I could through the rooms, peering under every bed, looking in every closet.

Downstairs in the living room, photo albums jammed the bottom shelf of the bookcase. I pulled out the fattest one and leafed through it, the plastic covers on each page curling, the sticky backings striped an ancient umber. When Charlie's mother was dying, he and I had sat together on this very couch, him pointing out his favorites, like the one of two wiry blond boys, one with curls, both with round blue eyes and smiles that twitched the right side of their mouths, before expanding, brightening their entire faces. After that night on the roof, I never saw Eli smile like this again. But Charlie—thousands of times, maybe even millions.

He would have had a hard time smiling at Eli, in the condition he must have been in. At some point, the two of them would have stood out on the deck together. Just up the street from the Moss house, directly across the bluff, a man who'd made a fortune with some sort of computer-related invention had built a house so large that it looked like a Carnival Cruise ship riding the night sky. He wouldn't have been here in September, but the floodlight he'd installed to light his American flag shone year round, damaging the view of the stars. Charlie might have complained about this, pointing out to Eli the new difficulty locating the Milky Way. Or he might have gotten to business directly. "Eli," he might have said. "We said you couldn't stay here unless you were taking your meds. It's obvious you're not, so you need to leave in the morning." Just then Eli, his rage stoked, might have seen the long-handled hammer, left on the plank of the ladder. Charlie never put anything away.

I turned the page of the photo album. There was a photograph of the two boys sharing some kind of drink, a soda or a milkshake, their heads pressed together—Charlie already a lanky child, Eli still with the chubby limbs of a toddler. Here was the era of Sylvia, pictures of her smiling, usually with Eli in her arms. In later pages, the brothers posed with trophies, tennis for Eli, sailing for Charlie. Charlie was taller than Eli, and stronger. That day on the lawn Eli's skin had looked pasty and white, his muscles slack from disuse, whereas Charlie's skin was brown from the sun, and fine sinewed muscles pulled taut along his arms. If Eli had come straight at him, Charlie would have stopped the hammer.

Perhaps Charlie took a moment to lean against the railing and complain about the change in the sky. Maybe he lit a cigarette, something he did occasionally to keep Eli company. He might have said something about me, the reason I wasn't there. "Brett could tell from the last time you called that you weren't taking your meds."

What might Eli have said at the mention of my name? That a hundred years ago I would have been a prostitute? In frustration and sadness, Charlie might have dropped his head into his hands. Or just narrowed his eyes and looked down to snuff out the cigarette in the seashell ashtray. Enough time for Eli to grab the hammer and bring it down with lunatic force; not enough time for Charlie to stand up straight, turn around, and exert his superior strength.

One blow to stun Charlie sideways, lurching and surprised. Another blow to bring him to the ground as he tried to stagger upright. With the second blow, the blood began, and then a third that sprayed country fair splatter on Eli's white shirt. There was a picture in one of the photo albums of Eli making one of those spray paintings, squirting paint from a plastic ketchup bottle into the whirling vortex, his head bent, serious and intent.

The coroner said it was the fourth blow that killed Charlie; by then, he would have been on the ground, unconscious. For this killing blow, the perpetrator turned the hammer around and used the claw. There must have been some sign from Charlie—a final gurgle or cessation—to signal that the attack could stop. And then the killer returned with the knife.

I turned a stiff, glue-stained page, and a picture of a child-hood dog, a slender-nosed collie, reminded me that I'd forgotten to insert Lightfoot into my imaginings. Where had she been? In the open doorway, watching Eli do it? Or maybe on the lawn, in Eli's arms as he watched someone else. She would have struggled against his grip, broken free, run to the spot beneath the front porch where I'd found her. At the base of my skull, the headache started to form, not far from the location where Charlie had received his first blow. Enough. I started to slide the album back into its place, then changed my mind. One day Sarah would want to have it.

Walking down the beach with the photo album tucked under my arm, I looked out at the water. To my left, the Huber's beach steps, in great disrepair, whole slats missing, some clearly rotten in the middle. Charlie used to sneak up and slide their kayak from underneath the deck, sometimes hauling it over to our house for months at a time, always returning it before Memorial Day and the family's annual return. No doubt the Hubers wondered about the new pings and scratches. Or maybe they didn't—judging from the steps, they didn't pay too much attention to light maintenance. Or heavy maintenance, for that matter. I imagined Charlie walking up the stairs, his foot slicing through any one of the sagging, rotting boards. And then I noticed a step toward the top, sliced clean through, its innards only a pale brown—whereas the other splintered boards were black with months or years of exposure. I put the photo album down on the bottom step and headed up, walking very carefully, placing my feet on the edges so they wouldn't break through. Kneeling by the broken step, I pressed my fingers against damp and splintered wood. Then I stood and headed up to the house.

The Huber place was much like the Mosses', gray-shingled and modest, standing low to the ground. Wide windows facing the water for lovely views. It also had the look of a house shut up for winter, all the outside furniture gone, curtains drawn, the driveway empty of vehicles. Days upon days of quiet gathered, settling in around me. I walked over to the deck and peered beneath it. In the wide, dusky space, I saw a few scattered beach toys, a disrupted pile of life jackets, and a rusty old hose attachment. But no paddles and no kayak, only a white smooth space where once it had rested, now slid away from its winter resting place.

By the time I got back to Daniel's house, Sarah was wailing and protesting my long absence. I could hear her from down on the beach. When I got up to the lawn, it wasn't Mrs. Duffy but Daniel holding her in his arms, walking her back and forth while jiggling her in an inexpert attempt at calming. Sarah cried with deep, shuddery sobs, stating the problem over and over: "Mommy, Mommy, Mommy."

"I'm right here, baby," I said, throwing the photo album onto the grass and holding out my arms.

Daniel couldn't hand her over fast enough; he looked almost as despondent as she did. "I think she's tired," he said as she wrapped her arms tightly around my neck, her sobs growing louder instead of subsiding. Her diaper was heavy; Daniel wouldn't know to change her.

I yelled over the noise. "I don't think Eli did it."

Daniel's hand was raised, about to smooth his disheveled hair back into place. Instead he stopped and just placed his hand on top of his head, a perplexed *what do I do next* expression crossing his face.

"Something you don't know," I yelled over Sarah's crying. My voice was so loud that she stopped, abruptly, leaning back in my arms to examine my face. She wouldn't understand anything I'd say next. Still, I tried my best to say it in code. "Ladd and I. The day Charlie left. We were together. Here, in his cottage."

What I had meant to tell Daniel was about the kayak, how it was missing, how someone had been up there very recently. How Eli would have ignored the pile of life jackets and pulled the kayak out to the water. It had been a clear day, better than any you'd see during the official summer, warm enough for short sleeves, the sun determined but muted by the barest amount of cloud cover and an even slighter autumn breeze. Hardly anyone walking on the beach to notice the man, paddling too far from shore, heading toward Provincetown, the curled tip of the flexing arm that made up this spit of land.

I meant to tell Daniel: How frightened Eli would have been after seeing Charlie killed. How a knowledge of himself as suspect—

or simply the old resistance to hospitalization and the electric mis-calculations in his brain—could have caused him to flee, paddling through the day and into the night, and stopping short of Prov-incetown, maybe in Wellfleet. I imagined him heading to the trails he used to love to bike. Not much of a place for hiding. Maybe he hiked out to Lieutenant Island at low tide, letting himself into someone's summer home. Row after row of seasonal houses would offer changes of clothes, and beds, even food. He could hunker down, living on canned goods and bottled water, house to house, until one day he decided a walk was in order before it got too cold. Or else until he forgot the reason he'd run away in the first place, and paddled back, to find me.

"I know," Daniel said.

Sarah dropped her head onto my shoulder. I swayed from my hips, moving her back and forth, feeling her dreamy gaze out to-ward sea, and knowing her eyelids were closing. I wasn't sure how much I'd said aloud, how much I'd only thought.

"Ladd told me," Daniel said. "I saw you that day, driving away. And I asked him about your visit. He was very upset, even before what happened to Charlie. He told me."

My eyes stung. I nodded, wondering if Ladd had told him about Deirdre. And then I said, "I feel like I should tell the police."

"I already did," Daniel said. "And so did Ladd."

"Ladd told them?"

"Yes, right away. That day . . ." He trailed off, looking at Sarah. Not wanting to say *The day Charlie died*. "They came to the house to interview him, and he told them everything."

"But then, why didn't they ask me about it?"

"Because," Daniel said. He stepped in closer and reached out his hand. For a moment, I thought he was going to touch me, but instead he stroked the top of Sarah's head, her breathing slowed to sleep. "Because you're grieving. And you're not a suspect. Neither is Ladd."

I could hear Daniel's voice, powerful man, in third person instead of second, instructing the police not to bother me with this detail, all the details, of Ladd and me. *She's grieving.* What would he have said to keep them away from Ladd?

Daniel's face looked so calm and sympathetic. Forgiving me. But I didn't want to be forgiven. I wanted to know what happened to Charlie. If I told Daniel about the kayak, he would walk into the house and phone the police. One more piece of information, one more thing they knew to look for.

"Look," Daniel said. "All the evidence, including your own eyewitness. It's very clear. Who did this."

"It's not clear," I said. "It's not clear to me." I thought about mentioning the other possibility, something Deirdre-related, but the thought of Daniel's knowing about that, Charlie's betrayal, was too awful.

He stood there, quietly, staring at me, feeling too badly for me to contradict what was obvious to him, what was obvious to everyone. Except me.

"So what happens," I said, not wanting to argue any further, "when they catch him?"

"I imagine a trial. And then a hospital."

A hospital. And what sort of hospital would it be? Even before this—before being accused of a crime—the wide and rolling lawns that Daniel had paid for were far behind Eli. People grow weary of mental illness. The way it rises, again and again. The way it never gets cured, never goes away. I had grown weary of it the day I left Charlie alone at the house. I couldn't handle the reappearances of Eli, in all his various states, the way we'd martial ourselves to get him hospitalized, to get him well, get him working, only to land in precisely the same spot, over and over again. Eli's hospitals had already gone from private to state. And now they would end with the only permanent one possible: for the criminally insane. If he landed there, would it feel any different to him, from all the other incarcerations, against his will? *The unspeakable horror*, he once wrote to Charlie, about mental hospitals.

Unless Eli managed to paddle away, to somewhere else. I nodded to Daniel as if I believed him and headed into the house, his hand sliding off Sarah's head, so that finally he could reach up and smooth his hair back into place.

I PUSHED THE DOOR to our room open with my hip, the sleeping child draped heavily over my shoulder, to find Ladd there, sitting on my bed, his legs resting sideways to keep his shoes off the covers. This the only indication of politeness—he looked agitated, angry.

"What was that?" he said. "What the hell was that?"

"Shh," I hissed, waving my hand toward Sarah, though she was out cold.

Ladd swung around, placing his feet on the floor, and I laid Sarah on the bed. "Get me a diaper," I said to Ladd, jutting my chin toward the bag in the corner.

He stood up obediently while I unsnapped Sarah's onesie and peeled off the soaking diaper.

"You shouldn't be in here," I said as he handed me a clean one.

"Eli didn't do it?" Ladd said.

I wondered how he possibly could have heard—through which open window. Had he already been waiting in my room? Or maybe he'd been standing on the deck or skulking in the bushes, watching me.

"Shhh," I said again. I lifted Sarah and placed her up toward the head of the bed and then built my little barrier of pillows around her.

"That doesn't seem safe," Ladd said, his voice shifting to normal. "Shouldn't you put her in the crib?"

"What the hell business is it of yours?" I all but shouted at him. We both paused, startled, then looked at Sarah. She didn't stir, her cheeks crimson, her little chest rising and falling.

"Maybe it's not," Ladd said in a fierce whisper. "But that other business. You can say it's not mine all you want, but that doesn't make it so."

"You can say Eli did it all you want. Everyone can say it. But *that* doesn't make it so."

"Who then," Ladd said. "If not Eli, who."

I sat down on the bed, placing one hand on the flushed rise and fall of Sarah. "I don't know."

"No suspect?"

I didn't answer. Ladd should have been able to figure it out, my mental list of possibilities.

"Me?" Ladd said. He pointed to his chest. "Seriously? Have you gone that crazy?"

"No," I said, knowing full well what crazy looked like. "I haven't gone crazy, not at all."

Just at that moment, Daniel appeared in the doorway. I wondered where the dog had gone, probably cowering downstairs under some furniture. Ladd stepped back, away from me, and looked at his uncle.

"Ladd," Daniel said.

Ladd raised his hands in surrender and stalked out of the room. For a long moment, it was just the three of us, Sarah, Daniel, and me, silent in the scar of Ladd's angry departure. It hit me then, the isolation there, the lack of neighboring houses. I felt myself longing for Amherst, the reliable rows of residences, people living side by side—strangers, but there if you needed them. To hear, if you should happen to call out for help.

When I finally went downstairs, Mrs. Duffy handed me a glass of sun-brewed iced tea with a sprig of mint. The glass felt cold and alien in my hand. So strange that all these cheerful substances insisted on continuing, existing, expecting me to enjoy them. I carried it out to the deck. From where I stood, I could see Daniel's car was gone, and I could also see Ladd, out on the beach, sitting in a lawn chair and reading a book. How long had it been since I'd known he was back from Honduras? More than two weeks, and I hadn't yet gotten around to asking him what it had been like or what he planned to do next. Ladd was the same age as Charlie, after all, and hadn't managed to get himself any more situated in a career. I guess I'd never thought about that much, partly because Ladd had enough money of his own to stay afloat, even if he only ever wafted from one adventure to another. Or maybe I'd just never thought about it because I wasn't married to him.

I saw exactly what happened. What had Eli meant? And why could I never stop trying to attach meaning and sense to the things he said when by now I should know better? My mind cataloged the things that Eli could and could not have seen. He couldn't have seen me climbing into Ladd's lap and kissing him. But he could have seen someone lowering the hammer. Did Eli think it was me? Years ago he had tried to warn me. Maybe he thought that now, not heeding his warning, I had reached my breaking point and killed Charlie myself.

Whatever Eli saw, or imagined, or hallucinated. The day Charlie died, he arrived before sunset. The two of them could have walked down to the water. Afterward Charlie might have sent him upstairs to shower, and maybe that's when Eli wrote his letter, slipped it into my book. I closed my eyes. Most likely it was a coincidence that he would accuse me of something on the very day I'd committed a crime. If he had even written it that day. Misfiring synapses for once getting lucky.

Out on the beach, Ladd turned a page, his long pale legs stretched out in front of him—they might be sunburned when he came back up to the house. I thought of his aspirations of being a great good man, and how I managed to get in the way, even all those years after leaving him. Upstairs, he had declared himself a suspect by denying that possibility. And I understood the impulse, both of us guilty.

Ladd closed his book and stood to fold the beach chair. I went back into the house and hurried up the stairs, out of sight.

OVER THE NEXT FEW days, pictures of Sylvia began returning to frames and tabletops. Sarah discovered the first one on a side table in the living room. She picked it up in both hands and frowned, deeply disappointed to find the lady in a place where anyone in the world could see her. After returning the picture very carefully to its spot, she opened the drawer beneath it. The little leather envelope remained, but Sarah closed the drawer, then toddled toward the sliding glass door, Lightfoot click-clacking behind her. Sarah placed her hands against the wide pane, staring out at the deck and scrub oak abutting the bluff—too small to see over the dunes and down to the beach. The dog stood beside her, staring out in the same direction, her tail wagging, not understanding why anyone would leave such a door closed.

A loud voice from Daniel's study made Sarah turn away from the glass door and I took a moment to study my daughter's face. She looked a little like Eli just then, with the little dog at her heels and the expression of surprise squinching her eyes at the corners. When I first knew Eli, he had reveled in the unexpected. He'd been so unafraid and so kindhearted.

Sarah's hand traveled from the glass to rest on the top of Lightfoot's tiny black head. My fingertips lingered on the frame. This house, without insulation, was meant for summer habitation, the walls and floorboards mere partitions. Sound carried so easily. I could hear Daniel talking on the phone in his study.

"It's preposterous," he said now. "We're talking about one man, who can't string a coherent sentence together. How can it be that he's still at large?"

A moment later, Daniel called to me from his study. I walked down the hall. The door was open, and he sat at his desk. "Come in," he said, gesturing at the chair opposite him as if I'd arrived for a business meeting. Sitting down, I noticed another framed picture of Sylvia, perched on the desk.

"I'm going into Boston," Daniel said, "to meet with a private investigator. The police obviously aren't accomplishing anything. This guy will look for Eli full-time. Then you can get on with your life."

I nodded, wondering what that would entail. Returning to Amherst and finishing my dissertation? Applying for teaching jobs? Or staying here, with Daniel? I pictured an eternity within these walls, on this beach, traveling back and forth between the two houses, never venturing beyond appointed ground.

"I'm going to spend the night there," Daniel said, "and take care of some business I've been neglecting. Mrs. Duffy can stay here at the house if you're not comfortable being alone. Or Ladd can."

Was it my imagination, or was this last offer a test, some faint challenge in the moment before he blinked? "No," I said. "We'll be fine." And then, picturing the empty house, just me and Sarah, I amended. "Maybe, if Mrs. Duffy doesn't mind staying, that would be better."

It didn't occur to me until after he'd driven away that I should have thanked him. In these last, long days I'd come to accept everything he did for me as a matter of course.

SARAH AND I WERE downstairs watching *Blue's Clues* when I heard a car pull into the driveway. Sarah sat on my lap, damp blonde curls tickling my chin, her hands resting on mine as she stared intently at the TV. The door banged open awkwardly, and in walked Ladd carrying a large cardboard box. He dropped it in the doorway between the foyer and the living room. The top flaps yawned open, revealing a mound of clothes, and instantly I recognized the collar of a white linen shirt. I put Sarah on the couch beside me, then got up and walked toward the box and knelt beside it, opened the flaps still wider.

"Daniel said you wanted his clothes," Ladd said. "I figured I better go by there and get them before they start clearing the place out."

I didn't think to ask how he got in. The clothes, such basic day-to-day items only a few weeks ago, felt like remnants from a long lost time. They weren't carefully folded or neatly stacked. Instead they lay in a tumble, as if they'd been grabbed from drawers and off of hangers, and thrown in carelessly. The way Charlie himself would have packed them.

Charlie! A scent that had been lost to me these many days rose from the box: of sandalwood and garlic and rosemary and saw-dust. I plunged my arms into the box, cradling the garments, each sleeve and pant leg and button delivering a particular image, a particular day. There were the scrubs they'd given him at the hospital when Sarah was born. His Aran sweater, the one my mother sent him, itchy and damp with lanolin, his face across the table, ladling out Portuguese fish stew. For the first time, I realized that I didn't have his wedding ring, which was also my father's wedding ring.

Sarah slid off the couch and walked over to inspect the box herself. She pulled out an old Herring Run T-shirt worn to silken thinness, with a fine line of holes stretching from one shoulder blade to the other. She examined it for a moment, then pressed it to her cheek like a security blanket. I heard Ladd retreat, closing the door behind him. I kept my face buried in the clothing and didn't picture Ladd walking across the lawn, to the path between the scrub oaks, back to his cottage.

I pictured Charlie. I pictured Charlie. I pictured Charlie.

Once in the fall when I was hugely pregnant with Sarah, Charlie and I walked along the beach from his father's house to the bluff right below Daniel's house. He wore these jeans and that flannel shirt. We found a fox, dead on the rocks, its fur a brilliant and burnished orange, its bared teeth gleaming white and perfect. He wanted to pick it up, float it back out to sea, but I didn't want him to touch it. "Anyway," I said, "it will just end up back here, won't it?" Later we called the Audubon Society, and they said it had probably drowned trying to navigate the rocks at high tide. It had already floated out to sea and then returned. In the morning, Charlie walked back out and dragged it up, beyond the rocks, in the dunes where the tide would not be able to reclaim it. I wondered if its bones lay there still, bleached by the sun, the teeth still gleaming, sharp and curved as if they were carved out of marble.

Sometimes I'd thought of our marriage as happy, and sometimes I'd thought of it as troubled. I'd imagined it continuing and ending in both veins, I had felt exalted and I had felt trapped. And in the midst of those pivotal moments—dramatic or tumultuous or romantic—there had been simple everyday pieces of life, lived out beside one another. These were the pieces I couldn't imagine living without. I couldn't give them up when I found out about Deirdre. I didn't see how I could give them up now.

Neither, it seemed, could Sarah. She hung on to his T-shirt all day, mostly pressing it to her cheek, but sometimes just slinging it over her shoulder, much the way Charlie used to cook with a dish towel over his.

AFTER MRS. DUFFY MADE dinner and then went to sleep in the room down the hall, I lay awake for hours, watching the overhead fan rearrange the darkness into regular, swirling patterns. Earlier, I had remembered old photographs of the Lindbergh kidnapping, the ladder leaned against the side of the house, and closed the window. But enough air had entered during the past few days that it still smelled salty and fresh. In the moving shadows, Sarah's face looked perfectly at rest, a faint smile turning her lips upward, her little fist closed around the collar of Charlie's shirt. She looked very much like the ultrasound photo I still had, somewhere, perhaps tucked into one of the Emily Dickinson books or perhaps back at the Moss house. A fierce imperative rose in my chest, the same instinct that led me to close the window, as if I needed to protect her not only from imminent danger but my own compulsive reordering of the past.

Because no matter how I arranged things, it felt like my whole life unfolded in a series of interactions with Eli, all of them creating a string of worry beads in my mind. I could roll each bead one at a time between my thumb and forefinger before moving on to the next. Starting with that first day I ever saw him, trying out for the musical, mirroring each other's movements across the dance studio. Summoning me to the party where I met Charlie, or filling my room with balloons, or rescuing that scraggly kitten. Holding my newborn baby. Pacing the lawn, decorated in Charlie's blood.

Lying there in the dark, listening to the absence of Daniel

beneath me, I felt flooded with a clear and certain knowledge that another bead had been added to the string. Maybe it was Lightfoot, who jumped up, skittered to the window, and placed her paws on the sill. Her little tail started to beat, back and forth, slowly at first and then faster. I sat up and placed a hand on Sarah's heart. Then I took off my nightgown and pulled on a pair of jeans, a bra, a T-shirt—before going to the window and seeing exactly what I knew I would: Eli, making his way down the path between the scrub oaks from Ladd's cottage, heading toward us.

My purse sat right by my elbow on top of the little desk. I could have reached in and grabbed my phone. But instead I left it there. I picked up my flip-flops but didn't put them on, one more thing to risk waking Mrs. Duffy. Even with Lightfoot at my heels, it seemed to me I made almost no noise at all, already a ghost.

I could have gone into the kitchen and used the old-fashioned wall phone. Dialed 911, made the world converge here. How long would it take for the police to arrive and arrest him, or worse? I didn't bother finding out. I just opened the front door, letting the dog burst through and onto the grass. Lightfoot ran down the hill to greet him. I stepped outside, locking the door behind me. The night air stood close and dark, one note of chill amid the dense summer breeze. No, I realized, not summer anymore, but deep enough into September that it had officially become fall. Beach grass swayed beyond the manicured lawn. Eli had bypassed the path to the house and now stood under the eaves of the shed. The sky sat clear and dark above us, the air dry, but Eli's posture suggested huddling away from rain. I could see him, stringy blond hair hanging down his back, his shoulders hunched. Lightfoot ran in joyful circles around his feet, then stopped to jump up on his legs, stretching toward him, asking for a return greeting. But Eli didn't bend to pet her. He looked so helpless, a forlorn shadow leaning against the shed. When could he have last eaten, or slept in a bed? I wished I'd thought to grab some food before leaving the house and felt acutely aware, these past few weeks, how well I'd been tended, first by Maxine and then by Daniel and Mrs. Duffy.

"Brett?" Eli said, into the darkness. His voice sounded hoarse and garbled, unpracticed, and still just exactly like himself.

"Yes," I agreed, loud and clear, no mistaking that he would hear me. "It's me. It's Brett." I left the path to walk across the grass, my arms outstretched before me as if I meant to embrace him. Eli had somehow managed not to trigger the automatic floodlight, but as I walked toward him it detected my movement and washed the lawn with a faint yellow glow.

His face looked wolfish, starving, with a patchy, unsuccessful beard. At the sight of my approaching, he let himself break into a smile. I knew it would just be one moment of the old Eli. But that was enough to let me muster my courage. I dropped one arm but kept the other one in front of me. As I approached he reached out and clasped my hand, and we stood there, facing each other in the eerie slant of light, examining each other's altered faces, the careful and fascinated way you greet a friend you haven't seen in a long time—someone you knew when you were very, very young.

PART FOUR

In this short Life
That only lasts an hour
How much—how little—is
Within our power

—EMILY DICKINSON

15

Three boys grew up on a stretch of beach, summer their most important time of year. Each one looking forward, through the drudgery of school, the slushy forever of northeastern winters, to the lush and persistent light of June, widening above sand and shore. The tide pools with crabs and periwinkles. Sea stars clinging to the rocks under the jetty.

Twice a day an ice-cream truck pulled into the beach parking lot and summoned the children away from plastic shovels and boogie boards. Of the three, Charlie probably missed the truck most often, walking out to the very end of the jetty, jumping from rock to rock, waving to the other two when he reached the end, standing out in the thick of the bay. Ladd would have been more civilized, swimming in races, and sailing, playing tennis. Eli played tennis, too, but what he loved most was mountain biking through the trails behind Daniel Williams's house, balancing in the deep sand, ducking his head under arches of tree branches.

All his life, when Charlie had no place to go, and no plans left, he came to Saturday Cove. When Ladd was finished with his travels, he came back to Saturday Cove. And Eli. The boy who built sand castles out on the rocks at low tide and watched as the ocean swept in around them. The boy who won science grants, and wanted to be a doctor, and laughed with his whole face, and loved to throw parties. That boy had seeped out of his original shell. Where he had gone I couldn't say. I only knew that the connective tissue between those three men and me was Eli, just enough left of him to come back to this place, to Saturday Cove, like a homing device that someone else had left behind.

Together, we walked down to the beach.

THE SAND STRETCHED FAR out toward the ocean, littered with seaweed and beach glass and pebbles. When I'd first known Eli, he'd carried a citrusy scent, somewhere between lemon and grapefruit. Ever since he'd gotten sick, even when he was medicated— even when he'd just showered, and wore clean clothes—he carried with him an odor of anxiety and decay, as if the lemon had begun to rot. When we got to the bottom of the beach steps, and he stopped just beside me, his sour sweat overpowered even the low tide. Away from the bath of Daniel's floodlight, it took a few minutes for my eyes to adjust. Grime caked and pooled in the hollow of Eli's collarbone, his hair was matted. But the clothes he wore, a white T-shirt from the Cape Cod Museum of Natural History, an unbuttoned denim shirt, and khakis, were clean. And they were Charlie's. Eli couldn't have been wearing them since that day three weeks ago. Maybe as early as this morning, he had been at the house. Maybe he had been there, hiding, when Ladd collected the rest of Charlie's clothes. There was no writing on the khakis, but Eli's hand kept moving as if he were scribbling, an imaginary pen clutched in his right hand. I remembered the jeans he'd been wearing the last time I saw him. What would the writing on them reveal to me if I could manage to decipher it?

"Eli," I said. "Where have you been?"

He didn't answer but turned and started walking, toward the public beach, the opposite direction from the Moss house. Darkness settled comfortably around us, but I didn't want to walk too far and let the morning find us exposed, out on the beach, for everyone to see.

"Eli," I called, to his departing back. I wished I'd thought to grab my car keys—though the noise of the engine might wake Mrs. Duffy or, worse, Ladd. A stream of words tumbled out of Eli, buzzing around his head like a cloud of mayflies. I said, "I'm going this way."

I jogged toward the rocky stretch of bluff, which we'd have to pick our way across. Eli lurched around, bone-thin and lumbering, all his natural grace gone. As he walked toward me, I tried to imagine where he'd been, how he'd been eating—if he'd been eating—and how he'd avoided getting picked up by the police.

"When did you get Charlie's clothes?" I said when he reached me. "Where have you been?"

He waved his hand, shooing my questions away. "Are you

ready?" he asked as we stood facing the direction of the rocks, the dark, his childhood home.

I presented my beckoning hand outward, toward the bluff, a ladies-first gesture in reverse. The truth was, I didn't feel afraid. It was Eli. Even now, he only scared me in theory. Even now—in this florid state, incomprehensible, alarming. I was used to him. Which didn't mean I was willing to turn my back.

"After you," I said.

As I TRAVELED IN the dark behind Eli, it was impossible to imagine the sun would ever rise. Words from his stream floated back to me in a paranoid staccato. Lightfoot trotted along cheerfully, overjoyed by the midnight outing and the reunion. Out here on the rocks, under the sky that hung low around us, we were surrounded by the detritus of animals that had met timely or untimely ends. Withering skates, and the abandoned husks of horseshoe crabs. Tiny snails crunching beneath our feet as we stepped, and for a moment the oppressive scent of a seal carcass, battered by the tide and sun, now seeping into the air. Eli didn't seem to register any of it. He kept his shoulders hunched, his voice low and persistent. I had the feeling I could take him by the shoulders and point him in any direction, and he would just maintain this posture, muttering and walking forward like a windup toy.

All I held as fact were the sand and rocks and debris beneath my feet. The sky above my head, and the ocean traveling its way all those thousands of miles east. A million worlds surrounded me, and the only one I cared to know occurred weeks ago, less than a mile in the direction we now headed. *What happened?* Maybe if I listened hard enough, the answers would spill out from Eli. Maybe they already had, in some nonsequential order, and I'd missed them.

By now, we'd crossed over the rocks and alighted on a clear stretch of sand. Eli stopped—not just moving but talking. It startled me, the sudden cessation of that voice. He turned toward the water, staring out toward the tide, and I stopped walking, too.

"Brett?" he called in a long and questioning syllable. As if he couldn't see me through what little darkness stood between us.

"Yes," I said. "I'm right here."

And then the words started spilling out again. Words that peppered and repeated. Important words like *Charlie* and *blood*, and my own name, jumbled together with enough other words that I couldn't begin to put them all together.

"Eli." I walked forward, right next to him, and put my hand on his shoulder. He jerked his head sideways, toward me, and shrugged my hand away.

"Brett," he said, his voice newly sharp and clear.

Just behind him I could see the roof of his house rising above the bluff. I stepped back to give him room. This would happen sometimes. A break in the stream. Moments of conversation, like logic had broken through the flood. It wouldn't last long. Above us, the slightest shift in the dark sky, the fading of stars, a hint toward gathering light. I needed to get him inside before morning.

"Why did you kill Charlie?" Eli asked.

"Me?" I pointed to my chest, feeling a flood of relief. Finally someone was accusing me of the thing I had done. And here we stood, out on the beach alone, nobody in the world even knowing enough to look for us or to worry about me. Sarah lay sleeping, safe upstairs, far down the beach. Would Daniel keep her if I never came home?

"Eli," I said. "Let's go up to the house." And then, thinking he must have some sense of being pursued to have remained undiscovered so long, I added, "We can hide there."

He nodded and ducked his head, then brushed past me. I followed him up the stairs and across the lawn. He marched straight to the deck, bypassing the low stairs to step directly onto it, then put his hands on his hips, surveying. I stopped on the lawn. In the days since I'd last been there, someone had started to rebuild the deck. To the north lay a pile of the discarded boards, dark gray, replaced by fresh slats, their pale brown color visible even in the darkness, the scent of fresh wood settling around us. Eli stopped at the precise spot Charlie had fallen. He knelt and pressed his hand to the boards.

"Here's where he died," he said. Then he stood and walked to the rail. He leaned forward, crossing his elbows, and dropping his head on top of them, exactly the way I'd imagined Charlie, braced for the first blow.

"Here's how he stood," Eli said. His voice should have been muffled, pressed against his arms, but it came out clear. "Just before you got him with the hammer."

I walked up onto the deck. A wintery breeze blew in from the direction of the discarded boards. It would leave a film of dew on every leaf, and then the light would come. Not impossible to imagine the scenario, me killing Charlie, so much more directly than I ever could have imagined. I was still so hurt, and so angry. Maybe I'd done it in my sleep. Maybe I'd used these past few weeks to rearrange all memories in favor of myself, forgetting this unspeakable act.

"I should have stopped you," Eli said.

"Where were you?" I asked. I almost wanted to add, *I didn't see you there.*

"Just over there. With the dog." He looked down at his feet as if seeing Lightfoot for the first time. She wagged up at him and he knelt to pet her. "Hey," he said, the lucidity gathering. "Hey Lightfoot." She put her paws on his knee and licked his chin.

"Charlie was surprised," I said. "By that first blow."

Eli looked up. "He fell sideways. He lifted up his hands. But he didn't want to hurt you. Neither of us wanted to hurt you."

Eli didn't say what happened next. Two, three. And then I turned the hammer around for the fourth blow, the one that finally killed him, but it wasn't enough. Because how could he have done it, when I loved him so much, and when I'd tried so hard? I didn't know Eli was watching. By now, the dog must have fled, already cowering under the front porch. I went inside, got the knife, brought it back, and slid it across Charlie's throat. The blood flowed slowly, arteries no longer pumping.

"Except," I said.

Eli's window of clarity was closing, his words starting to spill forth again. The dog backed away as he got to his feet and started pacing.

"It wasn't me," I told him. "I didn't do that. I wasn't here. I was at my friend's."

If Eli heard me, he didn't give any indication. In front of my eyes, shifting in his capabilities, the outside world registering or not. And who was there left to protect him? Charlie was dead, the blood-soaked boards already replaced, the world moving forward with brash insensitivity. I thought of Charlie's wedding ring and wondered what Bob had done with it. I had to get it back from him, for Sarah. I had to figure out a way to deliver Eli to help, to safety. I had to find a way to live, and continue, and survive.

In a way, it would be easier to believe I could have been here, that I could have killed him—and let them take me away. No more decisions or responsibilities. Nothing but penance to pay.

I sat down and pressed my back against the wall. Lightfoot trotted over and plopped down in my lap. Eli stopped again, and came to sit next to me. When I saw his hand reaching out, toward me, I couldn't help it. I flinched. But he only grasped a strand of my hair, his fist closing around it, but not ungently.

"Your hair," he said. "It wasn't like this."

It seemed like morning should have arrived by now. But it hadn't, nothing close, not even the light from the millionaire's flagpole. He must have given up, or else the bulb had died. Eli closed his eyes, done speaking for the moment. Maybe I'd miscalculated the hour, because even this time of year, birds should have stirred as the gloaming approached. Eli didn't say anything more about what my hair *had* been like, the night I'd killed Charlie. But I knew it had been long and fine and very blonde.

"It wasn't me," I promised Eli.

But he wasn't there to hear, not really, his eyes open now, but staring off toward who knows where. While I understood exactly what had happened, and could press my face against my knees, seeing it all, until the first signs of light arranged themselves in the sky, and I managed to blink into the world around me. Eli was gone.

A LITTLE WHILE BEFORE—PERHAPS an hour, perhaps less—Sarah reached out for her mother in the searching nighttime way she had. I can picture her exactly, the way she would have sat up in bed, accustomed enough to the dog to be additionally affronted by her absence. "Mommy," she called into the darkness. It would not have occurred to her to climb out of bed. She expected prompt and attentive service. "Mommy," she called again, and then once more, before bursting into anguished and indignant sobs.

From down the hall came Mrs. Duffy in her nightgown. "My heart stopped when I saw you gone," she told me later. She picked up Sarah and gave her a kiss, bounced her for a moment, then carried her through the upstairs, opening every door, even the wide closet. I imagine Sarah still holding on to Charlie's shirt, pressing it to her tear-swollen face, because that's what she did for the next few years—held on to that shirt, cuddled it and clung to it, until it was frayed and worn to near transparency.

Sarah was too sleepy and upset to object to Mrs. Duffy's carrying her, with one careful hand on the railing, walking down the steep steps, and then peering into every downstairs room. In the kitchen, Mrs. Duffy dialed Ladd's cell phone, but it went straight to voice mail. So she called the police and then took a flashlight from the utility drawer and walked outside in the predawn, down the path to Ladd's cottage, where she found the light on, Ladd unable to sleep, sitting at the table composing a letter he never did manage to send me.

I WALKED ACROSS THE grass, now damp with dew. Light-foot was nowhere to be seen. When I crested the top of the beach stairs I could see them, down by the rocks, Eli pacing barefoot in the surf, writing on his pants with that imaginary pen, while the little dog gamboled around his feet as if it were a game. When I got down to them, she took a break to run and greet me, her face ecstatic, a family reunited. Whereas Eli didn't seem to register me at all, his eyes on the ground, muttering and pacing in an increasingly smaller circle, until he was practically pivoting on one leg.

"Eli," I said, longing to break through so that he could tell his story when someone else arrived, and be believed. Instead Eli put his hands over his ears again and roared, loud as an injured lion. A sound from the Serengeti, here in the placid American night. Was there anyone in the neighboring houses to hear? If they did, would they stand and go to their windows to investigate? And then would the innocuous sea air, the comforting sound of the ocean, allay their fears and send them back to bed? As if the sound existed only in their dreams.

Down here on the beach with Eli, there was no immunity to the sorrow that roar contained, for his murdered brother, or his ruined psyche, or both. Eli stood quiet a moment, staring out at the waves, as if he had silenced the voices for at least a moment. I walked toward him and stopped just short of the surf. And then another sound, a voice or echo. Along with the sound of sirens.

"Brett," someone called, from up above. I took another step

backward, toward Eli. I didn't want anyone to find us, not out here. I needed to be able to intervene, and explain. My hand reached backward, hanging there unanswered for a moment before Eli's fingers closed around mine.

Once, across many years and miles, Eli told me that if you lay very still in the grass, on a day when the sun shone bright, you could feel the earth spin on its axis. We had walked together to the stretch of lawn behind the library, by Boulder Creek, and lain down under the heat of the day. I remember the sound of water, and every molecule of my back reaching toward the ground, trying to capture the sense of motion. The way it always works when you're not trying you succeed; as Eli and I stood together on the beach in Saturday Cove, I could feel it, the tilt of the world, so sudden that for a moment I thought I might fall off, plunging out into the universe like a thirteenth-century sailor.

Instead my feet clung fast to the ground. I could see Ladd, standing at the top of the steps, at first his silhouette as the light gathered and then further lit by swirling red-and-yellow lights.

"Ladd," I called out. "Don't let them come down. Okay?"

Car doors slamming, I couldn't count how many. I stepped backward, into Eli. It would look like he was holding me hostage, but at least then they wouldn't shoot, with my body in front of his. Standing there, I imagined a drama, guns drawn and people running, shouting, bullets and explosions. What happened itself was only Ladd, walking down the steps toward Eli and me, until a police officer called out to him. Ladd stopped, obediently, as officers sidled past, each with a gun in its holster, but none of them drawing. There was no need. Eli just stood there, behind me.

The police officers walked up to us. "Are you Eli Moss?" one of them asked.

When Eli didn't answer, I nodded, then cleared my throat. "Yes," I said. "Yes he is."

Two of them stayed in front of me. Two of them moved behind me. I could feel Eli's hand wrested from my own, and when I turned, his hands were behind his back, cuffed, as the police—with impressive gentleness—pushed him forward, marching him back toward the house. Eli went without struggling, accustomed to being handcuffed and led away to the hospitals that to him felt just like prison.

I followed. Ladd met me at the bottom of the stairs. He put his hands on my shoulders and stared into my face urgently, examining me, making sure I was all right, and for the first time in weeks I looked back at him. And then we walked up to the grass as the officers helped Eli into the police car, guarding his head with the same care you'd show toward an invalid, as if they already understood—as I prepared to spend the day telling them—that he'd not been caught, but found.

16

I had crafted a murder mystery where there seemed to be none. The information I'd discovered was not something to be delivered to the police, breaking the case wide open. My role was widow. Not investigator. So I wasn't aware that the police already knew Eli hadn't killed Charlie. His fingerprints were all over the scene, along with mine, and a strand or two of our hair. But the blood they found mingled with Charlie's belonged to a woman, a different blood type than mine. On Charlie's voice mail and in his deleted email, hundreds of messages from Deirdre, unanswered, anguished, angry. I imagined the emails I might have written him, years ago, if he'd had an account. Or if he'd chosen Deirdre instead of Sarah and me. Maybe they would have been incriminating, too.

Eli was no kind of witness. But he didn't need to be. What

Daniel had said about Eli's being the only suspect had been true at first. But then this other evidence began appearing. So instead of watching the Moss house, the police had been traveling to Amherst to interrogate Deirdre. To impound her car, and search for traces of Charlie's blood, which they found, in addition to the leather string Charlie had worn around his neck.

Meanwhile, Eli had been able to leave the Huber's kayak at Crosby Landing and walk back along the shore to his father's house. An innocent madman was not a priority. Why would they look for him at all once the real perpetrator was found? Eli was left to fend for himself, as he'd always been. It was only a coincidence that he turned up to find me the day before they arrested Deirdre.

I didn't know where in Amherst she lived. Maybe they arrested her there, or walked into the new restaurant where she worked, if she still worked in a restaurant at all. Maybe at some gallery, or a studio where she was working on a portrait of Margaret Garner. Maybe she was studying seriously now, painting more conventional subjects with a better practiced hand. The police would have walked into class, students looking up, a part of Deirdre relieved at being caught, because what must it have felt like knowing that Charlie was gone forever? Whatever happened to her now would work itself out over the coming months or years. Charlie and I had trained ourselves so assiduously not to talk about her. Now all I wanted to do was sit down with him and ask him if he ever realized she might be dangerous. In my mind, she had been so sad, anemic.

Charlie, I wanted to ask. Sometimes I wanted to ask him gently. Sometimes I wanted to shake him in accusatory rage. *Weren't you worried about what she might do?*

And then I remembered without him answering. Charlie never worried about anything.

LADD, LIGHTFOOT, AND I returned to Daniel's house in bright afternoon, a faint chill in the air, along with the thin scent of crab apples. All I wanted to do was collapse on the couch—the nearest spot—but Sarah barreled through the living room with Mrs. Duffy close behind her, throwing her arms around my bone-weary legs. I picked her up and lay down with her sitting on top of me. I waited for Ladd to leave us, but he didn't.

Outside a car drove up, slowly, and I knew it would be Daniel. I felt myself fill with the longing to see him, his confident stride interrupting the intimacy with Ladd, ready to do what needed to be done, entering the house with an expectation of completing necessary tasks, which in this case meant pouring glasses of whiskey without ice and distributing them. I sat up, one arm tightly wrapped around Sarah, who smelled wonderfully rich and clean, of baby things like diapers and soap, but also the scent that all infants and toddlers carry, a cousin of sweat but so much sweeter. A low-note fragrance, rife with the business of growing. Daniel had left the front door leaning open, allowing a cross breeze to move through the room. I took a deep drink, it tasted dark and medicinal, sending a little shudder through my body, along with a wave of anger at Charlie—that he had never told me about Deirdre's persistence, that he had brought her into our lives in the first place, that he was brilliant at talking everybody down from ledges except for the women who loved him.

I took another sip, and this time, along with the shudder, came tears. Sarah started a little, and then began crying, too. But instead of silencing me, her tears made me cry harder. Ladd stood up and took her from my arms. I let go easily, watching through a haze as he carried her—peering back at me over his shoulder, her face scrunched and sobbing—into the kitchen. I barely noticed Daniel as he got to his feet and then knelt in front of me.

"And now," Daniel said, placing his hands on my knees, and looking into my face. "There will be a time of crying. Lots of crying."

I nodded and then pitched forward, sobbing as I'd needed to sob for these past weeks, in somebody's arms.

DANIEL WAS RIGHT. THERE would be a time of crying, a long time, no doubt more complicated than his had been, all those years ago. When Sylvia died, he didn't have to take care of a small child or think about the fate of her killer. He didn't have to blame her, or himself, or worry about Eli, who stayed in the hospital for two months and then went to live in the Cape house, which Bob Moss took off the market. As the years unfolded, there would be more unravelings, more descents, and they would all belong to me. But for now a social worker and nurse came by, once every three weeks, to give him an injection instead of trusting him to take the meds on his own. So that on the one-year anniversary of Charlie's death, I drove from Amherst to the Cape, and Eli and I walked to the end of the jetty, where we smashed colored bottles as tribute, so that in another year or less they would wash up on shore as the sea glass Charlie loved to collect. Then we took some glass already smoothed over by years and the tide and left it on Charlie's gravestone in the Blue Creek cemetery while Sarah rearranged nearby flowers from a recent funeral.

But so many months before then, the morning of the night without sleep—the day Deirdre was arrested and Eli reappeared, after Mrs. Duffy fed us all—I took Sarah down to the beach, my eyes dry at least for this outing. It comforted me the way Sarah took the wide world in stride, and I picked her up and swung her to my hip. She didn't protest but let me carry her, one damp little fist closing around the strap of my bathing suit. The tide was high and gentle, turning the bay into the world's biggest swimming pool. The water felt cold, not summer anymore, but I persevered. Sarah screeched a little as it hit her feet, tightening her grip around me, but I pulled her away, my hands underneath her shoulders. I held her at arm's length and ticktocked her above the water, letting her feet skim through the surface. She laughed, and I pulled her back to me and continued walking. We had passed the low tide point and my feet sunk into silty ocean sand. I knelt down so that the water surrounded both our bodies, Sarah shivering but knowing it must be safe because she trusted her mother. With my hands pressed against her sides, she paddled and splashed and laughed under a bright afternoon sky. Part dolphin, like her father. We swam for as long as the cold allowed, then trudged back up to shore. I dressed her in a terry-cloth cover up and pulled on one of Charlie's sweatshirts, and we played in the sand and tide pools for a long time. The blood pumping through my veins felt new, thicker, allowing me to persist clear-headed despite the lack of sleep and everything that had changed since yesterday, and since the first days of September.

That night as I finally slept, my body contained the rhythm of the ocean, waves rising and falling beneath me. And I dreamt I was at a carnival. The light was insanely bright, nearly blinding, and the rides and people were festooned in festive hues of blue, red and yellow. Best of all, Charlie was beside me. Happiness doesn't begin to describe the emotion I felt when I saw him. Because he was *there*. He was so vivid, so exactly as he had been all those years I lived with him. Exactly as intoxicating as the first time I'd seen or kissed him. And he was so happy to see me, in his old Charlie way, picking me up off the ground as he hugged me. I could feel the teeth of his smile against my bare shoulder. Charlie was alive, and he loved me, and I loved him so much that for once I couldn't be bothered, measuring amounts against each other. He was here. My husband was back.

Charlie lifted his face from my shoulder and looked at me a while. There was still the air of a smile about him, but his expression had become serious. He looked intent, as if he wanted to make sure he committed everything about me to memory. So I looked back at him, realizing this might be my last chance. I took in the fair stubble across his chin, and the round blue eyes, and the unruly blond curls. More than that, I took in the Charliness of him, the aspect that transcended his features, and I realized with a rush of comfort that I didn't have to memorize him. That was already done, everything about him having long ago taken up residence in the system of tunnels between my brain and heart.

Charlie kissed me. The carnival noise swelled all around us. I smelled the ocean, and cotton candy. Girls screamed from a roller coaster. Bad music blasted from speakers, the first chords of "Smoke on the Water." While Charlie and I kissed and kissed. It went on forever, his lips on mine, the sense of beyond-joy rising rather than abating, until finally the crowd began jostling us apart.

I held on as long as I could. Charlie did, too. But before long we'd been separated so that only our fingers touched. I watched his face ride away on the sea of people, wanting to call out to him, and knowing I should feel sad, but still relishing this, the last moment I would ever see him.

"Charlie," I finally called out.

He didn't have a chance to call back to me. By now, I stood beside a low wall that bordered a river. Charlie stood a good hundred feet away. People of varying heights stepped in front of him, all around him. He kept moving backward. I got one last glimpse—clear as the last time he'd really stood in front of me. But this time I knew to appreciate the moment, to keep it and cling to it, for as long as I could.

And then the crowd closed in, and Charlie was gone.

Acknowledgments

Thanks to Peter Steinberg, who has worked so hard for me and has been such a trusted advocate from the very beginning.

Kathy Pories has been so smart and patient with this book. More than an editor, she's been a friend and collaborator, and I could not be more grateful, or feel more blessed.

Thank you, Chuck Adams, for helping me reshape my ideas about this story. Thanks to everyone at Algonquin, including Elisabeth Scharlatt, Brunson Hoole, Brooke Csuka, and Jude Grant.

Danae Woodward, as usual, read first and offered endless encouragement. Thanks to second readers, Abby Jones and Tara Thompson.

Thank you everyone in the Creative Writing Department at UNCW.

And thanks to David and Hadley, for everything, always.